# THE BOUCHARD LEGACY

## TED MAGNUSON

This book is a work of fiction. Incidents, names, characters, and places are products of the author's imagination and used fictitiously. Resemblances to actual locales or events or persons living or dead is coincidental.

Published by

Cascade Saga Press

Cascade Saga Press, LLC
13500 SW Pacific Hwy, Suite 58
Portland OR 97223

ISBN: 0-9800-1251-1
ISBN-13: 9780980012514

# THE
# BOUCHARD
# LEGACY

TED MAGNUSON

# CONTENTS

# I

## RANDY

*Before the Stockholders' Meeting*
*November 5, 1979*

Randy stared into the glass he held in his hand, gazing into its cobra eyes. A double shot of thirty-year-old single malt whisky. You can't be an alcoholic when you only drink top shelf. Right?

Before *she* drove his medical practice into bankruptcy, before the divorce, *before his life went down the tubes,* didn't he, Dr. Randall Bouchard Allen, have it all?

What did he have now?

*Jack shit.*

Oh yes, Father's scheme could put him back in the game…That's what Father said.

*Yeah, Father said.*

The same good father who helped him clean up the drug-dealing charges, the same good father who now wanted to strong-arm him after his screw-up with Cindy…

The same damned father who gambled away his college funds and started all the shit he had fallen into in the first place!

Man, that drink looked good…

A beautiful woman walked into the bar. There was something in the way her high-heeled sandals clicked when she walked. The confidence in her eyes as she scanned the room. Showing just enough knee—nice cleavage, too. Her dress was an impatiens red that some might call a little too "5:00 p.m." for the middle of the day.

How her presence lit up the dark oak paneling of O'Connor's Restaurant and Bar. She made eye contact.

Randy acknowledged the attention by straightening the drape of his sport coat, raising his glass…and blushing.

Who was she?

A gorgeous woman, certainly.

Waiting for someone or looking for someone?

If only Randy had the time. To buy her a drink, to watch her breathe as they talked. To smell her. It would be very easy to forget all his problems, if just for a few minutes.

But no, today he had no time.

He had to be at the family meeting. He had to find out what influence he had in *the way things were going to be.*

Randy lifted the shot glass again. He recalled how he'd offered a feeble excuse—something about checking in with his answering service—when his stepbrother (brother, Randy called him) left for the law firm of Benton and Allen.

Ha!

Barry wasn't on duty. So the new girl, Dorothy, served him the single malt.

He'd savor just this one…right?

If Barry were on duty—oh, Barry meant well, but what does a bartender know about pressure?

No, that wasn't fair. Everyone has challenges, right?

Randy lifted the glass; he admired the amber liquid. Just one drink to take the edge off the day. Just one drink to bolster his nerves before he followed Paul to the stockholders' meeting, where the fate of the family business—the Sunny Day Beverage Company—hung on—

What?

Did Randy seriously want to surrender his last shot at keeping his practice? Just so Paul could continue selling rock 'n' rye, cola, and the—what, fifty-seven?—other flavors of sody-pops? What future was there in that?

Oh yes, he had to be there.

That was the "easy" part.

He had to cast his vote.

That was the hard part.

What if he did stand with Paul and his bloody fifty-seven other flavors—and the motion failed? What then? He'd be principled all right: a principled fool. He'd be stuck even deeper back in the "animal soup of time." Isn't that what Ginsberg called crud like this?

And Father…forgive and forget? Right. And sugar plum fairies slide up and down the Gateway Arch on the Saint Louis riverfront all day long.

The problem was, he could no more picture himself telling Paul to beat it than he could imagine doing the same to Father.

Didn't he have it good until Cindy stuck it to him? The practice thrived. The respect, the service, the difference he made in the lives of people. The money. The glass was at his lips now.

"Damn! Don't do it, doc!"

The words came hurtling at Randy from behind the bar.

He looked up.

It was Barry. Randy hit the bar with his fist, the force of his blow spilling drops of whisky down his chin. He bolted down the drink, coughed, and wiped his mouth with the palm of his hand.

Barry crossed out from the door behind the bar. His fire-red hair, his ruddy complexion, and his long, bold strides brought him to stand in front of Randy.

Barry glared at him like a Baptist deacon. He gestured with his hand on the bar for Randy to give up the glass.

Leaning into him, Barry whispered, "You know what you're doing, man?"

Smiling, Randy liked to think he looked more confident than he felt. "I've got it under control. Those days are gone…I just needed the one."

"Oh," Barry sighed. He shook his head. "Merton was asking about you—just two days ago. When was the last time you saw him?" Barry wiped the counter with a bar cloth.

Randy cocked his head as if he didn't get the connection. Merton Jones was Randy's sponsor in Alcoholics Anonymous.

"Sure, sure," Randy said. "I'll call him. Get me the phone and some coffee too, will you? Really, it's no big deal. Just a taste. A sip. Anyway, drink never affected me like it did you and Merton. Shoot, you of all people. You should know drinking is here to stay. Prohibition proved that, didn't it?" Randy laughed, trying to make light of the situation.

Barry hovered over him, his breathing deep, slow, and heavy with coffee. He dialed a number.

Randy heard the receptionist coo "Vanderventer Realty." Barry thrust the cordless phone at him. Much to Randy's relief, Merton wasn't in.

"Have him call me, will you, please?" Randy said it like that just to play along—to give Barry some satisfaction.

"That's better," Barry said, placing a cup of coffee on the counter before Randy.

Randy breathed in the steam wafting up from the coffee cup. "Thanks," he said. "I needed that."

Barry appeared satisfied. Still, he looked over his shoulder several times on his way over to guide the lady into the dining room.

That's when Randy bolted. He'd go see the Russian. They weren't so particular about who they served at Ivan's Tavern, were they? And a nice buzz did wonders for a day, didn't it—insulating one from all the drub-a-dub-crud of things?

# II

## PAUL

*Before the Stockholders' Meeting*
*November 5, 1979*

Paul Elser waited with the rest of them in the conference room at the law firm of Benton and Allen.

When would Randy arrive?

How would he vote?

What influence did Randy have?

These were the uncertainties that roiled Paul Elser's stomach. Even so, he remained sitting bolt upright, breathing slowly, breathing deeply as he studied the faces of the others in the room. The chiseled features of his ebony face, the easy penetration of his gaze. He would wait until the time was right. He surveyed those gathered around the massive, dark, teak wood conference table. Did their faces offer any clues of confidence or lack thereof? Like Daddy, seated across the conference table, Paul was Lou Rawls dark, trim, and not prone to ramble in conversation.

The sheer curtains drawn to mute the sweeping view of the Mississippi River implied something nefarious about today's business. The Colonel, Margaret's father, was an especially hard read. "Colonel" Elijah Bouchard wore a white linen suit and a turquoise bolo tie. From time to time, in the stillness he imposed on the group, the Colonel would glance out of the corner of his eye at his gold-tipped ebony cane where it rested by the dictionary stand. Did he plan to rise to greet someone? He was hardly ambulatory, and the only other one expected was Randy. Yes, the Colonel was hard to read.

Fidgeting and drumming his fingers on the big table, Henry Allen screeched, "Why are we waiting for my son? Let's get this over with!" He looked hot and agitated, stripped to the shirtsleeves of his crumpled white dress shirt, tie at half-mast. "He's got enough going on in his life. Besides, his only interest in the beverage company is to see it sold."

"No," Colonel Bouchard said. "We shall wait for the young man. Randall can speak for himself, Henry. Our Mr. Elser Junior has just seen Randall B. So," and here Colonel Bouchard's voice whistled, his bushy white eyebrows rose, "we know he is on his way."

Stuart Benton sat back in his chair, polishing his bifocals with a cambric cloth. He wore a gray, Italian three-piece suit. "Easy there, Henry," he said. "You, me, Doctor Randy—we'll be in Palm Beach Wednesday night. Wait until you get aboard my new blue water sailing yacht…Do you know if Violet picked up the tickets yet?"

*What posturing*, Paul thought.

Margaret and Bruce sat together. Margaret wore a gray pinstripe pantsuit; Bruce wore glen plaid that complemented the black man's complexion. Both scowled at Henry's comment. Daddy Bruce said, "Randy is aware, Margaret, of what Sunny Day means to you. He'll be here."

Margaret looked out the large plate glass window and clutched Daddy Bruce's hand. "Where is my dear, my only son?" she asked.

This deal—this sale—Paul knew it would retire his daddy and his white wife Margaret on a pittance.

A pittance for nearly twenty years of effort, sacrifice, and soul.

Nothing for their dignity.

Nothing for the flair they brought to the business.

Nothing!

Yes, Paul thought. He, Daddy Bruce and Margaret were primed to fight this sale.

How he wanted to honor their work, to carry on and continue to build on what they had already achieved.

He could do it, too, but for Henry and Stuart and whatever schemes the two of them had fed Colonel Bouchard to foist this damn sale.

The tension in the room was so taut you could almost feel the Mississippi River a hundred feet below scraping its riverbed.

Paul shot to his feet. He walked over to the window. He pulled the drape aside. He could not stand to look at Henry and Stuart for one more second.

Oh, Paul knew this family. He'd grown up in it. Margaret, Randy's mother, had married Daddy Bruce-Paul's father. It was a second marriage for both. Henry Allen, Randy's father, was still—believe it, still—a stockholder, thanks to Margaret's father, the Colonel. Why couldn't the Colonel honor his daughter's choices? Why couldn't he honor his daughter's achievements?

Paul would like to pace, but he dared not show one jot of anxiety. He would bide his time.

It was a tangled mess. Those assembled had a long history; three generations and more of entanglements between the lawyers at Benton and Allen, the Bouchards, and the Sunny Day Beverage Company. But today, all that could change. The meeting had been called to sell the Sunny Day Beverage Company, the final casualty of the divorce.

As Paul understood it, Margaret's first marriage to Henry had been the mistake of her life. She'd been a fool to take counsel from her parents about Henry, the so-called "golden boy" of Saint Louis society. Some golden boy…Margaret put the sleaze through law school. What a philandering bastard *he* turned out to be, and not long into the marriage from what Paul had heard from Randy. And how many times had Henry been brought up on ethical charges before the Missouri Bar?

Now the motion before them all was to scrap the mighty profit engine—this Sunny Day Beverage Company—which Paul and Daddy Bruce had found rusting and misused—the one they had refitted and relaunched to where it surpassed every former glory it ever had.

The sellers would sail away out of Manalapan Bay while the managers, namely Margaret, Daddy Bruce, and himself, got little more than a song. Margaret turned to the Colonel. "Are you comfortable, Grandpere? Can I get you anything?"

He gave her *the look* and then again turned to look at his ebony cane.

As quickly as it rose up, the anger within Paul seemed to ease. He returned to his seat. He remembered how he came to be a member of this extended family. How it all began. Though it had been twenty years, *it seemed like only yesterday…*

# 1

## MARGARET AND DADDY BRUCE

*Paul*

It had to be the most vivid memory of my childhood. Man…twenty-one years ago…1958. Daddy Bruce taking sister Ellie and me to a businessman's picnic in Tower Grove Park. *It was Eden. Tall elm trees, vast stretches of lawn, flowers; the neighborhood stood high above the stark streets of The Ville*, where we Elsers lived at the time…

*Shortly thereafter, the lady who invited us to the picnic hired Daddy as a salesman for the Sunny Day Beverage Company. Nobody went thirsty, not with Daddy Bruce on the job.*

Daddy Bruce and Margaret Bouchard had so much in common, building the business together. Was it any wonder they married—despite the fact that Daddy Bruce was black and Margaret was white?

*I, Paul, contributed to the biz, too. Sunny Day Snacks and the Lindy Health Bar; both were my ideas. And now Linda, Bruce, Junior, and I lived at 37 Fern Street—in the old Bouchard family home.*

# 2

# HOME FROM COLLEGE

*Randy*
*Monday, August 13, 1968*

Randy didn't know what to do about Paul. *Sure,* he thought as he drove to the Stockholders meeting in downtown Saint Louis—*We were kids once, but now we're playing in the bigs; we're adults.*

Possibly once he downed a few at the Russian's, he'd steel his nerves and know what he had to do. He pulled his car to the curb in front of the seedy bar on Vanderventer.

He turned off the ignition.

*Wait.*

*What the hell was he doing?*

*Who was he fooling?*

You can't find answers in the bottom of a bottle of booze. He didn't need another goddamn drink. No, he needed a clear head and a sharp tongue. Resting his forehead on the steering wheel, Randy looked at his watch. If he got it together right now, he could just swing by his condo, pick up the broker statements, and hardly be late to the meeting at all.

Randy started the engine of his Buick Riviera. He pulled back out into traffic. And then the history he shared with Paul Elser came pouring into his memory. Childhood friends. Children together; that's right, the last sanctuary of innocence...

Paul and he—especially the high school years—pitching on the Sunny Day team in the city league...

Then the college years, their twenties...

Yes, there it is...

Junior year. Summer. Coming home to Saint Louis. That's when he first became aware of this whole dynamic, this power play, this situation that had now become a crisis…

Mum.

The Colonel.

And the Elsers.

That's how it all began.

Way back then-in that long ago college summer. Even when the Amtrak crested the trestle bridge as it crossed the Mississippi River into Missouri. He knew, he just sensed *something* in the air. How the wheels squealed like the goddamn Valkyrie warriors descending on Donelson, as the Colonel was wont to describe "chaos when it came calling."

How strange Saint Louis looked to him that long-ago summer.

His years of premed at Columbia University had been tough. Now, to see the skyline of his hometown framed by the window of the train, by the steel girders of the bridge, and finally by the tall chrome spans of the Gateway Arch.

His home, his birthplace, looked so bizarre…like a painting on the wall that the wind just might blow away.

A strange sensation like electricity flowed through his body. His teeth felt like he just bitten into the aluminum wrapper on a stick of chewing gum.

What was the matter with him?

*Loneliness?*

*Coming down from all the coffee and Benzedrine that fueled his all-night study sessions at college?*

Immediately, the two little girls across the aisle began squealing *again*. Randy, blessedly distracted from his cares, watched as the girls, sisters, possibly twins, tickled each other uproariously. No older than eight, fair-skinned and blond, dressed in red gingham check…when did *kids that young* start looking so strange?

Their Daddy-o took no notice of the girls' commotion until he looked up to see Randy staring at them.

"Cute kids," Randy said with a smile.

Looking over the top of his readers, Daddy-o dusted off his white polo and spoke softly to his children. "Settle down Bethany, Susan," he said. "Look! Why, there's a big…*croquet wicket* over there."

The two girls all but hung over Randy's shoulder, looking, as they were, through the window at the Gateway Arch. The woman (their mother?)traveling with them, put down her paperback.

They were close to the Arch now.

The stainless steel rainbow soared majestically into the sky above the Saint Louis riverfront.

*The oohs and ahs of the children.*

"Is it really a giant's wicket, Daddy-o?" one of the girls asked.

"What else could it be?" Daddy-o sounded pleased. His girls had found a focus to their zeal.

"It isn't a wicket," the younger one said. "It's a staple to keep the sky attached to the earth."

"No, it isn't," big sister said, slapping her sister's shoulder.

"Easy, Susan. Can't Bethany be the clever one every now and then?" Daddy-o laughed.

When Randy turned to look again at the Gateway Arch, he saw the Barnes Hospital Complex beyond it. How the sun glinted on the shoulder of the building, giving it a dazzling light. After graduation, after his residency, Randy planned to staple his diploma to a practice in the Medical–Dental Building in the Barnes Hospital Complex. He sought out the building now. There it was—right across the street from the Barnes. He put his finger on the train window as if to touch his future practice.

*Yes, sir. Life after med school would be one smooth ride. All he needed do was tough it out through his studies and he'd be there—sitting pretty.*

At the station, Randy waited for the car to empty before grabbing his suitcase. He buffed his oxblood loafers with a tissue by placing first one foot then the other on the seat cushion. His madras shirt and chinos— they were a bit wrinkled, but presentable.

On the platform, Randy inhaled. The air was a mixture of oil, sweat, jumbo pretzel, and hamburger. It was August 1968.

Now to find Mum.

Inside, the grandeur of the barrel-vaulted ceiling caught him by surprise. Yes, he'd been to the station before, but only now did the artistry of the vast ceiling catch his eye. He admired the craftsmanship.

The strange vibe that startled him crossing the river came back to him. Reunion with the family could wait two minutes.

What would his life have been like if he had lived back in the days when travel by train was the vogue? Take his present journey. Maybe if it were 1898 he'd be returning from…a medical convention…or having just treated the wounded from what, the Spanish-American War? Someone must have been wounded when Teddy Roosevelt took San Juan Hill…

Teddy Roosevelt on horseback; wasn't that a more robust image than soldiers jumping from a hovering helicopter into a Vietnamese rice paddy? That had been the AP photo on the front page of yesterday's *Times,* now tucked in Randy's travel bag.

Yes, the present day definitely paled in comparison to the majestic past. Teddy Roosevelt on horseback, Lyndon B, Johnson pulling his hound's ears. TR roaring to start a third political party, the Bull Moose, out to reform the world. Sour-puss Prez. Johnson on network TV mouthing, "No thanks, I won't seek nor will I accept mah party's nomination to run for president." Well, admittedly, Johnson already had six years in the job since he took office right after Kennedy's assassination.

Yeah, 1968 was the pits, all right. JFK's brother Bobby and Martin Luther King Jr., both murdered, assassinated. A hell of a time to be stepping onto the adult stage.

For Randy, the best part about keeping up with the daily news was putting down his newspaper, turning off his television, tossing the magazine. His problems paled by comparison with the trumped-up version of the world dished out by the media.

But now, flinging his rambling thoughts against the magnificent brocade of the ceiling, it seemed he had become privy to some wondrous cryptic message—like the great complicated electronic circuitry of society could be readily deciphered by those who knew the *scheme of things.*

A female voice chirped, "What do you see? Is there a bird up there?"

Randy looked about him. "Huh?" he said.

The young woman, a hippie chick, touched his wrist. "It's me, down here. What were you looking at? A bird?"

The girl wore a granny dress, a tiny blue forget-me-not print. Early twenties, like him. Her straight and delicate hair plunged halfway to her waist. Plump breasts-the size of peaches or maybe even navel oranges.

She sat forward on the long waiting room bench. Next to her, he saw a ragged knapsack. "What were you looking at?" she asked. Something in her manner invited Randy to sit down next to her on the bench. He did so, sitting a bit closer to her than she might have expected.

"Do you mind?" Randy asked softly. "I'm sorry." He remained seated quite close.

Her eyelids flew up in surprise but then settled. She said, "It's all right."

"Well," Randy said, getting comfortable, "I was just admiring what a great ceiling this place has. Isn't it incredible?"

"Well…" the girl replied, scooting away, but only a little. Just the tips of his fingers were under her thigh. "I don't know. Are you an architect or with the maintenance company?"

"Neither," Randy countered, running his finger up her arm as he pointed his palm toward the ceiling. "I'm an admirer of beauty. Isn't this ceiling beautiful? How many of these people walking through this room today even notice it?" His hand was now behind her shoulders, resting on the bench. He noticed she was a deep breather as he watched the rise and fall of her breasts.

"An admirer of beauty, huh?" the girl said. "I'm an artist."

"What's your medium?"

"Pottery."

"Has anyone ever told you that you look like Katherine Ross?" Randy said. He touched her leg with his other hand and left it there.

"Oh puh-lease!" the girl said, adding, "Easy on the touch." She put her hand on top of Randy's. She had beautiful teeth and intense eyes.

The quickness of this intimacy excited Randy. But something in the furrow of her brow told Randy to back off. He inched away from her, but only a little.

"Oh puh-lease," the girl said. "Yes, they do say I look like Katherine Ross—though I don't know why. My hair is lighter than hers." She brushed her hair back to reveal more of her face for the comparison.

"Still, it's striking," Randy said. He fingered her hair very lightly. "My name is Randy."

"Randy, my name is Kikeena."

He looked around.

How he would have liked to linger there with her, to hear her story, to ask where she came from, where she was going. She seemed so free, happy and willing to…reveal intimacies. But instead, he looked at his

Omega wristwatch. "Kikeena, it's a pleasure to meet you. Thank you very much for saying hi. I needed that." He reached and squeezed her hand.

Her eyes. She seemed unwilling to see him go. "Have a nice day," she said, "wherever you're going."

Out on the street, Randy called Mum's office. Syrupy but abrupt, Myrna, Mum's secretary, screeched, "She is on her way, Mr. Allen." Then, after what seemed like forever, Mum's 1960 Cadillac swung into the turnaround. The car still had its bright turquoise sheen, even if it was eight years old. The turnaround empty of traffic, the sidewalk all but abandoned, Mum spun in fast.

Coming to a stop, Mum put down her power window. She said, "I'm sorry I'm late." Once out of the car, wearing her big oval sunglasses and a scarf covering her hair, she hurried to the curb.

Randy greeted her with a hug. "I'm sorry I'm late, dear," Mum repeated. "That overpriced roofing contractor just would not take no for an answer. Finally, I chased him off. Well, here we are. My God, Randy, nobody travels by train anymore. Oh, we'll talk about the roof later. You look tired. Are you all right? And to think…I haven't been here in years. The place has really fallen apart."

Randy took the keys from her and put his bags in the trunk. Mum remained outside the car. "Are you ready to go?" he asked.

"No. Not just yet. Excuse me. There's something I need to do…so long as we're here. Why did you take the train?"

"What?" Randy asked. His mum had turned to walk across the street to the old fountain.

A vast bathtub of a thing some forty yards wide, it was filled with concrete fish, water fairies, and mermaid sculptures. It was bone dry. It looked like something out of a mason's nightmare. In the central piece was a man-sculpture with broken arms poised to dive at a female figure carrying a water jug on her shoulders. The fountain looked ready to crumble into dust.

Randy quickly followed Mum to the fountain.

"Oh, Randy," Mum said. "This old train station, this fountain… brings back so many memories. You don't mind terribly, if we linger here a moment, do you? Then we'll go someplace nice for lunch."

"Sure," Randy said, looking back toward the car. He had to laugh. All the life of the station depended on the train, and now with the train gone, the place was a graveyard. A sign next to where Mum parked stood in stark contrast to all the quiet. It said "No Parking-Loading Zone." About the only loading Randy could see going on were two winos sharing a bottle of fortified wine. What'd Mother see in all this decrepitude? The fountain was in worse repair the closer they got to it. Orange, red, and purple graffiti splattered all over the mermaids. A couple of the water fairies had been tipped over.

Even so, there she sat, his mum, Margaret Bouchard—corporate powerhouse and high-society insider—on a bench, gawking at the derelict monstrosity. Paper cups, crumpled newspapers, and food wrappers scudded about the dry basin, driven by the wind. Dandelions grew in the cracks that ran the length and breadth of the concrete basin, which was as large as the infield of a baseball diamond.

"I can't believe it's come to this," Margaret said. "Only just a few years ago, this place was the showplace of the city."

Randy had to lean in close to even hear Mum, her voice was so low. He didn't sit on the bench. It was too dirty.

Mum furrowed her brow. "Oh," she paused. "Oh, when was I last here? 1954, '55, '58? I can't remember. That must seem like ancient history to you. When the boys returned from World War II, oh my, this was the place to be. VJ day. Everyone so happy. The reunions. My, my, but those were some days. I wonder if the Chamber is even aware how bad things have become…"

"Maybe you ought to tell them," Randy said.

Mum perked up. "Me?" she said. "Now? No, Bruce and I are too busy now with our own business. We don't have near the time. Your grandpere would be the one…He's got the connections. It's just too sad that something this beautiful gets forgotten."

The wind picked up, sending litter scudding across the empty fountain basin. "Grand-pere? You mean the Colonel. I thought the two of you weren't talking. Has that changed?"

"No. Sadly, most of our communication has been through his CPA, Bernard Jeams."

"Involving the Colonel, hmm," Randy said. "That's not a bad idea. He's big on nostalgia, right?"

"Yes, he is." Margaret Bouchard laughed. "Oh, look at me. I've fallen into something of a funk, haven't I? Never mind. So how are you, Randy?

How are your studies going? She tapped the stone bench by way of suggesting he sit next to her.

"Schools great," Randy said, pacing a bit. "But I don't think you and I just sitting here will bring this place back. Can we get out of here?"

"Yes, yes, of course, Randy. I just needed a moment. Now, see? I'm done. You being the age I was when this place was hopping…well, I'm getting carried away, aren't I?" Mum stood up and took his arm.

Randy led the way back to the car.

"I do so miss you living at home," Mom said as they crossed the street. "I guess I'm not ready to see you grow up and me grow old."

"You're not old—not in a bad way *old,* ah that is. You're elegant, esteemed *old.* There's a difference."

Margaret laughed. "I'll take that as a compliment, I guess. Young people today are so frank."

Randy suggested Balboa's Italian restaurant for lunch. Then he drove them both there in the vintage blue Cadillac.

\* \* \*

Once at Balboa's, Randy took satisfaction in again seeing the elegant face of the world…complete with white tablecloths, crystal goblets, and fine china.

They ordered a full four-course meal in honor of Randy's homecoming, complete with antipasto, a mixed greens salad, and veal parmesan for Randy and shrimp scampi for Mum. For dessert, the waiter promoted a "*bell-ee-seemo*" tiramisu, which he wheeled out on a cart with other goodies. They split a tiramisu between them.

As Randy looked about Balboa's, he thought this was what it was all about. Candlewicks floating in glasses of alcohol, orchids in vases, waiters with full-length aprons, full-length mirrors jazzing up what would otherwise be a dimly lit but spacious room decked out with ornate chair rails, massive cabinets, and raised felt wallpaper. Even the ventilation was tremendous, bringing a light floral scent into the room with just a hint of fresh-grated parmesan.

Margaret folded her napkin and set it aside. In a crisp businesslike tone, she introduced a more pointed line of conversation. "Randy, on the way to get you, I remembered how you and Paul used to work together at the plant."

Randy said. "That was years ago. Is that bottling machine still as noisy as ever?"

"Noisy? Not that I ever noticed. What you *may* have heard was the jingle of money. Though the new line has rubber bumpers. It's much quieter. But what I'm getting at is…the roof."

"What about the roof?" Randy asked.

"It leaks when it rains. Didn't I mention the contractor to you? When both Jimmy and Paul heard about hiring the job out, each of them said they thought we could do the job ourselves. I'm inclined to believe them now."

"Really? And we're talking about this now because…?"

"Well, Paul had offered to do the job, but it wouldn't be right for him to be up there alone." Mum struck a quizzical pose as if surprised Randy wasn't quite tracking with her.

"Where are you going with this?" Randy asked.

"I'm thinking of you, Randall," Mum said. "Will you work with Paul on sealing the roof?"

"Me? What do I know about sealing roofs? Other than it's got to be hot, dirty, and back-breaking? No, thanks. For that matter, what does Paul know?"

"I understand. Actually, if it were just the roof, I can appreciate your hesitancy. But there's more. I know how you men operate. It's better if you're doing something together when you *talk*."

"Talk? What kind of talk?" Something in Margaret's tone said a deep and weighty *talk*.

"Well, you know Bruce has been so good for the company. He's brought in so much business. He traces much of his success back to his army training as a Tuskegee Airman. Paul is following in Daddy Bruce's footsteps, the Reserve Officer Training Corp, to pay for college, and then…off to Vietnam."

"So what is it you want me to talk with Paul about?"

Margaret leaned in close. She whispered, "About life. The Elsers come from a different place than you and I." She took a breath. Randy had never seen Mum look quite so distraught. "It hasn't been easy for

Bruce and me, for us," she said. "The roofing companies are in collusion. No one will give us a reasonable bid. I cringe to say it, but…these stiff-necks can't stand a black man in what *they* call *white society*." Resuming a more formal pose, manner, and tone, Margaret summed it up. "Bruce truly is what I call a self-made man."

"You helped him some," Randy said, his position softened by Mum's show of emotion. Could tarring the roof be a stand against racial preju-dice?

"Yes, yes. Look, maybe we're getting off subject here. What I want to do is put this in perspective for you…I want you to build a bridge. Extend a hand. Maybe Paul's family does come from what some would call the wrong side of the railroad tracks, but they're *here* now. That's why I'm asking you to do such a *dirty* job. It will put the two of you on the same plane when you *talk*. Something is bothering Paul. I don't know what it is. If you were to get next to him, support him in his struggles…lighten his load…I believe he would gain from your insights."

"My insights? What do I know of *his* struggles? Much less how to solve them? I'm not a black man, or the son of a self-made man, or a sol-dier preparing to fight in an unpopular war. Were I to suggest he desert to Canada and he did it…hoo-wee…"

"No, of course! Don't you dare do that!" Mum sat up straight on that one. "Paul has too much going for him here. Look! I'm not asking you to *inflict* your beliefs on Paul or solve his problems like some little rainy day parlor game. Desert to Canada—and you raised Republican. For shame—"

"Republicans don't have any special exclusive on wisdom," Randy said. "As for Vietnam, why it ever escalated beyond the advisor stage is beyond me."

"Well yes, *of course* it's beyond you. What do either you or I know of such things?"

Randy began to feel quite warm. Mum could be so assumptive at times. "What do I know?" he said. "Excuse me, according to the civic books, isn't our country all about an educated electorate led by the best and brightest? Right? So I know what I should."

"Oh Randy, yes, of course that's the way it's supposed to be. We can have that discussion some other time, for all the good it will do us. When it comes to Paul, please don't pigeonhole him in some knee-jerk view of the world. Try to find out where he's coming from-isn't that the phrase? Life is all about relationships and what *actually* happens when people *relate*, when people understand each other. To see each other for who they are, not what we want or expect of them."

*Knee-jerk view of the world?* Randy could contest that, but instead he stayed on topic, responding simply, "I'm not sure I can do all that."

"Oh, dear. Of course you can. At least try. Now, you may be on to something...Maybe Paul does have concerns that our leaders are...misguided. Even so, again, our conversation is not about the strategic intentions of world leaders and our influence on them..." Her voice dropped to a softer level. "*Our* conversation is about the influence we have, the commitment we have to the people we know and love. Just spend just a day with him. That's all I ask. If it's as hard on you as you seem to think it might be, go ahead, walk out on him."

Randy bit his lip. Mum had done it. If he didn't do the job now, he might as well turn into some unfeeling...Precambrian trilobite. "Now hold on," he said. "I didn't say I wouldn't do it...yet. What's the problem? What's bothering Paul? Can you give me the slightest clue?"

"No. I want you to arrive at your own conclusions," Mum said. "He just appears to be down, he doesn't talk much."

"Have you brought this up with Linda?" Linda was Paul's special lady.

"No," Margaret said, backing away from the table. "I couldn't do that. She'd think I was a *nosey parker.*"

"*Touché* on that. Has anyone suggested he see a psychologist? No, wait a minute, he couldn't do that. It would blow his commission, as well as..." Randy's curiosity was now engaged. "Hmmm." He put a finger to his lip.

"I'm not asking you to get clinical with him..."

"I wouldn't..."

Margaret's face brightened. "Good, you'll do it then?"

Suddenly golfing, nightclubbing, and late mornings in bed struck Randy as trivial. He said yes to the job.

# 3

## TARRING IS THE PITS

*Tuesday, August 14, 1968*

Paul had just climbed down from his jeep when Randy swung a bright yellow Corvette Stingray through the gates into the paved yard of the plant. He slithered the low-slung sports car into a parking space in the back. The deep-throated glasspack mufflers reverberated even after the engine had been turned off.

Randy crawled out of the car, unfolded to full height, and turned to shut the door with a carefree slap of his hand. He strolled toward Paul with large measured strides. As he came close, Paul noticed the tiny embroidered alligator on Randy's navy Izod polo shirt, as well as the brand new deck shoes and the crisp crease in his chinos. *What a dude*, Paul thought. *He looks more like a man headed for the country club than a workingman's job.* In his hand, Randy carried a big plastic picnic water jug with cups in a plastic bag hanging from the handle.

"Nice wheels," Paul said after they greeted one another.

"Yeah," Randy shrugged. "Don't laugh. It's an automatic. My Dad bought a new Mercedes and held onto his old car for me to use while I'm in town."

"Nice," Paul said. His eyes darted between Randy and the car. He asked, "So what brings you down to the plant?"

"Don't you know?" Randy said. "I tried your number all last night, man. We're going to tar the roof together."

"You called *me* all last night?" Paul said. "Get off it."

Randy waited a beat. "Okay, I called you twice."

"Well, I wasn't home. We had a prep meeting for next week's training exercise. Anyway, yeah I heard you were going to help. I just didn't expect to see you here this morning."

"See me? I wouldn't miss it. Heeeere I am," Randy said, gesturing wide with his arms. He drew closer, lowering his voice. "So are you ready to do this thing?" He rested a hand on Paul's shoulder.

Paul stepped back. Randy. Did he really just complain–about driving a *used* Corvette? And what's the jab with the quiz all about? Tarring the roof or the ROTC maneuvers next week? Paul went with the roof. "Tarring the roof? It's nothing," he said. "But you've got to be kidding me if you're going to wear those shoes up there." Paul pointed at Randy's new deck shoes.

"Whoa, thanks," Randy said. "My old shoes are back in the car. I'll get them." Immediately trotting backward to his car, Randy asked "We can still get work duds from Jimmy, right? Cuz I just figured we could." He jabbed the air right and left. Jimmy was the production manager.

"Yes, Jimmy's got 'em. Meet you inside," Paul said.

"No! Wait up!" Randy said.

Over the clatter of the production line inside, Paul asked "Are you sure you Ivy Leaguers don't have better things to do with your summers than tarring a roof?"

Randy compressed his face into a feigned scowl. Then, in a stagey Mafioso voice, he growled, "Eh, I'm wid da family and like I said…I'm here to help." He tried to put Paul in a headlock.

"Get out of here!" Paul said, quick to dodge the attempt. "Get serious!"

Randy stared back in surprise. "Okay, okay. You're not a morning person. I can relate. You need your space."

"It's been a long time," Paul said. "We're not kids anymore."

They changed into work clothes and met Jimmy out in the plant's paved yard. A large yellow semi-truck had backed into the lot, its flatbed trailer loaded with pallets of tar buckets. Diesel fumes filled the air as a forklift with a tall mast came off the back of the trailer.

Jimmy approached the driver shouting, "First thing we do is lift that stack of empty pallets to the roof." He gestured with his hand, raising it emphatically in the air. "Roof's gotta parapet, a firewall around it. There's nothing to set a loaded pallet on ' less we put something behind the wall…"

The driver countered, "E'm not heah to do extra work."

"Not extra," Jimmy explained. "Part of the job."

"I'm only here to deliver da buckets."

The exchange went back and forth like that, faces turning red, voices getting loud. To Paul, the conversation had more to do with who had the power or blowing off steam, ranting for ranting's sake…anything but getting the job done. Eventually, Jimmy won the driver over. Jimmy, a short swarthy middle-aged man of Greek descent, wore a faded denim jacket. He hobbled over to where Paul and Randy waited while the driver loaded the stack of three pallets on the forks of his machine.

"Hey, wait up!'" Jimmy shouted to the driver, running his finger across his neck emphatically. Then, once the driver stopped raising the pallets, Jimmy said to Paul, "C'mon, we're taking the elevator to the roof." Jimmy laughed as he climbed atop the pallets and gave Paul a hand up. The two of them rode the pallet stack up to the roof.

Randy gladly took the stairs instead.

\* \* \*

By the time Randy got to the roof, Jimmy and Paul had already stacked the empty pallets up next to the firewall. They were guiding the first load of tar buckets to rest on top of the pallet stack. Randy had rushed up the stairs far too fast. It took him a few minutes to catch his breath.

Two more pallet loads of tar buckets came up. Once it all had been delivered to the roof, Jimmy pulled a long screwdriver from his back pocket. He pried open the first bucket with the screwdriver and poured the tar into a tar trough.

"Here's what to do," Jimmy said, giving them the "quick strokes tool talk" as he called it "on the skills of sealing roof."

"First, you start at far corner of roof. Don't paint you-self into a corner. You end by the stairs." He punctuated each of his comments with a laugh, a wave of the big screwdriver, and a piercing look from his gray eyes. Then he assembled the applicator brush. It was much like a push broom with a long handle and short, hard bristles on the wide brush end. With another hearty laugh, Jimmy handed an applicator to each of them. "Have to it," he said. "Try get most of tar on roof." Another laugh.

The job had begun.

Paul jumped into it, working hard, fast, and keeping to himself. But not even a half hour had gone by before Randy stopped and leaned against his applicator brush/broom. "It is soooo ho…o…o…t up here," he said, dropping his applicator brush to the ground. "Hey! Slow down, man. Look at you, Paul. Take a break. Who do you think you are, John Henry, the original steel-driving man?"

"No, John Henry had a hammer," Paul spoke softly. "I'm all about getting this job done, as soon as I can, as fast as I can." He worked even as he talked.

"You keep humpin' like you are, and I guar-ohn-tee you'll be done. Heat stroke done that is, by lunch. Hey, what do you say? Let's start at 5:00 a.m. tomorrow. It'll be cool then—at least for the first few hours."

"You here at 5:00 a.m.? No way! You were late getting here when the job started at 8:00 a.m."

Randy nodded agreement and continued working at his own slow pace. Compared with Paul, Randy's method of attack featured many more stops between strokes and plenty more double and triple dunks of his brush into the trough when it came time to recharge his brush. Paul went for the quick dip and then slathered the tar on the roof. He was not much in the conversation department. Randy, however, had quite the monologue going. First, he was all about reliving old company league baseball games. Then he went into plant life. As Paul's college was in Saint Louis, he worked part-time still at the plan. Randy asked about "the little old lady from the local mission." "Does she still come around with her little red wagon to change empties for over- and underfilled bottles for the homeless shelter?"

Randy talked about anything and everything. Paul worked in silence.

After the trough had been moved and refilled three times, Randy removed his glove and wiped his brow with a handkerchief. "Hey," he said, "it's been an hour and more. I'm all for taking a break? How 'bout you?"

"No," Paul said. "I'm not ready for a break. But go ahead, you take your break, if you want. You do know, don't you, that company policy is only one break between start and lunch?"

"Comp'ny policy?" Randy said. "Doesn't apply here. We're not on the production line."

Randy leaned his broom against a ventilator shaft, walked over to the stack of pallets, poured some ice water out of his thermal jug and returned, setting a chunk of cardboard on a roof vent to sit down. "Tarring is the pits," he said.

Paul thought it odd Randy took his break so near to where they'd been working. He said, "That sucker's hot, isn't it?"

Randy shrugged, slapping the cardboard. "That's why I'm sitting on cardboard." He wiggled his butt. "But I do feel the heat. Good for piles, if you know what I mean."

"Hemorrhoids? No way," Paul said, smiling at Randy's exaggerated sigh of relief. "You're going to burn your buns."

Randy gulped down some water, refilled the cup, and held it out to Paul. "Wanna drink?" he asked.

Paul nodded. He took the cup. "Yeah, thank you, I am thirsty."

Although Paul took the drink, he continued working. Randy persisted in his attempts at conversation. "I can't believe it's been near a year since you and I last saw each other."

Paul worked the tar into a crevice. "So? Where're you going with all your talk?" He stared at Randy as he recharged his brush. *Here we are,* Paul thought, *acres of roof, hours of work, and the guy sits there with his thermal jug like he was on a picnic.*

"Oh, I just remember how we used to talk about everything," Randy said. "We were going to play ball for the Cardinals when we grew up? Remember that? Hey, they're looking good again this year."

Paul paused, leaned hard on his broom and shook his head. "You can sit there talking nonsense while I work my tail off? Well, don't hold your breath. This year's Cards are nothing like the '64 Cards."

"What!" Randy hooted. "Hey! You're down on the Cards!" He stomped his foot and clapped his hands to emphasize his disbelief.

"I'm not down on the Cards," Paul said. "I just got better things to do than blather. Kids dream fool things. Forget it."

"Uh-huh. We've still got Flood, Gibson, and Maris, don't we?" After each name, Randy slapped the palm of his hand. "Tell them they're fools."

"Which conversation are you trying to start? About the Cards' chances in the World Series or about old times?"

"Huh? What? Hey, I'm just trying to reach out, man. Talking just helps the job go faster for me. Don't you remember how it was the year the Cards were in the World Series? You and I couldn't wait to get all suited up, walk out on the diamond at Riverside Stadium—man, we were going to smash one out of the park for the Cards." Randy was star-ing now, looking at Paul in an intent way.

"Oh man!" Paul said. "Give it up, will you? You start off on me about your metal-flaky Corvette having an automatic tranny...then you sit there frying your butt on that roof vent prattling on about kids' stuff while I'm sweating away. While I'm doing all the work What's with you?"

Randy stood up and walked over to Paul. He put his hand on Paul's shoulder. "That was hard, man. Maybe you should take a break. It's hot up here. C'mon, the roof job can wait. I'm not kidding. Heat stroke is nothing to sneeze at. What gives? Are you sure there's not something going on with you? Something we could talk about? There's something strange going on with you. You seem...I don't know...closed down, clogged up, angry."

"I don't want to talk about it," Paul insisted.

"Talk about what?" Randy asked. He did not ease up on studying Paul's face.

Time seemed to freeze for Paul. Should he spill the beans or not? As for strange—yes, Paul could admit it, at least to himself—life had turned strange on him. It wasn't just how he saw Randy today. Hell, who knows, the guy may even have a purpose in his quirky little fishing expeditions, trying to strike up a conversation on just about...*everything*.

"Look," Randy said. "What gives?"

"You wouldn't understand," Paul answered.

"Understand what? That you've got problems?" Randy said. "It may surprise you, but even us rich white preppy guys with our hand-me-down Corvettes got problems. Sorry you didn't get the memo." Randy turned and crossed back over to the pallets to return his water jug to the stack of pallets. Oddly, he carried his applicator brush with him.

"Hey! Where're you going?" Paul demanded. The contrast between them hit him especially hard. "Are you staying and working, or not?"

"Of course, I'm here, aren't I?" Randy said. "Why do you ask?"

"You took your brush with you."

"Oh, so I did," Randy admitted, his voice carrying across the expanse between them. "Guess I'm feeling a little worked up. So go ahead. What would I not understand about you?" he said, resuming his seat on the roof vent. "Talk to me."

"You really want to know?" Paul shifted his weight, leaning on the broom. "About being black? About stuff eating at me you don't even know about. Talk about it with you?" Paul struck a defiant pose. "What's that going to do? Problems don't just go away."

Paul paused as if he actually had to decide where he was going to go at that moment. But whatever little meditation he did wouldn't even bend a hair's breadth of time. He blurted out, "Time heals all wounds… things work out…people forget. Everybody moves on." Paul stepped to it, dunking the broom in the trough and returning to work with a vengeance. Then he stopped and thought better of it. He plopped the broom in the tar trough. An energy, an anger, grew within him as he stepped toward Randy. He remembered how earlier Randy had tried to put him in a headlock. Randy backed away hurriedly and Paul said "Gotcha," as he kept on walking, heading to the supply pallets area and the water jug.

"Now where are *you* going?" Randy asked as he followed. Paul felt good. Maybe he did put a scare into his white brother.

Paul asked, "Do you *mind* if I get a *real* drink of water out of your picnic jug?"

"Hell, help yourself," Randy said. "That's what it's there for." He sounded amused, surprised, tensed up.

Paul sat down on the wall at the edge of the roof.

As Randy approached, Paul said, "Anyway, I'm tired of it." Opening up the insulated jug, Paul drank right from it, not bothering to use a cup.

Water dripped down his face onto his work-duds.

Yes, clumsy or not, Randy had broached the subject.

After setting the jug back down, Paul said, "All right. I'll tell you what's up with me. Just don't let it get back to the ROTC, okay? I'm supposed to be a tough guy, right? You swear you'll keep your mouth shut?"

"No problem." Randy remained standing, as if unsure where he should be.

"It could blow my commission, but hell…what's the use? I'm not sure I even want it any…" Paul stopped.

Then he lashed it out: "Walters's death, that's what bothers me! Why'd he, of all people, have to die? Why is it so hard for me to deal with it?"

"Who's Walters?" Randy asked. He sat down next to Paul.

"I still feel sick about it." Paul's breath was deep and automatic as if beyond his control. Dizziness came over him. For the briefest second, he thought he might faint or vomit.

Once again Randy asked, "Who's Walters?"

Now Paul felt more in control of himself. "Walters was battalion commander my freshman year," he said. "A great guy. Always had a zippy thing to say. Liked to come around and talk with each squad, with each cadet. The way he put it all together…made sense, man. Always encouraging. He wanted to go all the way. Be a general. Then oh, I don't know, two weeks, a month ago, we're in formation, at attention. The commandant tells us Walters got killed in action—KIA, Vietnam." Paul put his face in his hands.

Randy shook his head. "So you've been carrying that around for how long? Who've you shared your…distress with…over this thing?"

Paul admitted, "I really haven't talked about it with anyone. It was just too intense for me to even think about, much less talk about. I didn't even tell Linda. It's just not something we're encouraged to do. In the corps, it's all strictly stuff-it-and-forget-it. In a way, the stuffing of it has got to me more than the event, as if Walters was violating orders when he got shot down. But his being killed really got to me. More than I realize."

"Thank you," Randy said. "Thank you for trusting me with that. It's pretty deep with you, isn't it?"

Paul nodded.

"Hey, I know we joke around a lot, but man, some things are for real, like death." There did seem to be a quality of disbelief in Randy's face, like it was news to him too, that good soldiers died.

"Yes, it got to me," Paul said. He perked up. It felt better now, putting into words the thoughts that were haunting him. He had been so afraid that admitting his discomfort would brand him as a coward. He felt none of that now. "It gets complicated. Besides the macho soldier thing, there's the whole antiwar thing. Why are we fighting in Vietnam? At first it was campus weirdos, dopesters, and graffiti. Now, even the news reporters have turned against the troops. Walters gave everything, and people, they don't care."

"You care," Randy said.

"Yes, I do!" Paul said. He thought Randy's comment was spot on. "More people should care."

Randy said, "I'm very sorry for your loss, Paul. So what are you going to do now?"

Paul continued. "I don't know. It's different now. I know that much. The military always appealed to me. Maybe that's why I admired Walters so. He was *it*. I remember during my freshman year, I'd polish my shoes in the dorm, spit shine. I'd look down and see my face shining back in a mirror shine. I'd have a crease in my pants sharp enough to split hairs on. I'd be in my uniform cruising off across campus to drill or military science, looking so strack…that's what we call it in the corps. Studly, to you.

Paul caught his breath. "But those days are gone. It is different now. We wear civvies on campus and keep our uniforms in the locker room. The corps even has them laundered for us. That way we avoid any hassles from student who shout out crazy things like 'Baby killers!' or 'ROTC, what's that stand for? Robot oafs to command?'"

"I've heard some of that talk," Randy said.

Paul continued. "So what am I going to do now that Walters is dead? What can I do? Denying he died is no answer. Until you and I talked, that seemed to be the approach everyone took. But you and I talking about him…it's like he's living on…in my heart. Does that make any sense?"

"Perfect sense," Randy said. "Look, I don't have your military aptitude, but I'm sorry for your loss. Hearing you talk now, it sounds like some healing is taking place."

Paul nodded. "It helped bringing it out in the open. I'm starting to see him living on, like he's bigger than death… Anyway, he's not forgotten. What he stood for, what he strived for."

"All right. Good," Randy said. "I'm glad we got that squared away." Sounds like a start anyway…a way to begin coping with it," Randy said.

They continued working.

After grabbing a bag of burgers from a fast food place for lunch, and before resuming the job, Paul walked along the edge of what they had sealed that morning. A little less than a fourth of the job had been completed. "What d'you think?" Paul said, kicking the untreated roof. "Will this new coat of tar stick to the old? Will it be watertight?"

"What? Watertight? I haven't a clue," Randy said. "Been so busy up here all morning playing shuffleboard with you that I haven't had a chance to think on that one." Randy sat down to finish his burger. Paul had been in a hurry to get back to the job.

"Funny," Paul said. "Seriously, doesn't the roof sag a little over there? What about here? There's a gash in the old coat where the tar shrunk or something."

Randy shrugged. "No problem. Just take your shuffleboard stick and poke more tar there, right? Isn't that what Jimmy told us?"

"No! Listen. No more shuffleboard jokes. This is serious. What does Jimmy know? The more I look at this roof, the more convinced I am that you, me, and even Jimmy know zip about roofs. What if the roof collapses or if a leak damages stock or machinery?" Paul prepped the trough with more tar.

Randy shook his head. "How can you say that? You of all people? You're working like a man possessed. Jimmy said the roof was inspected and prepped by the maintenance company. They were the ones who said it just needed a fresh coat. You're looking for problems that aren't there, man."

Even while Randy spoke, Paul walked a bucket over to where he saw the gash in the roof. He poured the tar right into the crack in the roof. Without looking up, he said, "Once we're done up here, I'm all for getting the fire hose out. After soaking this place with that, we could find out real fast if we've got that watertight seal."

Randy laughed. "Ha! Listen to you! I get it. You think you're the new owner, right?" Randy doubled over. Then he clapped his hands at his own joke. Paul didn't care for the humor. "What's so funny?" he said. "Why not keep the business in the family? Man, I've been thinking about that lately. If I were in charge, I'd work so hard—"

"Get off it! Never happen."

Paul put the empty bucket back where they'd been collecting them. He stood in front of Randy. "What do you mean? You're studying to be a doctor. Other than myself, I don't know of one person in the family interested in taking over, when the parents step away from the scene, I mean. Years down the road."

"Eeeh, I hate to rain on your parade, but are you kidding? You think this place could just be handed over to you, on your say-so? Wrong! This place will be sold. Gone! Finito, Benito! There's no way the Colonel would just give it to you. He isn't even giving it to Margaret, and she's his own daughter."

"She's running it now. What's wrong with keeping it in the family? Look at all Daddy Bruce did to build this business up. The place was about to be sold for scrap. Then he went out and built up the customer base. That's the story I heard." Paul was holding his brush, but they hadn't resumed working. Randy was finishing his burger, leaning against the wall at the edge of the roof.

"No question," Randy said. "Your daddy's a good businessman. He's been good for Mum, too. But hey, news flash. The Colonel isn't about family. He isn't about hard work. His thing is *ownership.* Colonel Bouchard calls the shots, and when he bleeds, it's green stuff that oozes out his veins, not warm fuzzies for duh widdle fambwy-wambwy. So far as he's concerned, what little love he had for family disappeared when Margaret divorced Henry."

"Man, I don't believe that. You're harsh."

Randy smiled. "No. Just realistic. Sorry to be the bearer of bad news, bro." Randy took the last bite out of his hamburger, tossing the wrapper.

Paul rolled the handle of his applicator around. He took a breath. He did not like the position Randy took on his just-revealed secret. "Obviously," Paul said, "I'm not talking about now. I'm looking way down the road, when I'm thirty, forty, or so, and the folks are ready to retire. I'd be ready to take over. I'd work out a payment schedule. Daddy Bruce owns some stock. I'd be buying it on time. You don't need to worry. You wouldn't even miss a dividend payment."

Randy shook his head. "Ain't going to happen. Look, I'm on your side. For all the good it will do, if it helps, I'll even buy you a New York Lottery ticket."

"Is that some kind of crack?" Paul had risen to return to work. But now he turned and glared at Randy, who remained seated on the wall at the edge of the roof.

"It's no crack," Randy said. "I'll be blunt. You have about as much chance of owning this joint as you do winning the New York Lottery. Or hey, I'm easy, the Missouri Lottery."

"Missouri doesn't have a lottery," Paul said. "Anyway, why're you patronizing me like that? Is it because I'm Afro-American?"

Randy stood now, too. "No, no. Well sure; that's part of it. All I mean is forget that stuff about love making the world go round. You want to get ride on the success express, you've got to pay your own way. I'm not telling you anything different than anyone else would. Sure, I mean you're family to Mum and me, but well-who else knows about your hopes and dreams? What are they telling you?"

"I haven't talked about it with anyone," Paul mumbled under his breath. He gripped his applicator tightly. He shouldn't have said a word… *but now the cat was out of the bag.*

"Well, you *say* it's nothing," Randy said as he refilled the tar trough. "But your attitude screams the idea is *core* to you. Go ahead, check it out with Mum or Daddy Bruce. Let me know, will you, what they think of your expectations, OK?"

# 4

# GETTING WITH DADDY BRUCE

*Paul*
*Tuesday, August 14, l968*

That evening, Paul visited Daddy Bruce in the Bouchard house on Flora Street. The large colonial had been the family home since 1890. When Paul revealed his ambitions to "one day to become the CEO of the Sunny Day Beverage Company," Daddy Bruce sighed deeply.

They were meeting in the wood-paneled study off the front hall. Until then, Daddy looked like the picture of command. The large roll top desk, the ledger book, the stone fireplace, the map of the Upper Midwest with various colored pins marking customer locations, and the prints of the P-38 Mustang fighter planes on the wall all testified to the man's success.

"Your ambition is admirable," Daddy Bruce said. "But let me tell you something about life. When I was your age, if someone drove me up to this house and said to me, 'Mr. Elser, in twenty-five years, you will be living here,' the idea would have struck me as madness. I would have laughed in that man's face."

This disturbed Paul. He said, "No, you can't mean that!"

For Paul, Daddy's marriage, Daddy's livelihood and success all had an inevitable ring to it. Otherwise, what did the preacher mean when he talked about things like predestined, foreordained, and born again?

"I understand," Daddy Bruce consoled. "This place has been part of your life much longer than it has mine. Remember the day we first came to this neighborhood? You and Ellie were shunned by the other children at the picnic...the roughs smashed my headlights when we left the park...it hasn't been easy. The point I make here is that I kept my head down, I worked hard and quietly at the responsibilities given to me. When an opportunity presented itself to me, I stepped up and took a grasp on it.

"Now, why do I tell you all this? Because given our circumstances, you are going one hundred miles per hour in school zone…or a speed trap. You've got to live your life one day at a time, Paul. Your studies. Acing your tests. Serving in a combat zone, in what, a year or less? Those are the things you should be wrapping your head around now. See what I'm getting at?" Bruce Elser had served as a Tuskegee Airman in World War II.

No, Paul did not "get it." He did not agree with Daddy Bruce's approach to life. Even so, he said, "Yes, I understand perfectly." He swallowed hard.

On leaving the house, Paul knew his life was far more tangled, far more complicated, than the face he'd put on things for Daddy Bruce. A scream welled up within him.

# 5

## KNIGHTS OF THE TAR PITS

*Wednesday, August 15, 1968*

The next day on the roof, when Randy finally did arrive, Paul greeted him with a growl. "Where've you been, Mr. Five O'clock in the Morning?" Paul had already opened, poured, and spread over half the first bucket of tar.

"Didn't we put the kibosh on that?" Randy said, slapping his cheek to help wake himself up.

"Yee-esss," Paul said. "But that doesn't mean you don't show up at the regular time, turkey. You can just pour the next tar bucket yourself, you think it's so funny."

"No can do," Randy moaned. "My back is killing me." Bent over, hand pressed on his back, Randy turned to fumble together a fresh applicator brush.

This did not sit well with Paul. He made to lunge toward Randy.

But taking a cue from Paul's actions, Randy said, "Cool your jets. I'll pour the next bucket all by my lonesome, so you can kick back and take it easy. But if you ask me, somebody didn't sprinkle enough sugar on their corn flakes this morning, did they now, sunshine? Just lighten up, will you?" Randy waved off Paul's peevishness as he went looking for his applicator brush.

Paul laughed. More weighed on him than Randy's slapdash manner this morning. Walter's death hadn't just affected his attitude. It interfered with his schoolwork, too. As a result, Paul's grades had slumped. Daddy Bruce had called him on his attitude last night. This got Paul to thinking: how would he cope with combat?

What about his business ambitions? They looked fine in the privacy of own mind, but to air them in front of Daddy and Randy?

How dumb can one person get? Paul should never have said a word.

Later, Randy asked, "You ready for a break yet?"

Paul shook his head "No," he said. "Don't take too long. We both need to put in a full day today—or we'll be back tomorrow."

"I won't take that long," Randy said.

The morning went back and forth like that. Every conversation, such as they were, bordered on breaking into argument:

Paul: "Students at my school went on strike. They want a new constitution."

Randy: "Really? That went down at my school last year."

Paul: "The demands are ridiculous. Don't parents have a right to view report cards? Coed dorms? Liquor on campus?"

Randy: "Students are older these days."

When a church bell rang ten o'clock, Randy set his brush aside. "Man, these fumes, this heat…this job is getting to me. I need fresh air bad." He walked to the edge of the roof nearest the Mississippi River. "I am so looking forward to a round of golf this afternoon," he said. "Do you play?" Randy continued to scan the river.

When Paul didn't answer, Randy turned around. Paul stood in a lunge pose, wagging his fully charged brush at Randy's pants.

"Do I play? Oh yes, I love to play. Let's play Get Back to Work, slacker!" There was a crazed look on Paul's face. "You're the slacker. And I'm the enforcer."

"What!" Randy said, setting his water cup down. "That sounds like a lame game. What's got into you?" He looked Paul up and down, sizing of the nature of his threat.

Paul dropped his tarred brush on Randy's boots. "It isn't about what's got into me. It's about what's going down with you! There! Now your shoes are all brightly tarred. You don't have to worry about keeping them clean anymore or avoiding fumes or anything! Get. Back. To. Work. Now!"

Did he catch Randy off guard? Paul couldn't tell.

*How would Randy call it?*

*How would Paul respond?*

Then Randy's eyes rolled around in their sockets. He cried out "You messed my shoes! I'm going to get you!"

Feigning left and cutting right, Randy dived for his own applicator brush. He'd left it leaning against the tar trough.

Armed now, Randy took a fighter's stance. "I forbid you to tar this roof!" he said. "You are not worthy of this noble calling!"

In no way did Paul expect such a full-bodied response from Randy. Backed, however, by a robust repertoire of antics built up over their childhood and high school years, Paul rose to the occasion. "Sez you? I'll tar this roof with your long shaggy hair if you don't pitch in and *work! Right now!*"

What was with Randy? He looked like a caricature of anger gone haywire. Images of a mad scientist flashed through Paul's mind.

Snarling and shaking his brush, Randy said, "Oh yeah! Defend yourself, Knight of the Tar Pits!" He lunged at Paul.

"Defend yourself, crazy man!" Paul said, parrying the attack with his raised brush, pushing Randy back toward the treated area in an effort to box him in.

The fencing match was on.

Tar splattered everywhere, speckling both their faces. In reckless abandon, the horseplay drew them away from all focus on the job. The adrenaline rush, the scrimmage, the dueling tar brushes may have lasted ten minutes, or it may have just lasted for a very long ninety seconds, but however long it lasted, it ended in bursts of laughter from them both.

"Defeat!" Randy cried. "Or at least time out for water."

Sitting at the parapet wall, they parleyed for peace.

"How's your back now?" Paul asked once they sat down together on the parapet at the edge of the roof. "You were complaining about it earlier."

"Better now," Randy said. "When you snuck up on me and put tar on my shoes, it gave me such a jolt…I think my vertebrae popped back into place."

"Well, glad to be of service," Paul said. "Hey, ah, if you can be serious for a minute, there's something else. You remember yesterday when I told you about Walters?"

"Yeah." Randy looked at Paul carefully. His eyes darted about, as if he might not want to hear or know what Paul would say. Then, more businesslike, he asked, "Is there more to the story?" A cool breeze swept across the roof.

Paul nodded. "You could say that. I let my grades slip. I didn't mail my draft report back either. So anyway, I got *notice* last night. The draft board pulled my student deferment because I'm on academic warning."

Randy said, "Oh man. After all you've been through? Are you sure? They can't draft you, can they?"

"Well, yes they can. They're the draft board. That's what they do. Anyway, what other choice do I have?"

Randy swung away from the parapet wall. He stood up. He paced. He swung his arms about. "What choices? What about your original choice? First thing I would do is check in the head of your mil sci department. See what it would take to get back in the good graces of your program."

Paul said, "That's just it. As an officer, I'd responsible for the men. I'd have to explain to them why we're over there fighting. I can't do that. Not the way Walters did."

"Paul! Screw that. Hey, news flash. *Second lieutenants don't have to justify wars to anyone.*" Randy went over and leaned on the sill of the parapet wall. He got eyeball to eyeball with his brother. Then he resumed his full standing height while Paul remained seated on the parapet. "All I'm saying, true Knight of the Tar Pits, is you got to take your lumps and git on with it, finish ROTC if you can."

"I thought you were a dove."

Randy shrugged as he resumed his seat on the parapet. "Me? This isn't about me. It's about you." He put his arm around Paul's shoulders. "Wars, dear Paul, are here to stay. I'd rather have sensible people like you and the way you described Walters drawing up the battle plans than some trigger-happy, war-mongering military-industrial complex fiend like Eisenhower warned us against. I know you like your Daddy. The two of you get along fine and everything. But being old does not necessarily give *everybody* an edge on being wise, all-knowing, and on-target. You've got to be your own guru, and you've got to be true to yourself. You don't just back down because the going gets tough."

Paul scowled. "You know about Eisenhower saying that?"

"Course I do. He was president of my school, wasn't he, before he became president of the US?"

"So," Paul said. "What are you saying with all your gobbledygook? Do and die, don't reason why, be a hawk or what?"

"No," Randy said. "You can't pin me down like that…what I think or whatever buzz the media has going. It's totally your call. What I'm hearing you say, the one thing that keeps going through my mind when I hear your misgivings, is this: a tiger doesn't change its stripes. I remember how senior summer, you and I sat down for a break right down there on the loading dock, over there." Randy pointed down by the plant yard where the trucks came in. "You told me this story about how you wanted to study ROTC at college. You said how there was this Zulu warrior situated up in an acacia tree, standing watch over the savannahs of your mind."

"Zulu warrior?" Paul put down his cup of water. "You're memory is a little shaky, my man. He was and is an Ashanti warrior. He's my good luck champion."

"Yeah, well, you told me about him and it stuck. You don't want to mess with him, right?"

The job continued even as the temperature on the roof climbed to 110°.

# 6

# LEAVING HOME

*Paul*
*Sunday, January 15, l970*

A crystalline frost coated the grass and bushes of his Saint Louis neighborhood the day Paul Elser left home for infantry officer Basic Training at Fort Benning, Georgia. Awake hours before sunrise, restless, his wife Linda and he walked to Forest Park, marveling at the transformation that had fallen upon the Central West End. The trees, the houses, and the power lines glowed in the surreal light cast from the streetlights and reflected from the frosty ground. The curbs, stairs, and other dark spots along the way were easily illuminated by the flashlights they each carried. Linda still had a year to go to graduation; she would remain in their apartment, close to campus. Kings Highway was crossed with ease—at 5:00 a.m., the thoroughfare was deserted. No traffic in either direction. The insulating quality of the frost combined with the stillness in the air silenced all but their footsteps. They walked on moondust.

While Paul's pending departure weighed heavily on their last moments together and their thoughts, it was a pleasure to be out alone together. "We've got the whole world to ourselves," Paul said as Linda reached for and squeezed his hand.

They wore the tracksuits she'd bought them for Christmas, both cardinal red. Linda wore a rabbit fur hat that covered her delicate ears and a scarf around what Paul sometimes described as her long, Egyptian neck. A morning jog was customary for them, and continuing that routine helped to normalize an otherwise heavy-hearted day. Only a hard rain or the kind of silver thaw that coated the pavement with black ice would keep them inside, so dedicated were they to the practice. So, in a sense, this unique day was every day even as Paul would soon be living a full-time military life. A time when they would be apart for months on end.

One of the best things about spending time out in the cold was returning back inside where it was warm. Returning home was especially welcome in that way. Good to go out, good to be back. In the dark of winter, a brightly lit room also does wonders for the spirit. Paul started a pot of coffee, and Linda got out the makings for an omelet she'd prepared the night before. Then they showered together and returned to the bedroom for an intimate farewell.

Breakfast consisted of a large omelet with green and red peppers, diced onions, cheddar cheese, ham and mushrooms, plus fresh squeezed orange juice, followed by oven-baked croissant rolls that Linda snapped out of a tube. They talked of what their first house would look like. How big the kitchen, how tall the living room ceiling, and what neighborhood they'd buy into. The morning had a special flavor to it, like Christmas, a birthday, or another kind of celebration. Then, as if on cue, John Denver's "Leaving on a Jet Plane" began to play on the radio. Paul put on his uniform, and Linda drove him to the airport.

As their Mustang coup pulled off the highway onto the airport drive, Paul said, "Please, let's just say good-bye at the curb."

"But I'd like to see you off," Linda protested.

"It'd be better at the curb," Paul said. "If we both start bawling, it'd give national defense a bad rep."

"That is the lamest excuse…are you serious?" A quizzical look came over Linda's face.

"Please?"

Linda laughed and accepted the request. In truth, Paul did not want Linda to see the abuse soldiers in uniform were likely to receive from the war protestors who often patrolled the ticket lobbies of airports all around the country. He did not even want her to *know* that particular gauntlet even existed.

In those days, anybody could accompany a passenger out to the gate. All the well-wisher need do was to submit to the metal detector inspection at the head of the concourse, just like the ticketed passengers did.

Once Linda pulled the Ford up to the curb, she turned to face her man. She clutched Paul's hand. She squeezed it. "I'm so proud of you," she said. They embraced inside the car and kissed and then embraced outside the car also.

Then it was good-bye.

That past November, only two or three months before Paul reported for duty, the cover-up on the My Lai massacre had been blown. The newspapers ran red with the story. This outrage fueled protestor's outrage against the war in Vietnam. The My Lai massacre occurred in this way: On March 16, 1968, four hundred or so civilians—women, children, and elderly men—had been shot, tortured, and buried in My Lai, South Vietnam. A chivalrous helicopter pilot and others attempted to intervene during the event and afterward, to bring the matter to justice. It was actions of this nature that added fuel to the fervor of the war protestors, raising the frequency and the intensity of exchanges between the antiwar demonstrators and soldiers traveling on civilian airlines.

Paul did not condone the massacre, the cover-up, or any other action that tarnished American prestige, but what could he do about it? His issue at this point was simply to march right up to take his seat on his airplane, preferably keeping his Class A uniform looking clean and orderly all the way to Fort Benning.

But when Paul saw the man in the army field jacket standing in front of the security gate, he knew there'd be trouble.

Soldiers on active duty never wore field gear, especially battle-worn and tattered field gear, while traveling on civilian aircraft in the USA. To the contrary, war protestors seldom wore anything else but such a battered old field jacket. As Paul approached the man, he saw this particular coat, which was tattered, greasy, and bedraggled, had seen combat, even if the man had not. The old army field jacket was festooned with a short-timer's calendar marking off day to DEROS (Date of Expected Rotation for Overseas), an embroidered peace sign, and a spattering of buttons on the lapels. Among the buttons, Paul recognized Frank Zappa, Jerry Garcia, "I Piss Goldwater," and "Nix on Nixon." There were marijuana leaves on his sleeves where hashes (marking years of service) would be on a regulation field jacket. Then Paul saw the man's eyes. He could only guess what those eyes had seen. Vacuous, yellowed, set back in a well-weathered face. The man stood stiff and motionless as his gaze in on Paul. The man appeared traumatized—his brain possibly fried on heroin. A white man or possibly Native American   he did wear an

Indian style headband—he stepped toward Paul. He raised a hand. His fingernails were cracked. He appeared about to speak. He appeared to be mouthing words. By his expression, it appeared to be something like "Don't do it, man..."

On either side of the man were two women dressed in loose, floor-length floral print dresses. As the three approached Paul, he asked, "You okay, brother? Need anything?"

The women carried daisies in wicker horns slung from their shoulders. One of the women stepped in front of the man to stand before Paul. Almost simpering, she handed Paul a flower. "Do you know where you're going, soldier?" she asked.

Paul picked the delicate flower out of her hand. He saw the Americal Division 'horse blanket' unit patch on the shoulder of the man's jacket. "Is he getting any help?" Paul asked.

The woman handed Paul another flower. He looked at each of the three of them in turn. "How will it feel to kill a baby suckling at her mother's breast?" she asked.

Paul maintained unblinking eye contact with her. "Unconscionable," Paul said. He handed the flower back to her. It fell to the floor. "I'm sorry for your pain," he said and moved on.

The woman stepped back, Paul's answer appearing to surprise her. Did she expect anger, disgust, or arrogance? The man in the tattered field jacket put his hand on her arm. He said to Paul, "You take care, man. Welcome to the insanity."

As Paul continued to meet his flight, the vacuous gaze of the man in the tattered field jacket stayed with him. The strange mission of the group... haunted him. What had the man seen? Who were the women? Why did they feel compelled to confront soldiers in airports? What purpose was accomplished? The man had clearly fallen into a pit, but as to who, how, or even if he could pull himself out...Paul had no idea. *There but for the grace of God go I.*

Paul grabbed a *Saint Louis Post-Dispatch* to catch up on sports scores. But Vietnam, the Cold War, the grip of the Military Industrial Complex on the economy, etc., was sprawled all over the front page. He found himself searching for information, for background to the drama he had now committed his life to.

In one story, Sen. Gore, a Democrat from Tennessee, urged increased production of submarine launch missiles "to keep pace with Russia's 230 SS-9 missiles." While in another story Sen. McCarthy, Democrat from Minnesota, discussed trade relations with the Soviets in Moscow. Paul found the contrast puzzling; it seemed almost like the senators were playing a scene from *Dragnet*, interrogating the Soviets in good cop/bad cop style.

The story about the downed helicopter in Vietnam would have to wait. Paul heard someone call his name. It was Linda. She had parked the car and come to join him in the boarding lounge.

Paul set his paper aside and greeted her. They laughed, whispering of love, affection, and missing each other. He reminded her of his leave after training and then again after six months in-country.

Linda summed it up: "That's forever away." She touched his chin.

"Don't I know it," Paul said. His voice seemed especially deep. When the boarding call came, Paul felt Linda shiver. He kissed her good-bye. She said, "Stay safe, I love you, dear."

Once on board the plane, the flight attendant welcomed Paul with a seat in first class. He sat next to a stout man in a blue suit with a double chin and an anchor tattoo on the back of his hand. Looking out the window, Paul saw Linda standing in the big plate glass window of the terminal. He waved slowly to her until she saw him in his tiny window in the big plane. She waved back.

Paul's seatmate did not intrude on this private moment. Once the plane taxied away, he introduced himself, saying his name and "six years navy, Korean era." He was "proud of his service, his country, and to be sitting next to an active duty soldier," adding with a soft nudge, "Your lady is a looker."

Paul put his seat back and enjoyed the comforts of traveling off to war, first class, compliments of Uncle Sam and Bravo Airlines.

# 7

# SAIGON

*Paul*
*Wednesday, March 4,1970*

If the only problems with the mess hall at Long Binh/Saigon were the puke green walls and the reek of too much bleach, it wouldn't be half bad. But on his second day in-country, Lt. Paul Elser arrived early for dinner anyway. The officers' mess stood desolate with the exception of a group of NCOs and junior officers sitting by the windows. A man from the group stood up. "Come here and take a load off, soldier," the man said, waving Paul over. He wore a nineteenth-century cavalryman's hat. His remark set off a chorus of "Oh yeahs" from the rest of the group.

They were all laughing and joking as Paul pulled a chair out to sit down. But no sooner had he reached for his silverware than a second member of the group shot to his feet.

"What'd you go and invite him here for, Jim?" the lieutenant said to the first man, removing the man's cavalry hat to swat him with it.

Jim placed his hat back on his head, deadpanning, "Don't tell me we're all leaving now!" He dropped his jaw and then covered his gaping mouth with his hand. "I'll bet this maaa-yan feels bare-assed awful, getting invited to sit at an empty table with all these dirty trays around him." With a hearty laugh right in Paul's face, Jim bumped his tray against Paul's. By then, the others were also standing up. They also pushed their trays into Paul's. These "comrades in arms" had no intention of inviting him to dine with them. They'd left him alone in the midst of their dirty dishes and leftover food. The deliberate, vicious, and mocking way Jim stretched out the word *man* was not lost on Paul either. The blatant implication—a black man was less than a man? How could Paul fall for such a stupid joke.

Calmly, Paul placed his napkin on his lap. Other than quietly promising himself to eat later, Paul did as little as possible to acknowledge their prank. Would his field assignment ever come?

As the rowdy crowd left the officers' mess, Paul heard chairs shuffling out in the enlisted men's mess. Looking past the six trays of half-eaten food and through the large archway, Paul saw the source of the commotion. A group of black enlisted men had locked their gaze on him. The intense expressions in their eyes, the way they appeared half out of their seats, confirmed for Paul they'd seen the harassment and they might even be inclined to confront the punk officers. As an officer, Paul couldn't sit with the enlisted, but he appreciated their solidarity. He stood up and walked to the archway. "It doesn't mean a thing," he said.

When Paul returned to his tray, a Vietnamese orderly had begun cleaning up the mess. He said, "Jeb Stuart's raiders number ten." He held his nose in disgust.

"For sure," Paul said. "An appropriate name, I guess. Reliving the Civil War in Vietnam…"

The orderly held each plate and utensil at arm's length, as if they were all infected.

In the midst of this, Captain Choi Kim of the Republic of Korea (ROK) Army appeared. A fireplug of a man, the collar, cuffs, and placket of his uniform shirt neatly starched, he asked in very crisp English, "Will you join me, Lieutenant? We'll sit over here, while Tran cleans up that mess."

Besides commanding a ROK tiger unit, Captain Kim held a masters in international business from USC. Eating a rushed dinner, the captain said, "Please excuse me, I have a presentation tomorrow. I would, however, like to invite you to dine with me off base tomorrow evening. I think you will find the fare at the place I have in mind far more digestible."

Provided neither of them received orders the next day, they agreed to meet at the officer's club at 1830 hours.

The next evening, after winding through the twists and turns of narrow streets of broken or nonexistent pavement, adroitly avoiding bicycles, scooters, pedestrians, and even a few cars, Captain Kim pulled the jeep to a stop in front of a chest-high stone wall on a cobblestone street. Only the heavy scent of ginger, garlic, and beans cooking revealed that a restaurant or household expecting a host of hungry guests lay hidden behind the lush plantings of cilantro and bamboo. "Come," Captain Kim said as he led the way down a stone path through the foliage up to the stairs to the porch and the front entrance. There, a thin man in a white silk jacket stepped forward. "Chào, Danh-tu Kim," he said. The maitre d's appearance declared "company is expected"—despite the discrete appearance of the Maison Pierre from the street. The ROK captain bowed and offered a similar Vietnamese greeting.

Three others of the family had also greeted Captain Kim by the time they arrived at their table. The room featured thick stone pillars set between large open-air windows. High up in the ceiling, paddle fans helped to move and cool the air. The day had been oppressively hot, the evening not much cooler, but the Maison Pierre was delightfully cool. There was a timeless quality to the place far removed from the temporary barracks at Long Binh, the American presence in country, and Paul's one-year tour of duty.

The dining room could seat perhaps thirty people. That night, only two other groups, a young couple and a family group, occupied the place.

"When next you check in with MACV, you should request the An Hoa Basin," Captain Kim said as he broke out his napkin and placed it on his lap.

"Oh?" Paul said. "And why would I want to do that?"

A waiter came to fill the water glasses while another brought "a bottle of wine Danh-tu Kim and his guest were sure to like."

As the waiter poured out two glasses, Kim said, "The region offers you an interesting adversary. I should know. My Tiger Division has been up there many years. There is a former French Legion Officer in the area of operations, a Senegalese named Lang, an African. When the French left, he sided with the Viet Cong. He has a tactic you may find challenging, in light of last night's mess hall embarrassment."

When Kim did not proceed, Paul said, "How's that?"

"Lang is a Negro like you. He has ordered his men to shoot only white soldiers. I understand this selectivity is not lost on the white American troops. It destroys unit cohesion."

"You've seen this firsthand?" Paul asked.

"I throw no bull, nor take any either," Kim said. He sipped his wine, smiling in a wry way. The captain peppered his speech with such misapplied American clichés.

"On the face of it," Paul said, "to truly test Lang's tactic, black soldiers could be ordered to take more risks to see if this Lang truly oper-
ated the way you describe."

"Would your black troops comply with such a tactic?" Kim asked.

Paul split his roll open and buttered it. "It would certainly test the
theory. A more interesting method would be for the whole platoon to
appear to be colored; white soldiers with blackened faces would become
colored. Who would Lang's men shoot then?"

"You would make this Lang a challenging adversary. Would your
white soldiers obey such an order? Isn't it the white man's pride that he
is not colored?

"White soldiers under my command would best take more pride in
my intent to keep them alive than in the color of their skin. Racial preju-
dice will have no place in my unit. My men will know that. It diminishes
combat effectiveness."

"Well said, Lieutenant."

The *pissaladière* onion tarts were served for the hors d'oeuvres course.
As Kim lifted the tart tray, the gold cap on one of his teeth showed off
to good effect in the dimly lit room. "Go ahead, you are my guest. Have
one. I'm pleased to see you are not one to be easily riled. I saw that about
you last night at the mess hall. A level head will serve you well in the
bush. Yes, a good strategy. Racial prejudice gets the boot, interferes with
combat effectiveness. Staying alive is the higher value."

Then, with an abrupt change in tone, he said, "Tell me, Lt. Paul,
what is your understanding of the American presence here in Vietnam?
I should tell you before you answer that I have spent all day in a briefing
with a group of American officers—all of them bitter your Congress will
not fund a continued American presence here in Vietnam."

"My understanding is we are here in Vietnamese officially on two
levels: to help the South Vietnamese survive as a country, and to fight
communism encroachment on the Third World."

"And unofficially?"

Paul groaned. "Your guess is as good as mine."

"Do you plan, then, on a military career?"

"No, sir. It's just four years in and then I'm done. Uncle Sam paid for
my college and then I came here at his request to show my appreciation."

"As you should. It is very kind of your government to watch out for you like that. You wear your cavalier attitude well. It is not so easy for me. It is a very old profession you are engaged in for a season, and I for a career. Warriors. Tactics, strategy. Outfoxing the enemy. I daresay these elements will appear for you in whatever pursuit you follow. Yes, life lessons are here for the wise to see. How does the saying go? Hold your friends close, your enemies closer."

"It sounds like you have something you want to say, but I'm not getting the message," Paul said.

"Ah yes. Boldly put. My point is only this, Lt. Paul. Yes, communist China does have an interest in this conflict…in this region. I for one, in my little country, would not care to see an angry, unrivaled China follow in the expansionist footsteps of Russia. Their ambitions, Red China's, must be contained. Will China be contained if America stays here in Vietnam? Will China become more bold should America leave? What will an expanded China look like on the world stage? Surely, we have seen Japan filled with imperialistic notions a generation ago. What language do the nations use when answering questions like this? Diplomacy? Atom bombs? Conventional warfare? Trade agreements? Your President Nixon talks of peace with honor. What does this mean? When he says these words, what do the different interests hear? The Americans? The Chinese? The two Vietnams?"

Paul said, "I hear what you are saying. Your view of the situation is more immediate than mine as your country is so much closer to the scene. When you talk, I see there are countless futures possible depending on the many different actions of world leaders. I am here from eight thousand miles and more away. Eventually, all this fades in memory for me. While for you, this is your neighborhood. You are here to stay.

"Me a citizen soldier, you a careerist. I see China as a very isolated place, surrounded by its Great Wall, impenetrable. You see something else, I'm not sure what."

Kim laughed. "Yes, I know this about Americans. Even next year, no make that next month, seems unthinkable. It is all about today. History? Not a dinner topic conversation. Yet in the East, the continuum of time is a much more tangible commodity. I represent all the generations of my family that preceded me and within me is the seed of all my family yet to be. I know this as a constant fact and a daily source of meditation."

Paul smiled. "Now, to me, thinking like that is best saved for a very private time, cut off from the action of daily life. More power to you that you can pull it off, but for me, it would take some doing."

The onion hors d'oeuvres were gone. Paul took a long draft of water and savored a sip of wine.

When the next course came, Paul was pleased that he had cleansed his palate. The lobster bisque had a very subtle taste that might have been lost if his mouth still burned from the onions of the earlier course.

Captain Kim had studied international business at the University of Southern California in Los Angeles. He had great admiration for American ideals, which he quipped could be summed up as "E Plurius Unum and In God We Trust (all others buy on time). Look, it's even written on the money."

Other Americanisms alarmed him. Captain Kim did not care for "Nuke them till they glow and shoot them in the dark." The chief aim of man, he said was "Gratitude to the ancestors for life, and duty to the progeny by tending the garden earth."

The main course was steak tartare, a very rare piece of meat, possibly the most tender Paul had ever eaten. In total, the meal must have either set Captain Choi Kim back a month's pay or he had done a great favor for the family that owned the place—Paul never found out either way. He did, however, thank Captain Kim for a welcome break to the Spartan military life.

As Lt. Paul Elser returned to barrack that night, he thought the conventional wisdom had it all wrong. The East was no more "inscrutable" than the West. What was inscrutable were the ways of war.

# 8

# TALKING ABOUT MY GENERATION

*Randy*
*Summer of '69*

Randy left the sidewalk in front of Butler Library to walk out on the quad. It was the first warm afternoon in the spring of '69. Anna Toth, a woman Randy knew from his public health lecture, had waved to him from out on the lawn. She sat there with a man who rested on his side, propped up on his elbow. He laid on some kind of military issue trench coat.

As Randy approached, he could hear the man regale Anna with laughter and tales of police brutality at the Days of Rage, the protests outside the International Amphitheater during the 1968 Democratic National Convention in Chicago. Yep, the man, Joel Scroggins had been "at Chicago." Anna knelt on her knapsack, stroking her hair over her shoulder. She wore a long denim skirt and looked as comfortable in the awkward pose as only a yoga devotee could. She smiled and cupped her hand in a subtle wave to Randy as Joel continued his tale. With Randy towering over them, Joel's gaze began to bounce between Anna and Randy. "I got shoved to the ground," Joel said. "Just for *being* there. Tear gas…have you ever been tear-gassed? I can still feel the burn in my throat, the rasp in my eye. The police knocked a newsman's big video camera off its tripod. Then one of 'em whaled on it with a sledge hammer! What were they afraid of? The right of assembly, man. The people will be heard. It's constitutional, man. You would not believe the rumors." Joel stopped for breath. In a high-pitched mockery of a whine, he continued, "Somebody gonna put an eye-dropper of LSD in the billion-gallon water reservoir? Ooooouuuhhh, poor babies. The whole flipping city flipping out in a Peter Max hallucination, people floating away in flower bubbles? Too outrageous, man. What are the cops flipping afraid of?"

The grass had some moisture, but Randy was committed now so he squatted on his haunches. The guy was a card. It pleased him that Anna had waved to him. He would get her phone number. Ask her out for a study date, a coke, anything.

Joel fingered the joint stuck behind his ear. "What's the country coming to, Anna?" Joel whispered. "Remember Martin Luther King's March on Washington in '63? I have a dream. That's what the man said. The people want sanity. Then, bim, bam, bong, race riots in Watts, Newark, Detroit. At Days of Rage—that's what they're calling the Chicago DNC thing—Major Daly gave the police commissioner orders to *shoot to kill arsonists and shoot to maim looters*." Joel lit a reefer. His brow dropped considerably during his rant. "What are you looking at?" he asked Randy.

"I'm cool," Randy said. "Wanted to talk with Anna for a minute. But go ahead with your story. What were you doing in Chicago?"

"Showing my support for McCarthy, protesting the war, what else, man? Just being there, standing with *my generation*. Nobody looting and burning...that's bull." He laughed before offering the marijuana cigarette to Anna. She waved it off.

Randy said, "We really shouldn't be smoking out here." They were right in the middle of the quad in front of Butler Library.

"Why not?" Joel said. "It's good stuff, man. Acapulco Gold. You want a hit? No one's going to come out here. Too wet."

"Sure," Randy said. All the other students were keeping to the sidewalks, weren't they? Randy wouldn't have been out on the lawn either—except he saw Anna. So that's how Randy met Anna. Joel was just a bonus.

*Joel*

Despite his bohemian ways on the quad, Anna assured Randy that, in the classroom, Joel presented himself as clean-talking, polite, and polished as anyone. He had extremely curly hair like the singer Tom Jones, a delicate nose, and he was not very tall. Joel, an erstwhile pharmacist in training, paid his way through college selling marijuana, hashish, and speed.

Later that summer, Joel went to Woodstock. "Three days of peace, love and happiness. You should have seen the place," Joel said after he sat down with Randy and Anna at the Bean Sprout on Amsterdam Avenue. "Out-flipping-rageous. Even the rain, and it rained hard…thunder… nothing could dampen the energy, the vibe, the happening. Nude swimming, nude *lovemaking*. Right out there in the open. Let the people jump up and dance for joy. Oh yee-AH! The speaker boxes they set up for the music. All over the field. Way up on towers. You could hear Joan Baez whisper at six hundred yards and when The Who wailed out on 'My Generation,' the sound ate everyone. Up. Alive."

Joel on his own time, the joker prince of joy. "Woodstock, man, the ultimate nuclear fusion where everybody came together mucho gusto." To Joel, nothing said Boomerville better than Woodstock.

Joel had been to Woodstock.

Randy had not.

Yes, Randy liked rock music.

But until he heard of Woodstock, phrases like "my generation" and "Baby Boomers" meant little more to him than the Demographic Bli*p*, the upsurge in births occurring between 1946 and 1964. Indeed, the way Randy saw it, calling grown adults babies insulted everyone involved.

As a result of hooking up with Anna (and maybe falling not just a little under the influence of Joel Scroggins), Randy hungered to be part of "my generation," out to change the world through peace, love, and rock n' roll. Tune in, turn on, and—figuratively speaking anyway—drop out.

What did it all mean?

How could he catch the "vibe" and find out what "my generation" was all about? The generation that had created such a buzz on campus, in the news, everywhere around the world. And so the stage was set for Randy to take part in a "my generation happening," He did not have long to wait.

# 9

# WHAT'S IT ALL ABOUT, TRICKY DICKY?

*Randy*
*Wednesday, October 29, 1969*

College life took a major leap forward when Randy moved out of the dorm into an apartment he rented in an old walk-up building on Riverside Drive. Jacobs, his first roommate, something of a slob, moved out shortly after Anna moved in. Randy and Anna didn't mind the increased privacy one bit. It was all good. They split the rent and started taking more of their meals in. Anna cooked up goulash and Italian, giving Randy the opportunity to develop his talent for cooking the pasta to the perfect *al dente* consistency. Anna's salads were garnished with vegetables Randy sliced and diced.

The Wednesday before Halloween, Randy read the *Village Voice* to Anna. "McCarthy, McGovern, and Martin Luther King's widow will be at that rally in Washington we've been talking about."

"Widow? You mean Coretta Scott King?" Anna said.

"Yes, of course," Randy said. "Sounds like you've heard of her."

"Yes, I have. Besides being married to Martin Luther King, she's quite an activist in her own right." Anna studied sociology in a joint program with Barnard College. "I understand the busses are filling up fast. If we're going, we'd better sign up soon."

Randy scowled. "Go by bus? No, thanks." He looked about his apartment on Riverside Drive. How many guys, even at Columbia, shared a two-room apartment with a chick? Five or six hours on a bus? Diesel fumes?

The rally had been the high-water mark of efforts by the 'National Mobilization Committee to End the War in Vietnam (MOBE), a coalition of anti-war activists who had already staged a number of rallies around the country.

Anna put some more turbinado sugar in her coffee. "Nothing. How else could we get there?" she asked.

"By train. And Joel? What's his plan? Sleep in a church basement? Forget that. Surely Washington must burst at the seams with hotels."

"Hmm," Anna shifted in her chair. She didn't show the enthusiasm for comfort Randy expected. "Isn't the shared sacrifice, our generation being all together, kind of the whole point of the thing?"

"Of course," Randy said. "I get that. We'll all be together at the rally—while we're listening to Mrs. King and the others." Randy shook his paper to another column. "A widow of a downed pilot and William Sloan Coffin, a chaplain at Yale, are leading a march from Arlington to the White House—the March Against Death, they're calling it."

Anna sipped her coffee. "Hmmm, it's not like you, Randy, to talk about widows so much. Feeling a little kinky this morning, are we?" She pinched his side.

Randy grabbed her hand and held it. "Coffin, cemetery, widows. It does sound a bit ghoulish, doesn't it?" He nodded and grinned at her.

Smiling, and quite excited, Anna said, "Are you serious? So we're going? I thought you had to study for a test?"

"The test? No problem. I can study on the train, right? Anyway, trains and hotels work for better for me than busses and sleeping on some church floor."

Anna's face brightened. "Hotels? Could we stay at the Governor's House Hotel? Eileen and I had high tea there last spring when we went to visit the Smithsonian."

"High tea?" Randy said. "That sounds like five stars."

"I don't know how many stars it has," Anna mused. "But you did say hotels."

Randy moved his jaw around as he thought this over. At that point, Father's monthly stipend was generous and with the interest-free student loans he took out just to collect the interest…why not start living the doctor's life early? "OK, I'll call and make a reservation."

"Fantastic! Really? The Governor House? Wait until Eileen hears about this."

Randy nodded. Why Anna and Eileen were such buds, he knew not. Anna was tie-dye and sandals, she bought her sugar at a health food store. Eileen? Heels, make-up and high tea.

"It'll be fun, but do you really think it will change anything?" Randy asked.

Anna laughed. "The rally? It will change everything. It will show the people care about how their army is employed. It will show the administration they can't just charge willy-nilly all over the world killing millions in the name of the red, white, and blue. God only knows how long this tragedy could drag on if the politicians, the defense contractors, and their lobbyists keep milking and bilking the taxpayers…The rally will cut five years off this war. Oh! I'm so glad we're going!" Anna got up and knelt next to Randy. She put her head in his lap and looked up at him.

Looking down at her face, seeing her doe eyes pleading with him, Randy's pulse rose.

"I'm going to Bloomies and get a nice warm wool beret for the weekend," she said. She got up, sat in his lap, and kissed him hard. "God, I love you. I'm so glad we're going together."

"Moi aussi, mon cheri," Randy said. Gently he ran his hand over her body, and they retreated to the bedroom for a quickie before she darted off to Bloomingdales.

*In Washington*
*Friday, November 7, 1969*

It was much later than Randy would have liked when he and Anna stood before a folding banquet table in the basement of the Georgetown University Student Union. The MOBE volunteer behind the registration table wore a tattered army field jacket with the name "Bowen" stenciled on its pocket. He wore a black armband and kept adjusting his wire-rimmed glasses in a distracted manner—as if these particular John Lennon–style glasses let him receive visuals on wavelengths the average guy could not see. What with his thinning hair hanging down to his shoulders and the fatigues, Randy thought Bowen looked like a refugee from *Doctor Zhivago*.

"We've run out of New York names," Bowen said after his dexterous fingers had thumbed several boxes of placards before him.

Randy moaned. He had stood in line for twenty minutes to pick up a fifteen-inch-wide nametag to hang around his neck on a string. Boxes behind Bowen and the other two volunteers were stacked on the floor and table, each filled with placards sorted alphabetically by state. Scrawled on cardboard tacked to the wall above the boxes was a sign that read "We ONLY hold 'Will Calls' for the friends and relatives of deceased soldiers who have phoned AHEAD. Sorry for any inconvenience."

"Give me a Missouri name," Randy said.

The MOBE volunteer scrounged in a box, handing a placard to Randy. Randy turned to Anna. "Please tell me," he said, showing her the front of the card, "the placard doesn't read 'Second Lieutenant Paul Elser'?"

"There are no ranks printed on the cards," Bowen said. "A dead soldier is a dead soldier."

Anna studied the placard. "No, it's not your brother," she said. Randy turned the card over and read the name: "Alexander Morr." Randy wondered who Morr was and if any friends and relatives were standing in line behind him, hoping to walk his name in the line of people stretching from Arlington to the White House in this event the MOBE called the March Against Death.

Then Bowen asked Anna, "Would you like a Missouri name, too?"

"Ah, no...that's all right. Let's go." Before Randy could respond, Anna had turned to go back up the stairs, past the long line of demonstrators, and back up to the street.

There, out on the street, Anna looked about. Spying a taxi, she scampered toward it. "You go ahead now that you have your name. I'll be at the prayer vigil in the National Cathedral and catch up with you later... quick, there's the bus. A bientot, mon cher," she cried, walking backward, clutching her blue wool beret against the wind. She waved.

What could Randy do? He couldn't blame her, though splitting at the last minute wasn't right either. He hopped on the yellow school bus shuttle that would take him and other marchers across the Potomac to the Arlington National Cemetery.

Going over the Potomac Bridge, Randy watched the long line of marchers going the other way, back into Washington. Almost all the marchers were men. Rain, wind, and the dark of night…didn't Anna's decision to stay warm and dry indoors make sense for a girl?

In front of the Eternal Flame dedicated to John F. Kennedy, someone handed Randy a candle. Someone else muttered, "Gotta light, Jack?"

Randy began his own March Against Death.

He wondered when would he see Anna again? In bed at the hotel? How long would the trek to the White House take?

His placard around his neck, Randy joined the long, slow-moving single-file line that hour by hour flowed from the Arlington hillside, surging across the windblown bridge over the Potomac, past the Lincoln Memorial, through side streets to burst forth at the iron gates in front of the White House.

A very symbolic and surreal thing, Randy thought. Him, his lit candle, the others…all actors in a play. Ghosts. Randy, the ghost of Alexander Morr, the name on his placard, marching down from Arlington, past the Iwo Jima statue, goin' to haunt the White House, stepping front and center forward to hold the president and the nation accountable for the loss of life, for the cost in human lives of the decision to be in Vietnam.

The first bite of reality hit Randy as he stepped out from the lee of the hill onto the bridge. There, the full gale force of the wind coming down the river hit him. A volunteer standing close to the bridge repeated as the marchers went by, "No need to keep your candle lit. You can light your candle later in town."

A MOBE staffer standing on the bridge wall while holding on to a street light bollard shivered uncontrollably. Dressed in a very damp denim jacket, he shouted down at those walking by, "March on, my brothers!" His teeth chattered so hard Randy wondered if the man might bite off his tongue or knock out a tooth. "The president is home! In four hours, you'll be heard at the White House!" The staffer's hoarse rant continued, "We all will be heard! Keep the faith, my brothers. We will all be heard!"

The marchers cheered the MOBE staffer. Some reached up to slap hands.

A few feet beyond the staffer, a drummer beat out a slow funereal cadence.

The March Against Death had begun.

Randy pulled his trench coat tight across his chest. He was warm and dry, waterproofed against all inclemencies, according to the tag on his collar. How about that guy clutching the lamppost to cheer the marchers on? Doing a great job, but did he even own a raincoat?

Randy tightened his Irish walking hat against the wind. Soldiers might be used to such inclemencies, deprivations, and weather, but it occurred to Randy that unless his car broke down somewhere out in the sticks, he might never again in his life come this close to toughing it out in raw weather for so long.

A noise behind him startled Randy. He turned around. The marcher behind him looked up with a sheepish grin. He had scuffed his shoe. He was a short, skinny, bald fellow wearing clear plastic-rimmed glasses and no hat. His placard read "Charles F Montgomery." His shoes were thin moccasin-style loafers—more suitable for a day at the office than a night in the pouring rain.

The man asked, "Do you have another cigarette?"

"Sure," Randy said. The man must've seen him smoking earlier. He offered Charles F. a cigarette.

At first, the man didn't take the cigarette. It was getting wet. Instead, he asked, "Is it a regular cigarette?"

"No," Randy said. "It's filtered."

"That isn't what I mean…" The man was older and dressed well, but not for this kind of weather. Why was he so obsequious? "Is there any marijuana in it?"

"No, it's just a regular cigarette," Randy said, again offering the cigarette to the man.

The man's shoulders drooped as he took it. "What do you want for it?"

"Nothing. You can have it. Sometimes I bum a cigarette too, if I'm out. That's just the way it is with us smokers, right? Here, take another."

The man bowed appreciatively and pulled a book of matches out of the pocket of his trench coat. He lit up. "Thanks," he said. During the ninety minutes it took to cross the bridge, Randy had three cigarettes and the man had four, going through the same cautious routine each time. One time Randy asked, "Did you serve in Korea?"

Other than an emphatic head shake, Charles F. made no answer. He appeared nervous, hunched over, like he was doing something subversive and certain people should not find out about his being in the march.

On the fourth borrowing, Randy gave the man the rest of his first pack, which still had three cigarettes in it.

"I should give you two dollars for all the cigarettes you gave me," the man said. "Except I only have a five dollar bill."

"I'm sorry," Randy said. "I don't have change."

"Here then," the man said. "Take the five, please. I mean it."

So Randy took the five-dollar bill from the man, just to make Charles F. happy, though it made no sense to Randy.

Crossing the Potomac took forever. Other than Charles F. Montgomery, Randy talked to no one. He would take a step and wait, take a step and wait.

On coming off the bridge, the pace of march quickened. An olive drab army bus crept by the other way. Some of the marchers surged onto the street. The bus slowed down but did not stop. The marchers in the street gave way.

Soldiers on the bus rolled down the windows. "Peace, baby! Peace!" They were *cheering* the marchers.

Then the sergeants took control of their troops. Moving up and down the aisle in the bus, they smacked heads and barked, "Shut up, shitheads!"

"Silence!"

"Stow it!"

In the macabre humor of soldiers, the soldiers changed their tune to "Pussies, peaceniks, Commies going to eat your lunch, perverts."

The sergeants eased up their attempts at discipline. "All right, all right. Pipe down, soldiers." The windows on the bus were put back up, the driver revved the engine, and the protestors let the bus go through against the line of march, back toward Arlington.

Randy said, "Be something if they were going to march, too."

"No," the man in front of Randy said. "Must be the riot squad. Pigs are scared shitless we're going to storm the White House. Or what we're doing will spoil their game."

"How's that?" Randy asked. "Will Tricky Dick get a whiff of mari-hootchie and challenge Chairman Mao to a game of Ping-Pong instead of nukes at ten thousand miles?"

"Don't you wish," the man said. "Not gonna happen."

"So okay, I get it," Randy speculated. He enjoyed passing the time in conversation. "We're storming the White House with twenty thousand verses of 'This little light of mine.' Like that's really hardcore."

The man's lip rose into a leer. After a stagey Lon Chaney kind of laugh, he said, "Who knows what evil lurks in the hearts of men?"

Charles F. Montgomery lit up another cigarette.

After an eternity of hours, Randy, like the marchers before him, crossed the Potomac to parade down Seventeenth Street in the shelter of the tall buildings on either side of the street. Now out of the wind, with the rain easing, Randy felt much more comfortable. Theater ropes were set up to contain the line of marchers, while behind the ropes a crowd thronged to cheer the marchers on. Some of the onlookers handed the marchers cigarettes, cups of coffee, matchbooks, and pieces of bread and apples.

The candles were relit before turning a final corner.

Then there it was: the White House.

One by one, the marchers stepped up on a wooden platform set in front of the tall wrought iron fence that ran along the White House grounds. A MOBE staffer stood on either side of the platform as each marcher in turn stood alone on the platform, looked up over the black wrought iron fence, and uttered the name of their dead soldier.

Most of the marchers used nothing louder than a normal conversational voice, though sometimes someone would really sing out a name:

"James Johnson!"

"Arnie Stevens!"

Sometimes Randy saw a man stomp his feet before stepping up on the platform. Bam! Bam!

Then the klieg lights would go up and the marcher would shout, "Mr. President. Matthew Guthrie! Where has he gone? Why, Mr. President? Why?"

The crowd would then erupt in cheers.

"Right on!"

Things moved quickly. The urge to really sing out grew within Randy. His resolve became more and more certain. It was his turn now.

He mounted the steps to the platform. *Boom, boom.* This was insane. Sound off to the big man. He stomped his feet again. The strobe lights, the bright TV lights came on, brighter than day. Randy steeled himself. In the long line of march he had been anonymous. Now his words could be recorded for all the nation to hear. He felt dizzy.

As the bright lights glowed and photojournalists took pictures, Randy stared at the small second-story window where the MOBE volunteer pointedly said the president actually sat. What? Like a king on his throne, with subject after subject petitioning him for hours.

Only a split second went by, but it stretched out into forever. Randy cleared the muddled thoughts from his head. He shouted, "Why did Alexander Morr have to die, Mr. President? How many more soldiers must you march to their deaths before you satisfy your faulty peace with honor?" He trembled now; he burned as the adrenaline surged through his body. He asked, "Who'll be the last to die, Mr. President? Do you even know what the hell you are doing?" Louder and louder, until he was dying for a gasp of air. Stooped and winded, with the last of his breath, he shouted, "What's it all about, Tricky Dickey?"

That's when he realized he'd become so caught up in the emotion of the thing that he'd forgotten to inhale. He felt quite weak. The volunteers on either side of the platform reached up to help him down off the platform.

"You were great!" one of the volunteers said.

"Breathe deeply, you're among friends," the other said.

"Thanks," Randy said. He was quite dizzy. He thought he heard one of the photojournalists say "cover of *Time* magazine."

Randy liked that.

Down on the pavement, away from the TV lights, an onlooker said, "You said it, brother."

Randy took large draughts of the crisp night air and slapped hands down a reception line, stopping as some slapped him on the back while others clasped his hand "brothers" style, palms up, as he was debriefed from his encounter with the president and the media.

At the end of the reception line, another MOBE organizer appeared, urging Randy to deposit his name in a coffin by the Jackson Equestrian statue on the Ellipse, pointing out the direction. A volunteer further down the way added, "The names will be delivered to Congress on Monday."

Then Randy saw Anna stand up and walk toward him. She had been waiting by the White House fence. She greeted him warmly. "Your voice was so loud and deep," she said. "I loved it!"

Randy rubbed his throat. "Thank you," he said, dropping his voice to a whisper as he rubbed his throat. "Wow, I may have screamed too hard. My throat feels so raw now." They walked on to the square on the South Lawn, where Randy set Alexander Morr's placard in one of the many coffins that were filling up under the hooves of General Jackson's horse.

His duty discharged, tired but with a sense of accomplishment, Randy quickened his steps. Soon he was all but running. Anna kept up with him. They held hands, running down the sidewalk to the warmth of the Governor's House Hotel.

# 10

## HO, HO, HO CHI MINH

*Randy*
*Saturday, November 15, 1969*

Randy and Anna were up most of the night, talking and renewing acquaintanceships with each other's bodies. They arrived early on the Capitol Mall, where Randy spread out a picnic blanket within one hundred yards of the tall stage that had been set up in front of an outstanding backdrop: the Capitol building.

Besides going to the National Cathedral yesterday evening, Anna had gone shopping. Consequently, her canvas boat bag was stuffed with bagels, cheese, grapes, dry roasted almonds, watercress sandwiches, paper napkins, and Chablis with plastic wine glasses for later. For the morning, Randy's thermos contained strong coffee. In front of them, the atmosphere was like lawn seating at an outdoor concert. But not too far behind them, the rally-goers still stood. They stood row on row until eventually the crowd poured out way past the Washington Monument, three hundred thousand, four hundred thousand, half a million strong, depending on who did the counting.

Eventually the MOBE emcee came out on the huge stage, welcoming everyone as if we were all old friends. His voice booming over the large speakers and frequently interrupted by applause, he said, "AT&T donated these speakers. Let's give them a hand for setting them up in last night's rain. They're the same type of box used at Woodstock." His voice came through speaker towers the size of billboards, reaching hundreds of thousands, sounding soft, clear, and personable. The speakers bracketed the highly elevated stage and were mounted on towers every 150 yards or so clear back to the Washington Monument on both the sides of the gathering.

Wavy Gravy of the Hog Farm then stepped forward. "Hey! How're y'all doing? Isn't this amazing?" The crowd cheered. "Earlier, members of my Arizona commune, the Hog Farm, passed out thousands of kazoos. If you didn't get one, I'm awful sorry. We had no idea how many of you would show up." More cheers. "If you did get one, or if you didn't, you are about to take part in the world's biggest kazoo concert. C'mon, everybody, I know you know the tune. It's Howdy Doody time!"

Many of the crowd, Randy and Anna for sure, knew Howdy Doody as the puppet host of a 1950's TV cartoon show from their childhood. The instrumental version of "The Howdy Doody Show Theme Song" went over very well.

Next, a Dr. Benjamin Spock was introduced. "That's right," Dr. Spock said as he took the microphone. "I'm not the Star Trek Spock, but Spock, the one who helped bring you up. It has been said that many parents considered my *Baby and Child Care* the most consulted reference book in the house, more so than the dictionary and I shudder as I say this, the Bible. Oh, that many of these same people would listen to me—and to YOU—now!" More cheers from the crowd.

Anna whispered, "Did your Mum have a copy? Mine did."

Dick Gregory, the black comedian turned activist, and William Sloan Coffin, the Yale chaplain and co-organizer of the March Against Death, both congratulated the crowd on being there. In all, the event was well-orchestrated and peaceful to the point of mellowness. One of the speakers said, "This summer, Neil Armstrong took a big step forward for mankind on the moon. With this moratorium on the war, right now, democracy has taken a big step forward right here in Washington—thanks to you all."

When Coretta Scott King, widow of the slain civil rights leader Martin Luther King Jr. came to the microphone, she spoke in her husband's words on Vietnam.

She quoted him: "Don't let anybody make you think that God chose America as his divine messianic force to be a sort of policeman for the whole world. God has a way of standing before the nations with judgment, and it seems that I can hear God saying to America, 'You are too arrogant. If you don't change your ways, I will rise up and break the backbone of your power, and I will place it in the hands of a nation that doesn't even know my name.'"

"Wow," Randy said. "That's heavy stuff."

Anna agreed. They opened the Chablis. The day had warmed up. Randy took off his coat.

The Broadway cast of *Hair* performed "The Age of Aquarius" and the title song to the musical.

It was a good time. Randy and Anna stretched out on their blanket. Randy wore tailored jeans, Frye boots, and a suede jacket. Anna wore a cable knit sweater, a beret, jeans, and even a little mascara and blush, which was unusual for her. It seemed a perfect day, like attending a symphony in the park. The crowd applauded at all the right cues. Randy and Anna were good citizens, supporting a smooth and reasonable view of foreign affairs. Surely, Washington decision-makers could see all this. Some of them, Randy heard, were even in the crowd.

But even as the cast from *Hair* cleared the stage, mayhem erupted.

A long, single file of men dressed in deepest black snaked their way up to the stage from the far right, from 15th Street NW. As they marched, the men chanted low and deep, "Ho! Ho! Ho!"

The lead man carried a large red pole like a drum major would.

Given the wacky air of the day and the proximity to Christmas, Randy sighed, "God, what's this? Jolly Santa and his elves? Advertising from a local department store?"

Then the veneer of well-being vanished.

Shouting louder and louder, the intruders cried out, "Ho! Ho! Ho Chi Minh!"

The bunting on the red pole unfurled; it became a large red flag with a gold star in the middle. The leader waved it high in the air. The intruders stood in for the North Vietnamese!

"What are you jerks doing?" Randy shouted as he jumped to his feet. Their path would bring them within yards of where Randy sat with Anna sipping their Chablis.

Randy dropped his plastic wine glass. He bolted through the crowd. He shouted, "Get that flag out of here!"

He repeated it. "Get that flag out of here!" Others picked up his chant. "Get that flag out of here!" The refrain was repeated over and over.

Randy walked up to the flag bearer. He grabbed the staff of the flag. "Put it down!" he shouted.

"Ho, ho, Ho Chi Minh," the flag bearer said, a blond guy who looked more like someone you might find out surfing or laying out on the beach. Later, Randy read in an underground paper that the guy could have been Ralph Arnold, a UC Berkeley dropout, formerly from Whitebread, Nebraska.

The flag-bearer said, "Vietnam for the Vietnamese."

"Oh yeah?" Randy said. "You wanna be Vietnamese? Go to Vietnam yourself! Get that flag out of here!"

Others began to tear the flag away from its pole.

"Get that flag out of here!" said the people all around.

"Let's have order!" came the well-modulated voice of the MOBE emcee. "Security is being summoned. Security, the disturbance is up front, house right." The silence following the MOBE organizer's announcement had substance to it.

Then Wavy Gravy stepped up to the mike. "Everything is cool, my brothers and sisters. Softly now, let's get it together. We all know the words. Let's sing the song. 'All we are saying is, give peace a chance.'"

The intruders, the erstwhile North Vietnamese stand-ins, were accompanied off the Mall by the DC police to the crowd's vocal support.

Randy walked back to rejoin Anna. He was high on adrenaline, pleased the brouhaha had such an easy resolution.

Anna asked, "Were they armed?" Her face was tense. She did not look comfortable.

Randy shrugged. "Don't know. Didn't have time to ask. All I know is they were a strange cluster-clutch of jokers." He made a funny face.

They both laughed.

It was a sunny day. The peaceful assembly continued into the night but Randy and Anna took the 5:43 back to Penn Station.

# 11

## CAMBODIAN INCURSION

*Paul*
*In the field, III Corps, RVN*

*Wednesday, May 6, 1970*

After ten days on patrol, all Lt. Paul Elser and his platoon could think about was returning to the relative comfort and security of Fire Support Base Bunker. They'd be there soon, too. Lt. Paul could hear the thumping of helicopter blades in the distance. All twenty-three men were dug in by the edge of a clearing in the jungle west of Pleiku. No casualties. Praise God.

A shower and a change of uniform, a few hours of what passed for real sleep, and life would be good again.

They were three days away from their last encounter with Charlie, but in the bush, ambush was ever present. Charlie—the name given the North Vietnamese soldiers, for Victor Charlie, VC, Vietnamese communist—was everywhere. Only three nights ago, the platoon's night defense position had been attacked.

But as the helicopter sound drew nearer, it rose in pitch.

Sharpie, the radio operator, cupped his hand over his headset. He said, "They want us to pop green smoke."

"Pop green smoke," Lt. Paul said to Sergeant Archer. A flare spewing green smoke was launched into the air so the helicopter pilot would be able to spot the platoon's location.

What was up with that high-pitched tinny sound? They were expecting a much deeper sound—something dark and deep, whump-whump-

whump like the Huey helicopters—that had dropped them in the jungle seven days ago.

Then a solitary light observation helicopter (loach) flared overhead and set down in the middle of the clearing. As it set down, Lt. Paul saw seated in the bubble cockpit a pilot and a passenger: the battalion commander, Lt. Col. Francis Marion.

Yes, Lt. Col. Francis Marion, the Swamp Fox, an eighth-generation American patriot, the commanding officer of the battalion, had come out here. Why? No one considered Lt. Col. Francis a blowhard or a fool. No sir, the men knew Marion as right-on and always ready for the battle, the Swamp Fox. This Lt. Col. Francis Marion stepped down to the ground with a canty swagger.

*What's with this?*

Paul caught the glint in Lt. Col. Marion's eye. Despite his fatigue, Lt. Paul could sense it. Something was up. But weren't American troops being withdrawn daily? Wasn't the war rapidly winding down? Weren't old soldiers like Lt. Col. Marion supposed to be fading away? What was up with this strange appearance of the commanding officer in his garrison-best uniform out in the middle of the jungle, poised as if he expected everyone to stand at attention in the middle of the jungle, salutes and all?

No one saluted anyone in the bush. Hell, even rank insignia was low-key.

But this man, this American patriot, this Lt. Col. Francis Marion said, "Assemble the men."

Like ghosts, the men left the foxholes of their night-defensive position to huddle in what, under field conditions, could even be described as a parade formation! Only three sentry posts remained manned.

As if that weren't brazen enough, then Lt. Col. Francis Marion, lean, clean-shaven, haircut high and tight, snapped open his Zippo lighter and lit up a smoke right out there in Indian country!

What would he not do to draw fire?

"Gentlemen," the battalion commander said after taking a puff of his cigarette. "President Richard Nixon has authorized an invasion into Cambodia."

For an eternity of seconds, no one said a thing. Though everyone must have felt it. Lt. Paul sure did. No soldier's soldier he, but you didn't need to be in the bush around Pleiku long to know Charlie had a refuge, a sanctuary, in Cambodia. The American rules of engagement made it clear: Americans forces will honor the border. They do not cross into Cambodia. Until now. Until rule-breaking, garrison-gear-in-the-bush, cigarette-smoking-in-the-bush Lt. Col. Francis Marion shows up authorizing exactly such action.

Then radioman Sharpie, Cpl. William Sharp, spoke unofficially for the whole platoon. He said, "The son of a bitch."

Oh, Sharpie didn't say it loud. But his voice carried. All eyes turned to Sharpie and then to the Swamp Fox. Lt. Col. Francis Marion—days away from retirement—insistent on serving to the end of his army days in the field—how would the Swamp Fox respond to an enlisted man slurring the commander-in-chief?

The Swamp Fox scanned the eyes of the whole platoon. If you looked hard, the faintest of smiles, the wryest of crinkles, broke out on the face of this battle-tested veteran.

"That's right, men," the Swamp Fox said. "Our commander-in chief *is* a warrior. He has authorized one last blow for liberty, one last punch before we leave, to give our allies, the South Vietnamese, a toehold chance to keep their borders secure."

As this news sunk in, as fresh adrenaline appeared to seep into the blood of these war-weary men, Paul could even see the men standing taller, breathing deeper, and living larger. It was almost as if they did get their hot showers, their clean uniforms, their five-day stand-down, eating meals in comfort and sleeping in the relative security of a forward fire base.

Hit the NVA where they felt secure.

Destroy the Cambodian stockpiles.

Yes, sir!

Hoo ahh!

Yet, wait one. Why did the lieutenant colonel announce it here, in the field, especially to the First Platoon of C Company 3/24?

Could it be the First Platoon, C Company, Third Brigade, Twenty-Fourth Battalion would be sent on this mission? Immediately?

"Yes," Lt. Col. Marion said. "You men, First Platoon, C Company are the best. I want you to eat hearty."

As if at his cue, a second helicopter landed, a Huey this time, and it brought coffee, sausage, and French toast in mermac containers.

As the field formation broke, Sgt. Archer echoed Paul's thoughts. "The Swamp Fox is saying Cambodia and I'm hearing…we won't be seeing FSB Bunker today."

Paul gave Archer a knowing nod. Limber, quick, and clever, Archer had been the one who set the platoon up for the successful ambush a few nights ago. The product of a swashbuckling lineage of African, Mexican, and Polynesian blood, Archer called the army home for life.

Lt. Col. Marion's aide-de-camp had come in the Huey supply ship. He motioned for Paul to report to Lt. Col. Marion. The aide also brought the Swamp Fox some coffee.

"Lieutenant Elser," the Swamp Fox said as he began walking back to his loach, Paul sticking by his side and the aide-de-camp following. The Swamp Fox said it again. "Your men, First Platoon, Corsair Company, are the best the 3/24 has." He was shouting now, handing his coffee cup back to the aide. Over the thrashing of the rotors, the Swamp Fox added, "I want them to lead the assault."

"Yes, sir," Paul said. Then the Swamp Fox was gone. Paul returned to Sgt. Archer and to his now-cold breakfast.

"What'd Swamp Fox say, LT?" Sergeant Archer asked.

"He wants us to lead the assault on Cambodia," Paul said.

"Us?" Archer asked as his syrup-soaked toast dissolved in his mouth. "Our platoon? We're due to rotate in. What about Fourth Platoon? They're due out next."

Paul almost lost his bacon. He coughed as he washed it down with coffee. "I didn't see The Fox asking *them*," he said. "He came out here to see us. He said we're the best."

Now it was Archer's turn to choke. He horsed down his dried eggs. As shocking as this may have been to him, his voice was calm as he asked, "You want me to break the word to the men by squads, LT?"

Paul shook his head. "No," he said. "No. Not you. Let Kowalski do it. I don't want you going out on this one, Sarge. We've got to get you back to Saigon. You're way too short. Four days and you're out of here. Going home. You should be reassigned to warehouse duty or something, way away from fire.

"Then, once you're out of the Nam, get yourself some leave, be with your wife when the baby's born. Isn't this your first?"

The two men exchanged a glance. Talk of babies. They could almost be a couple of civilians talking in a coffee shop back in Saint Louis, Detroit, or somewhere back in the world.

Archer laughed softly. "Yes, sir," he said. "It is our, my, first. Oh shit, LT. What chance is there, really, of something like that happening? I'm all for it, but then again, I got to be there when Charlie gets his nose caught in the grinder." Archer groaned as if not being there would be a personal loss.

Paul took a deep breath. This was Archer's second tour. He called the NVA "Charlie" without malice, as if life and death didn't hang in the balance. "Let me at least put in the request," Paul said. "If it's granted, you will get the hell away from here. Understood, Sergeant?" Paul usually didn't take such a stern tone with either Archer or Kowalski. They were lifers. On patrol, they were the platoon's logistics, tactics, and survival. Sometimes, like now, Paul's job was more about being the voice of reason when confusion was the order of the day.

Archer's eyes widened. "Yes, sir," he said and passed the orders on to Sgt. Kowalski.

*Archer*, Paul thought. He took far too many risks for even a career soldier.

Sharpie, the platoon radio operator, never far from Lt. Paul's side, heard these last remarks. He fumed, kicking the ground.

Paul asked, "What's the problem, Sharpie? Leech in your boot?"

"No, LT. It's just…are we really cav assaulting Cambodia right away?"

"'Fraid so," Paul said. "The Swamp Fox didn't come all the way out here just to show off his shiny new brass belt buckle, you know. It's resupply now and CA (cavalry assault) at 1100 hours."

Sharpie made no audible reply.

"There you have it," Paul said. "He said *we're the best*."

Sharpie, a lank and nervous nineteen-year-old with an acne problem, pushed his glasses up the bridge of his nose. The strap that kept them in place was broken. *Sharpie*, Paul thought, *possibly the weakest man in the unit*. Yet he carried the heavy PRC 45 field radio in addition to his personal supplies and some armaments. He bore hardship coolly, but give him an idle moment and he became unglued.

So Lt. Paul gave him a task. "Did you take your orange bomber, Sharp? It's Monday." The "bomber" was an antimalarial pill the size of a plumb that everyone took weekly.

"I'm on it," Sharpie said and disappeared.

Up in the skies over Vietnam, the air was cool. With the platoon—thirty-two men in four Huey helicopters, bellies full, bodies rehydrated with hearty swigs of fresh water—Lt. Paul recalled his unit's last encounter with Charlie. After they set up their night bivouac, Sgt. Archer studied the foliage and the ground around the clearing. He brought a tiny Vietnamese coin to Lt. Paul. He said, "We're on a VC trail here."

Paul waited. "Go ahead," he said.

"I suggest we continue digging in, but about 2130, I'd like to—very quietly—move the men out to the west and northern perimeters of the clearing and dig in again."

Kowalski had used this tactic before, without action. But Paul trusted his sergeants. "Very well, Archer," Paul said. "Go ahead. We'll dig in twice."

Kowalski and Archer broke the news to their squad leaders, and the ruse was carried out. Out in the bush, that was the way to spread news like that, quietly, one to one.

This time the extra caution paid off big time. At around 0300 hours that night, Charlie rushed up on the platoon's old foxholes, rifles firing madly. Oh, they must've thought themselves the clever ones, baby. They must have thought they were beautiful, catching First Platoon napping.

Charlie paid dearly for his blunder. Twelve of them would study war no more…

And twenty-three Americans just got one breath closer to catching the freedom bird back to the World that sent them to exotic Vietnam, the place of the bizarre maneuvers.

Oh yes, Paul knew First Platoon Corsairs were the best. There were only two reasons why: their names were Sergeants Archer and Kowalski. As for this foray into Cambodia, Lt. Paul read what there was of the battle plans and studied the assault maps. What were they in for?

# 12

## EAGLE FLIGHT CAMBODIA

*Paul*
*Wednesday, May 6, 1970*

At twenty-five hundred feet over Vietnam, the air may have been cool and pollen free, but fresh it was not—the engine exhaust, the engine noise, and the buffeting of the ship in the wind saw to that. Lt. Paul and the First Platoon were in the lead four slicks of the air cavalry assault that tore down the valley at 125 knots directly over route 14A, straight for Cambodia.

Is there anything more primeval in intensity than charging into combat? Paul calmed himself by focusing on the numbers. At eight troops to a slick, the two thousand–some soldiers in Companies A and C made for a line of 125 Hueys all pouring into Cambodia on orders from the powers above that decided such things.

Once Companies A and C established the forward base, the other half of the battalion would join them. Even now, they convoyed up Route 14a to join them at the border.

Lt. Paul rode in the lead bird. From his perch between the seats of the pilot and copilot, he saw the headwaters of the Chhlong River to the north. The UH-1 Huey flared into a hover and dropped much like a hawk might on seeing prey below. Lt. Paul resumed his seat and did a quick check on his weapon. They came down to just above the treetops and crested a hill. Next to Lt. Paul on the bench, Sgt. Kowalski readied himself by the port door. On a hot landing, when the helicopter received enemy fire on setting down, Kowalski often charged out first. By doing so, he reasoned, the element of surprise still worked in his favor. Few soldiers argued the logic.

The column of orange smoke they'd seen from above appeared again on their low pass. This marked the landing zone. The forward air controller (FAC) must have spent an intense few hours preparing the landing zone…waiting for the troops to arrive…sweating it that the troops would arrive and fortify the zone before the NVA discovered what was up.

And the landing zone covered some ground. It had to be the size of the playing field at Riverfront Stadium, four times over. It was hard to believe the NVA did not know something big was about to shatter their stronghold. The place had been blasted out of thick jungle with Bangalore torpedoes, long thin pipes filled with explosives, and armored bulldozers called Rome plows. That's how the combat engineers did such things.

Not a quiet operation at all.

The 125 slicks set down in groups of eight, the men gushing out, the Huey slicks setting down and lifting off within seconds, clearing the way for the flight behind them. The machines flew in and out of the LZ smoothly and rapidly; the deployment of the 3/24 was thus established on the ground. A few of the platoons would stay behind to secure the landing zone. Others, namely First Platoon, Corsair Company, would move out, entering Cambodia in a matter of minutes.

With the troops landed, the forward air controller turned his focus to the small planes patrolling the area for enemy presence. He would coordinate any and all air defense of this place, called Landing Zone (LZ) Nathan. Air support for LZ Nathan and for the ground pounder into Cambodia would be provided by Cobra attack helicopters, "fast movers," or jet fighters, and "spooky," the C130 gunship outfitted with Gatling guns and napalm.

While all these precautions were as prudent as they were expensive, so far there had been no enemy fire.

Once the second half of the battalion arrived by truck with medical and commissary supplies, LZ Nathan would be reinforced and transformed to FSB Nathan.

The Swamp Fox presided over all these proceedings, hovering in his bubble cockpit loach. "Move out," he commanded.

Lt. Paul and the First/Corsairs began the march east. Yesterday, Charlie had sanctuary in Cambodia. Today, the self-imposed rules of engagement prohibiting US entry into the country had been suspended by the president himself.

"Clean out Charlie's Cambodian lair."

"Yes, sir."

The three platoons of the company fanned out, with Lt. Paul and First/Corsairs in the middle slot, assuring their participation in any firefights. Fourth Platoon was placed in the back to reinforce the lead platoons as needed or as "sweep up" to pick off any NVA who fled in their direction.

Still no enemy contact.

In fact, the village of My Thiet, Cambodia, offered the first contact with any people at all. The three lead platoons entered the village moving cautiously from covered position to covered position. Entering villages always called for extreme care. The dangers ranged from bombs to enemy fire to women and children used as shields by non-uniformed adversaries. It was not unknown for small children to approach soldiers with gifts that contained bombs…a gut-wrencher every time. While from a distance, My Thiet looked to be the same kind of subsistence farming village typical of those Lt. Paul had seen in South Vietnam—but Sharpie gave voice to the obvious difference. He said, "Look at all the military-age men here."

"They're not doing much farm work, either," Lt. Paul said as he scanned the thatched huts. These young men idled in the village, lounged in the huts, and squatted and talked among themselves. Typically when First/Corsairs saw men of this age and physique, they were armed and out for the kill. When they entered a typical South Vietnamese farming village, the village housed women, old men, and children. Military aged men? No way.

On rounding up the military aged men, more peculiarities became clear. Hair was cropped short, hands were callous free, and not a water buffalo among the lot. Yet they denied being NVA, neither could any weapons be found.

At that point, Swamp Fox, up in his circling helicopter, radioed, "Tire tracks to the northeast. Better take a look."

First Platoon Corsairs, 3/24, continued toward their objective, an arms depot linked into the notorious Ho Chi Minh Trail, which was actually a network of roads and dirt tracks used by the NVA to ship arms and supplies down from North Vietnam to support their offensive in South Vietnam.

These supplies included AKs from the Soviet Union and grenades from China.

The company fanned out as it entered jungle canopy, heading in the direction of the truck-tire tracks Lt. Col. Francis Marion had seen from his light observation helicopter. The Cambodian incursion ran rife with the thrill of the hunt, and Paul's senses responded with heightened vigilance as he scanned the terrain before him, listening and smelling for signs of danger.

The terrain was open enough at ground level, but dark. Little sunlight penetrated to the ground due to the thick canopy above. *What an exotic, beautiful place*, Lt. Paul thought. There was danger from the environment as well as the enemy.

The first enemy contact occurred at 1400 hours. A staccato burst of AK-47 fire opened up in front of First Platoon. Everyone took cover, dropping to the ground. Lt. Paul spit out a red ant.

Sharpie identified the source of the machine gun fire. "Spider hole at one-thirty, sixty meters," he whispered. A spider hole was a deep hole with brush on top acting like a flip-top lid that concealed an NVA rifleman—a common NVA tactic. The NVA soldier would pop up out of the spider hole, shoot, then conceal himself. One had to be quick to spot him or, if the light was right, the puff of smoke lingering to mark the spot.

That day, the light was right. The smoke lingered. Private O'Brian hit the spider hole dead on with a rocket-fired grenade. Then, about fifteen meters to the left, almost straight ahead, the explosion flushed another spider. Did he figure his position would soon be discovered by the approaching Americans? Whatever the case, he jumped out of his hole, running toward the approaching Americans and firing his AK from a running crouch.

"I got him!" Williams shouted. The NVA soldier fell.

Then O'Brian shouted, "Cover!"

The next NVA spider popped up practically beside the line of march. Shooting at him could backfire as there were friendly troops behind the spider on both sides. The NVA had the upper hand until Cpl. Cory loaded up an RPG. The spider abandoned cover, running down the slope, against the line of march. Private O'Brian dropped him with a burst from his M-16.

The company continued forward up a ridge that had started as a gentle rise, but now approached 8 percent. They passed several abandoned spider holes, the lids flung wide open. Captain Walters—his radio call sign Corsair 6, Lt. Paul's immediate superior—radioed, "Get ready. All those NVA won't run forever. They're jumping back to somewhere…"

"Affirmative," Swamp Fox echoed. His command and control loach helicopter offered an everywhere-at-once view of all the combat action. While he may have a great view, as Lt. Paul saw the arrangement, using the loach reminded him of a man seated on a dunk bench at the state fair. Lt. Col. Francis's front row seat carried just too high a price tag, so far as Lt. Paul could see. Talk about a single-minded adrenaline junkie. Hooo-eeee.

Although Lt. Paul had seen more enemy action when out on other patrols through the bush, the difference here was the size of the operation. The four platoons of C Company Corsairs, plus Dagger, Eagle, and Bravo companies, in total some seven hundred–plus troops, and all the air support from Cobra gunship helicopters and artillery—there really was quite a bit going on, all coordinated by radio. Sharpie was good at picking out the various frequencies. The Swamp Fox passed on the order for an artillery barrage to a forward air controller who spotted the action and called in the coordinates as he flew above the action in a single-engine plane. In an easy drawl, the FAC patched into Lt. Paul's radio frequency to give him an update: "How y'all doing? I'm going to walk arty up the hill for you, sweep off the doormat and ring the doorbell so Mr. Charles knows he's got company in a big way."

Paul, the platoon sergeants, and the whole platoon continued their climb up the ridge, being careful to stay a good 150 meters behind the curtain of 105 mm artillery shells that the artillery battery was now "walking up the hill" in front of the platoon. This barrage motivated more NVA spiders to evacuate their holes, though countless others received fatal concussions as they hunkered down in their holes.

As another spider abandoned his hole, running toward the approach of First Platoon, Sgt. Archer groaned. "Looks like Charlie'd rather die by a marksman's personal touch. No thanks on tha arty concussion stuff."

Damn! Paul felt his jaw clench. Archer shouldn't be here. And being here, he shouldn't carry on like some kind of action hero defying death one last time.

He, of all the platoon, should be keeping low. Four days to DEROS and going home. Four days to being with his wife, being there for the birth of his child.

The request for Archer's relief had been denied.

Then the shelling stopped. Sgt. Archer and his squad swung forward fast and low. They looked over the ridge from the left flank. Time crept by. Where were they? What did they see?

Then Cpl. Williams, Archer's radio man called: "Sierra Lima. Sierra Lima, we've found the swag." Sierra Lima was Lt. Paul's call sign.

"Affirmative," Lt. Paul said. "What's your pos?"

"We're on it! The Swamp Fox had it right!" Cpl. Williams gushed. "In the target area. We see the tire tracks. Over the other side of the ridge. More canopy. There are pallets four-foot cubed, crates of 7.62 ammo, Rooskie. Fifty of them, about ten meters apart, raised wooden walkways between them-a monsoon precaution maybe."

Paul cut in over him. "Archer, secure your position," he said. "Take cover." Damn! Why did Archer jump ahead like that? He was way too exposed. It sounded like he was not just observing the arms stash—he was in it!

The radio was crackling. On the battalion frequency, Paul heard Dagger Company found another stash cold, no enemy fire.

The caches were no surprise to anyone. They were a known commodity. But why were they abandoned? Were they rigged to blow up? Then too, what about all those military-aged men in My Thiet? Deserters? Dispersed for the duration of the American incursion? Discharged? Where were the officers? What should be done with the My Thiet lot? Were there other NVA lying in ambush?

Oh yes, those were all A-1 professional questions to ask, but the one that worked Lt. Paul over had to do with Archer. What to bloody do about Sgt. Archer? Why did Archer move his men so far out ahead of the rest of the platoon?

Lt. Paul did not like this at all. Then came the worst: Archer on the radio. "LT, we're taking fire."

"Where's the fire coming from?" Paul asked. Together he and Archer requested arty against the hill on the other side of the arms cache.

Sgt. Archer's squad got cut off. Then Cpl. Williams radioed, "We're low on ammo."

Williams! Archer! Short of ammo in an ammo dump? Lt. Paul keyed the mike. "Can you use Charlie's swag?"

"Negative," Cpl. Williams reported back. "Plenty of ammo, but the AKs are still packed in cosmoline." Cosmoline was an anticorrosive grease. It would take a good long rubbing with a cloth and plenty of gun oil to ready these guns for use.

Cpl. William again: "Medic! Medic! Archer's hit!"

No! Not Archer. Hell. War has fooled another man. None of us are as immortal as we might feel when the adrenaline takes hold.

*Two Letters Home*

Dear Linda,

The company secured a very large cache of enemy arms and supplies this week. Did you see us on the news? The TV cameras came out— along with just about every general in Military Assistance Command-Vietnam. Army life never ceases to amaze me. One day we were in a combat zone, the next morning, we're issued clean uniforms, shaving gear, and "It's Stan Mathers and the CBS Evening News live from III Corps, South Vietnam."

I'm blessed with a great unit. We don't take chances, we're soldiers doing a job. The men here are very dedicated to preserving liberty. Speaking of that TV spot, did you see it? Major General Ernie Vaulter, commander of all III Corp, comes over to inspect our enemy cache and speak with the news. Afterward, he addresses the troops saying, "You'll all be leaving this place, going home soon." Remember that shaving cream I mentioned earlier? Some of the men in Fourth Platoon used it to spray peace signs all over the trees in their area.

One of their troopers (ours are much more disciplined) shouts back to MG Vaulter, "Man, I don't ever want to leave this place. I love it here!"

As for me, I'm ready to leave this place yesterday. I count the days until I am home again.

Loving you babe,
Paul

Hey Randy,

Thanks for your thoughtful letter. We don't have much time here for reflection; it's all about action and orders, orders and action. But widening the war? No. It's not like that at all. We did capture quite a trophy this week: a big ammo supply depot in Cambodia. The action was designed, I believe, more to motivate our South Vietnamese allies than for America to take over all of Southeast Asia. C'mon, who's feeding you that bull? The South Vietnamese will soon run the whole show themselves. We're out of here. Let me respond frankly to something I picked up in your letter. We, you and I—everybody—none of us should ever take the rule of law for granted. There is too much in human nature working against it. The law may work in America today, and may it forevermore, too, amen. But it comes at a price. I'm all for fair play for one and all. If I've seen things here, and I have, it's chaos, barbarity, man's inhumanity to man. No thank you to all of that.

Speaking, in a general way as I am, of civilization (and giving me a chance to keep my penmanship up, it's been a while since I wrote a page) right now I'm at Cam Ranh Bay. We have ice here. Loads of ice. Let me tell you, with no electricity in the field, ice is a luxury. It is like gold. Rarely, ice may be flown out to a firebase but only in meager supply. To suck on one cube is a luxury in this heat and humidity. But these rear areas—the big bases back in Saigon and Cam Ranh Bay—have ice by the bucketful. Lovin' it here for that reason.

In closing, have you been to see the Cards lately? I dream often of being up there in the bleachers at Riverside watching Lou and Jose do their thing.

Peace,
Your bro,
Paul

# 13

## AT THE LINCOLN MEMORIAL

*Randy*
*Saturday, May 9, 1970*

Four college students were killed by Ohio National Guardsman at Kent State University.

"Outrageous!"

Randy B. Allen wasn't the only one outraged by this event. Hundreds of Kent State students had gathered at the central commons to hear fiery speeches in condemnation of President Richard Nixon's April 29 TV announcement. In the broadcast, he had confirmed and supported the "secret bombings" of Cambodia.

College students everywhere across the nation rose in protest. Kent State was not the only place to suffer casualties. Bonfires were lit; objects were thrown at police cars. In the eyes of college students and others around the country, the selling of the war fared no better than its prosecution.

"One of the women killed by the guardsmen only wanted to walk to her class. Just crossing campus. How rowdy is that? How does that justify her death?"

Randy heard a rumor that one of the guardsmen couldn't see too well. There were wearing gas masks that didn't fit over glasses. "What was he doing pulling a trigger? Was he being attacked-even with a baseball bat?"

No, not at all.

A slogan of the time said "War is unhealthy for children and other living things." About that same time, the Cuyohoga River caught on fire. It seemed even industry, the economy, had become unhealthy for children and other living things. The Cuyohoga wasn't the only geography rife with the offal of industry, either. "What kind of world are we building for ourselves?" Randy asked. "Where's the profit in being richest man on the planet when the world has become one big shit-pile?"

"Temper, temper," Anna soothed.

Like many young people who felt powerless facing a culture-turned-killing-machine, Randy and Anna looked for something they could do to defy the onslaught.

In lower Manhattan, construction workers laid down their tools at an office tower building site to go beat up war protestors. It was said the president commended the hardhats' "initiative."

The trip to Washington last November for the Mobilization to End the War in Vietnam (MOBE) had touched Randy's patriotic nerve. He quoted Jefferson: "When the people fear their government, there is tyranny; when the government fears the people, there is liberty."

Randy's read on Jefferson made Anna laugh. She said, "Dear one, Jefferson did more than vocalize versus the British. He urged taking up arms."

"Given our present circumstances, that's a bit extreme," Randy replied. "Democracy appeared to work just fine last November. And another rally will happen May 9. Let's go," he added.

Anna agreed to join him. "We're a little late for the cherry blossoms on the tidal basin," she added. "But it's worth a try."

Randy, more animated, responded, "Of course it's worth a try! I can't just stand idly by while the government raids Cambodia! Kills college students for what? In the name of submitting to the madness? No way!"

But no sooner did Randy drive his rental car by the White House in the early morning than he could see the city had changed. In May 1970, the hatches were battened down; the city prepared to fend off—a siege.

Parked bumper to bumper around the White House, a barricade of busses sealed the bastion of democracy off like a wall around a medieval castle. Yes, the hatches were battened down, the drawbridge lifted. No way was the casual visitor or tourist going to be strutting over to lay words on Mr. Prez.

As for cruising by the Mall, the grassy expanse between the White House and the Capitol Building, no large stage had been set up with a program including amplifiers, speaker towers, and acts from Broadway.

There would be no shout-out marches to the gates of the White House.

And no coffins filled with names on cardboard slips delivered to Congress on Monday morning.

Seeing the shape of things as they were, as Randy parked the car, he envisioned Nixon as a drowning man bobbing up and down in a life-preserver, thrown overboard in stormy seas.

As the sun rose, the crowd forming out on the Mall…that scene was freaky in its own way. It was pure chaos. People milled around with all kinds of signs, some of which made sense to Randy:

"Stop the Bombing, Bring home the Troops."

"Would you drink Cuyahoga River water?"

"Don't Fool with Mother Nature."

"Equal Pay for Equal Work."

"Greed is Gross."

But other signs were just plain weird: "Nationalize Now—Socialist Workers of America." What was that all about?

The crowd on the Mall seemed like a scene from a refugee camp. Had the Apocalypse occurred? There were groups communing together, sitting in circles here and there, some smoking dope, others quietly chatting. Blue jeans and army fatigue jackets were the uniform of the day, though Randy admired the occasional buckskin coat with leather-fringed sleeves, a look that was often topped with a wide-brimmed leather hat, a feather tucked in the hatband. More than one woman wore a halter top, making a marked improvement in the scenery. There was plenty of cussing and joking going on, as much a social as a political event.

At one point, Randy and Anna stopped to observe a bare-chested man wearing only blue jeans. He had a tattoo of a dragon on his arm. His long hair tied in a ponytail; he went about asking people, "What's so hard to understand? All we are saying is give peace a chance!"

His manner was open, his manner oddly tragicomic. His ability to command the attention of some he talked to was remarkable. In these cases, people would talk with him longer than others did, wrapping the encounter up with a hug. Others would just laugh and say, "I don't know, man."

When the man posed his question to Randy, Randy said, "It's okay, man. Here, let me lay some Panama Red on you." Randy offered the man a marijuana joint.

"No! No! No!" The man flung his hands up to either side of his head. "Don't medicate, placate, or educate me, man. We got to love, we've got to radiate love, man. Our love will change the world."

Then the man opened his arms again. He pleaded with his eyes. "May I? May I? May I?"

Randy put his joint back in his pill bottle. He embraced the man as he had seen others do before. It was a gentle gesture. The man then hugged Anna and staggered on his way to the sympathy of some and the puzzlement or apathy of others in the crowd.

"Oh man," Randy muttered. "That guy has lost it big time."

Anna would have said something, but then a woman stood before them. Her still manner changed everything. Her blouse featured dragon embroidery matching the man's tattoo. Silently, she offered them each a chubby oatmeal cookie from the wicker basket slung from her shoulder. Never had a cookie been presented with such solemnity. "All-natural ingredients," she said, adding, "No pharmaceuticals." She cleared her throat. "Allen was at Khe Sahn. He is moved to see so many people who care about the soldiers. Thank you for coming out today."

Suddenly, the man's once whacky antics ascended to a higher level.

Anna asked, "Are the two of you together?"

The woman nodded while Anna and she exchanged a telling look. Then Anna turned to Randy. "Can't we do something for them?"

Noticing an envelope in her basket, Randy slipped her five dollars. "I'm sorry for your loss," he said.

After the woman left, Randy asked, "In your work as a sociologist, do you see many people like him?"

"All the time," Anna said. "At the free clinic."

The crowd on the mall, freaky and disorganized as it was, amounted to about one hundred thousand people. Later in the morning, many of the demonstrators broke away to other things.

Randy and Anna also broke away. They walked to the Jefferson Memorial. "I wished we were here in time to see the cherry blossoms," Randy said as they lay down in the grass to talk of the city and the protest.

"Look at that tourist family," Anna said. "To them, this protest of the Kent State/Cambodia fiasco must be more an inconvenience to their sightseeing than an exercise in democracy."

"Guess it depends on where your head is at," Randy said, "Whose the self-absorbed one? We in the Me Generation?" "Ha" Anna laughed. "That's a stretch, isn't it?" She tore up some grass and sprinkling it on Randy's shoulder. "We've given up a weekend to petition the government. The family I pointed at are the self-absorbed ones. Visualizing an idealized past that never existed."

"Hey," Randy said. "I resemble that. Don't rain on my illusions. They're all I have."

A tussle resulted.

The Lincoln Memorial was within a two-minute walk. After climbing the steps up to the foyer, Randy spent some time studying how the sculptor brought out muscle groups, giving Lincoln a seeming energy as if he were about to rise. "Incredible," Randy said. He lit up a reefer.

A group with a guitar had taken over the floor space underneath the wall where the Second Inaugural Address had been carved.

Randy and Anna joined them. There was peace there, communing as they were with the presence of Honest Abe. As the hour grew later, Randy took up a collection for food for dinner. He walked to a sandwich shop on Virginia Avenue to get hoagie sandwiches and a bag of apples. On the way back, he also grabbed the picnic blanket from the rental car.

On his return, Randy asked the guitarist, "Do you know 'Blowin' in the Wind'?"

"Yeah, don't mean a thing, though, without the words."

"You sing it, I'll sing it." Randy opened his arms to signify the group. "We'll all sing it."

"All right."

"Right on."

"Let's do it."

Anna asked everyone to introduce themselves. Marijuana cigarettes made a few circuits around the group. Neither Anna nor Randy took a hit. They had a bottle of wine. Brian had a camera. He took photos.

The sun set, and night came. Cathy set out some candles. By the time "If I Had a Hammer" hit the song list, Randy was glad he had grabbed the food. It didn't look like this hootenanny would shut down anytime soon. Why leave? Who could sleep? It seemed like a vigil for the nation, a celebration of what the new generation was all about, praying with Abraham Lincoln for better times ahead.

At four o'clock in the morning, the Memorial Hall echoed with the clack of leather soles striking the marble steps with authority. Randy abruptly awoke. An entourage of men in trench coats appeared in the half-light of the portico. The newly arrived group stopped and silently surveyed the interior with flashlight beams, scanning for those who stayed the night in the hall of the Lincoln Memorial.

Cathy, she of the candles, jumped to her feet and ran to the new arrivals. "Oh my God," she said. "It's the president, everybody!" She clapped her hands. Later, she explained she had run to the men so quickly because she thought one of them was her father.

The Secret Service men grabbed hold of Cathy's arms, cautioning her to "Please be quiet." They took stations and did not appear easy as to the president's early morning constitutional.

"Hey, everybody," Randy said, rising to his knees, crawling around to nudge everyone to stand up to greet their visitor. "Get up," he said. "Check this out."

The group assembled and approached the president.

"Hello, ladies and gentlemen," President Nixon said, "I've seen your group camped out on the Ellipse. I've come by to talk with you. I admire your commitment to your civic duty. Where are you all from?"

"Syracuse."

"Ohio."

"Wayne State, Detroit."

Those were a few of the names Randy heard.

He and Anna introduced themselves. Flashes went off.

Anna wrapped the blanket around her shoulders. The president said, "The Orangemen, a great football team." This was directed to the person from Syracuse. "Being a Southern California man," Nixon qualified, "USC is my team." The president opened with an easy patter like that. Everyone seemed a bit stunned. His voice had a remarkable resonance that the marble hall set off to good effect.

Then President Nixon got down to business. "Look," he said, "I just came by to be with you young people, to let you know that I stand with you, admiring the great heritage we all share as Americans."

"Yes, Mr. President," Steve the guitarist said.

"When I was your age," the president said in a wistful manner. "I thought Neville Chamberlain was the greatest man alive, peace in our time and all that. Winston Churchill, a madman. Well, as we all know, Churchill was the wiser man and he was right. Hitler could not be appeased. It took blood, guts, and courage to stop him. There's a difference between wishing for peace and achieving peace. It is so important to understand history if we are truly to understand the present and to guide the future into what we want it to be."

Anna bristled at this. She grabbed Randy's elbow and whispered in a trembling voice, "Could he still say that were his daughter killed at Kent State?"

Stunned by her verbal attack on the president, the hootenanny crowd seemed to move away from Randy and Anna. Her voice must have carried better than she thought. A Secret Service man gave Anna a severe frown. "This is the president, young woman!" he said.

If the president heard the taunt, he did not respond.

"It is a very early morning," President Nixon said, "and I admire the vigorous discourse that characterizes our great nation. May God ever bless America." He raised his hand in a V-for-victory benediction and then he and the Secret Service entourage left. A slight breeze seemed to rush in to fill a vacuum left by his departure, and Randy walked out to watch Nixon descend the stairs—the persona of the man, his convictions, the weight on his shoulders. Randy wondered: how did the general public perceive Lincoln in his day?

Once Randy returned to the group, Brian said, "Wow. Anybody got a reefer? I'm craving my morning hit early today."

Randy pulled the pill bottle out of his jacket pocket, took out a reefer, lit it up, and passed another to Brian.

As the reefers were passed around, the group digested their early morning encounter with destiny's man.

"That was the president who just stopped by to say 'Hey, man.'"

"Yeah, he a college man."

"Guess all the schools got football teams and all the nations got armies."

"Yeah, I think that's what he meant."

"God bless America."

"That's what the man said."

"Amen, brother."

# 14

# WITHOUT A DOLLAR IN HIS HAND

*Randy*
*Sunday February 27, 1972*

It was early morning—2:30 a.m.—by the time Randy got home from a night at the disco. His head still rang from the music wailing at a jet-engine decibels. Inside, did the phone ring? Fumbling with his door keys…yes. Four rings, five rings…the door finally sprung open. Stumbling over the mail lying on the floor, not stopping to find the light switch, Randy grappled for the phone.

"Hello?"

"Uh, Randy, it's your father." A deep breath. "I've got bad news." The senior Allen attempted a nervous laugh.

"Is Mom all right?" Randy asked.

"No, it's nothing like that." Father sounded nervous, uneasy. Then he caught himself. "Where'd the weekend go? I'm sorry about the late hour."

"What is it?" Randy said, pacing past his Windsor chair to turn the floor lamp on. "Why'd you call?"

"I was coming to visit you, take in the Yankees game—"

Randy burst in. "Couldn't that have waited until morning?"

"Oh, all right. I'll get right to the point. There've been some financial reverses. Nothing that won't sort itself out in time."

"Dad, what are you not telling me?" It wasn't often Randy called his father "Dad."

Father continued, "Well, it's just this. Can you make other arrangements through the school for loans or grants or some other way to cover your tuition and college expenses?"

"What?" Randy asked. If his father had just made his point, no way could Randy wrap his mind around it. "Dad, explain yourself, please. You're talking next term, right? What's this all about?"

"No. No, this is a surprise to me, too, son. I'd meant to return your calls. I'm sorry. You see, the IRS is demanding immediate tax payments. Yes, that's it. They've frozen my accounts. I'll get it squared away…in time. Maybe next year, things will be different, but for now…I—"

"Next year!" Randy burst in. "Next calendar year? It's February, for crying out loud! What happened to the agreement we had?" Randy winced, thinking about his overdue bills. Father's February payment was three weeks overdue, and Randy had been spending most every dime living month-to-month. Tuition, rent, utilities, groceries…

Another deep breath. "Look, I'm sorry. It gives me no pleasure to ask this of you. As a parent, you've no idea the pride it gives me to brag about 'My son, the doctor.'" There was another nervous laugh and some babbling. Before closing the call, Father even extracted a promise from Randy that "Under no circumstances is Mum to know of the change in his situation."

Damn! In the silence following the call, Randy's head reeled. He wasn't just broke. He was in debt. The weekend at the Governor House Hotel started him tapping the loan money he'd planned to repay on graduation, with the interest earned while in school just a nice bonus "for being frugal." And since Anna moved out, he'd attempted to get another female roommate, with little success, unless one-night stands counted. And they didn't pay rent. Anna had been the last woman he had been with, but that had begun to fall apart ever since…well it was the May Day Tribe thing in Washington. They were blocking traffic and "shutting the government down…cuz they won't shut the war down."

*A little over the top, isn't that, Anna?*

That's where his law-and-order values got him. Call a cute free spirit on her counterculture extremes and "It's been nice, but it's all over now…"

What could Randy do? Now was no time for regrets. He looked about his well-appointed apartment on Riverside Drive. He simply did not want to give it up. Give up restaurant meals? Who would pay the bar bill now when Ed Jones "hosted" him at the New York Athletic Club… all that had to be maintained. Right?

Randy flung himself in his arm chair. Not tell Mother. Hells bells, it'd be the first thing to do—in seven hours.

But right now he had a more immediate problem.

He needed someone to comfort him—or he would go crazy. But who could he call at 3:00 a.m.? "Hello, I'm horny. Do me, please." Without thinking, he did call Anna. What did he have to lose?

Her phone rang once, twice, three times.

She picked up. In the background, Randy heard Roberta Flack singing, "First time I ever saw your face." My God, she was up, too. Then a male voice said, "Hello? Who's this?"

Randy hung up without a word.

*Shit.*

So much for Anna.

That's when Randy decided to go to a massage parlor.

He suspected they were open all night. *The city that never sleeps, right?* Down by Times Square. But what money could he use?

Brightening, Randy recalled the credit cards in the drawer of the beat-up end table. Jacobs, a long-gone former roommate, had sold some of Randy's pot to another student. The student gave Jacobs the unsolicited cards he'd received in the mail as security for the dime bag Jacobs stole out of Randy's stash. Who knows, the card just might work yet and be worth far more than the ten dollars Jacob had frankly stolen from him.

The cards neatly stashed in his back pocket, Randy dashed down his three flights to the street, out into a chill and bracing night. In his new-found frugality, Randy even took the A train instead of a taxi.

He arrived. Nearly silent streets. Aaahhh, greeting him like an old friend, a tout on Broadway suggested he frequent the Arrago Massage Parlor on Forty-Fourth Street, just off Times Square.

Randy rushed up to the top of the narrow stairs. There he met a man dressed head-to-toe in black, a watch cap perched at a jaunty angle over one ear, standing guard outside a massive battered metal door. After frisking Randy for guns, whips, knives, and God knows what all else, the man tapped on the metal door. It opened.

Inside, Randy presented his credit card to the madam. After a very long two minutes, a curtain parted and three girls appeared, each wearing melon colored leotards, stockings, and heels. Randy picked the only one who ground her hips while looking directly at him through strands of flowing hair. She led him into a room no larger than a closet.

After negotiating a tip, Theresa obliged him. Besides the sex, he sensed intimacy in her eyes, in the patter of her words. She did him right—he was "with someone," much more so than the business suggested. The electricity of this contact helped soothe the sudden loss of his college funding. He put the ten-dollar tip on the stolen card.

Downstairs, the Arrago Bar was being unlocked, and Randy decided he'd top the visit off with a drink. Remarkably, the young woman behind the bar wore a melon colored leotard much like the women upstairs, though Grace also wore hot pants.

Randy was the sole customer.

Pulling a videocassette out from under the counter, Grace said she "did art films. You ought to audition sometime."

She put a business card on the counter: "Arrago Productions." Hmmm, Arrago Massage Parlor, Arrago Bar, and now Arrago Productions. Randy looked at the title on the videocassette: *Tracy Does Manhattan*. He laughed, pocketing the card more to hide it than for any other reason. Hurriedly, he finished his drink. He didn't buy the video. Man, had he ever fallen into a strange little crevice of the world.

As the subway car clattered up the rails home, Randy regurgitated his odd midnight dislocation. Was it some bizarre form of sleepwalking? He had met people who catered to the baser needs in life. He could have been robbed, beaten, or both.

Would 10:00 a.m. ever arrive? Randy tried lying down; he tried deep, slow breaths. Yes, sleep would have been wonderful…perfect. But nothing worked. Finally, it was 10:00 a.m. Eastern/8:00 a.m. Central. Randy called his mum. She sat in her breakfast nook, eating toast and marmalade. Randy told her of Father's tax problems. "Could you help me with college expenses?" he asked.

"Tax problems!" Mother began to laugh. "Are you sure he didn't say 'lapse' problems?" Mother sounded neither sympathetic nor surprised. "Please don't be disappointed in your father, Randy," she continued. "Your father has a gambling problem. Casinos in Freeport, Bahamas, Las Vegas…Grand-pere tells me Stuart is trying to help him get it under control, but I'll see if I can scrape up six hundred dollars and mail it to you."

"Could you make it nine hundred?" Randy asked. "Father used to direct deposit twelve hundred dollars every month. Living in New York is expensive."

"I'm sorry, Randy." He heard the clatter of silverware in the background. "That's out of the question. Bruce and I put everything back into the business. Grand-pere keeps raising the franchise fees. Can't you transfer to a less expensive city, or take in some roommates? You're a smart boy. You'll figure something out. Why, I'll bet two boarders would be ecstatic to rent your master bedroom."

"I'm sure they would," Randy said, though he had other plans than twin beds for the master. With a little wheedling, he got her to go eight hundred dollars, "provided he sent home some receipts."

Phew.

At least Randy made up some of his lost income. Where could he get the rest? As he showered and reheated his coffee cup, it occurred to Randy he could call Joel. Anna had introduced him to Joel. Joel had been to Days of Rage in Chicago. He'd been to Woodstock. As a pharmacist tech, he sold uppers and downers that were supposed to be destroyed, thus paying his way to a pharm D. But Randy typically just bought marijuana from Joel. Not cocaine, not hashish.

"Coffee at the Union?" Joel said over the phone. "No problem, Randy. See you there. Take it easy, my man."

Now Joel watched NBC news, read the *New York Times*, and smoked menthol cigarettes. At the student union, Randy spotted him wearing a denim shirt with a brass peace button on the collar. His brown hair fell to his shoulders, and the scraggily growth on his cheeks didn't look like any kind of beard Mum would approve of—it looked inhabited. Splayed on the table in front of him, the headline of the *New York Times* read "Nixon in China." Randy put his finger on the picture of President Nixon, Secretary of State Kissinger, Chairman Mao, and Premier Chou En-lai. They were all seated in 1930's style vinyl arm chairs—just like the ones in the break room at the Sunny Day Beverage Company.

"Look at that," Randy said. It was always fun to get Joel going on the news. "Do you believe it? Isn't Nixon the ultimate Cold Warrior? What's he doing chumming it up with Chairman Mao?"

"It's just an end-run around Russia," Joel said.

"Oh?" Randy said. He knew he could draw Joel out better than that. He pretended to hold a microphone in his hand. He asked, "So how does President Nixon's visit tie in with the Domino Theory…China toppling the nations of Southeast Asia like so many dominoes…like the Russians did to Eastern Europe?"

*There*, Randy thought, *that ought to cue Joel up for some of his "Revolution Rap."*

Joel stifled a laugh. He lit up one of his menthol cigarettes before going into hipster mode. "You've got it all wrong, Ran-man. Tricky Dicky say dominoes, shmominoes. He just puts on his clever cammo commando gear, crawl over that crumbly old Great Wall of China, and sell Chair Mao all those stolen Cadillac cars running up and down his sleeve. No one's buying them here, man. Now Mao got no time fo' no revolution, he gonna tool around Chinee-town in he big American Cadillac, Jack."

"Is that so," Randy deadpanned. "Good one, Joel. I didn't know Nixon was that clever. Seriously though, another thing that gets me about this whole trip is, here at home, the president can't even cross the street without launching a four-car motorcade with twenty Secret Service agents, and there he sits in the capital of our arch enemy cutting a deal with Mao."

Joel shrugged. "Old Chinese proverb, my man. We live in interesting times."

*OK. Got the good vibes going. Good. Now, down to business.* Randy leaned forward and lowered his voice. "Look, here's the reason I called. A business deal."

At this, Joel put his hand over the leather pouch that lay on the table before him. A bag like that, Randy knew, usually held a few sample joints of the marijuana Joel sold. Joel Scroggins gave Randy a careful look. "Are you talking about the kind of business deal I think you're talking about?" he asked. Randy could see Joel's eyes click in their sockets. The man shook his head. "Oh, I may pick up some weed…a few pills now and then, but I'm no dealer."

Casually, Randy said, "I've heard you say you do a pretty good business at some of the other schools. What was that all about?"

With a tap of his finger on the table, Joel changed from punster to point man. "Are you sure you want to do this?" he asked.

Randy clutched his coffee cup. He matched the intensity of Joel's gaze. "No. I just need the money. Look. Isn't retail where a guy's ass is hanging out? Why take that risk when you can farm it out? I know tons of smokers and pill poppers here on this campus who would pay top dollar, but I need some kind of a break on price to make it worth my while. I can't do it for kicks anymore. I could easily double what I buy from you every week—if you can give me a break on price. What do you say?" Randy thought $75 a week would put him right back where he was before Father left him in a lurch.

"Hold on," Joel said. "You don't have to fuckin' flood the market. Be selective. Neither of us are going to like it if you get nailed by the narcs."

"No problem," Randy said. "I agree completely. It's a deal, then?"

Joel nodded. "Yeah, it's a deal. Look," he said, pushing the leather pouch across the table. "Here's some new killer weed that's going to blow your mind. Columbian buttons. Oh, and give me the pouch back next time I see you, all right?"

They shook on it. Randy hefted the bag and put it in his pocket. Deal done. Good. A new feeling was coming over him. He shouldn't feel bad about this at all. Man, he should be feeling really good. He was taking a big step toward independence. Still, there was that alarm bell ringing in his head. It was one thing to smoke dope and joke with your friends for fun—even to pop a bennie to cram for a test. But to do it for profit? Wow. That was a whole new ballgame.

Maybe, just maybe, that's why "adult" and "X-rated" were such weird synonyms. Maybe that's the ever-so-soft and subtle agenda of the college experience. Maybe legitimacy isn't the black-and-white, clear-cut distinction the world tries to foist on the innocents, the uninformed, the kids, at all.

No, "legitimacy" was a shades-of-gray spectrum best left to individual interpretation, to gumption, to guts. Look at Nixon. He hangs out with Mao, and he's a brilliant strategist. Man, you know damn well, people, if Edward Kennedy or George McGovern rang Chairman Mao's doorbell, there would be hell to pay. Talk about alarm bells clanging away to high noon. Talk about being arrested at the airport and slammed into the trial of the century. Sedition! Treachery! Heinous Communist sympathizers!

But you didn't have to wander too far afield for examples of hypocrisy. Take doctors. If doctors prescribe "rec" meds, that's okay. But when people "self-prescribe"? Yuck! That's drug abuse.

So where do you draw the line?

What is truth?

If he, Randy, sold uppers and downers, wasn't he only getting the jump on what he would be doing once he graduated anyway? Fake it until you make it?

Where was the fault in that logic?

Furthermore, as if to seal the deal, Randy reasoned: *I could have walked the straight and narrow, I was on course with my studies, with my ambitions, it's just that, damn it! My plans got thrown all in the shit basket when Father, Mr. Respectful himself, happened to overextend himself...and how? Cheat on his taxes or what? Let a credit card payment slip? Whatever the hell it was, he leaves me holding the bag. I'll show the fucker, I can take care of myself.*

# 15

# OPERATION HOMECOMING

*Paul*
*Monday, February 12, 1973*

Paul spent the last few months of his army tour at Clark Air Base in the Philippines. As the American presence in Vietnam dropped, Clark started becoming less a staging area and more a quiet backwater—until that is, Operation Linebacker II kicked into high gear. A new vigor shook up the flight line.

Bright brawny B-52s, air-tankers, and various other military aircraft flew in large numbers.

Tents sprung up on the athletic fields and the flight crews ran around the jogging trails and stood in formations under the mimosa trees. They drilled up and down the tarmac and stood stiffly in formation under the wings of their planes.

All through January, these big metal birds rolled down the runways, lifting off, punching big holes up into the sky. Operation Linebacker II was on task, doing its part to assist in the peace negotiations then taking place in Paris. While the North Vietnamese squabbled over the shape of the negotiations table, the B-52s made bombing runs over North Vietnam.

Incredible amounts of ordinance were loaded onto those bombers. Paul saw it. Day after day, the process repeated tirelessly.

At mess the night of February 11, Paul's friend, Staff Sergeant Vincent Morrison, asked "Do you have anything going on tonight?"

"No," Paul said. "I work day shift, counting boots, helmets and cases of 30.06."

"Well," SSgt. Morrie said "I know you take an interest in radio communications from your days in the field. If you're up for it, maybe you can help keep me awake. Operations at the radio shack tonight could be instructive for you."

Lt. Paul laughed, remembering the lifeline the radio had been in Vietnam. "What are you not telling me?"

"You've got to be there if you want to know," SSgt. Morrie said with a wink.

So Paul went. No sooner did he step into the radio shack than he sensed it: something big was happening. The electricity, the briskness, the energy.

Several operators were on duty with SSgt. Morrie. "We're patching calls Stateside," he explained. "They're coming from one of the three C-141 Starlifters in flight from North Vietnam."

"Did you say North Vietnam?" Lt. Paul asked.

"Oh yeah. The American prisoners of war are coming home."

The signal corpsmen were taking phone numbers from the repatriated prisoners even while they were in flight from Hanoi to the Philippines on leg one of the trip back home to the United States of America.

After witnessing a few calls, Paul began to dial and make the Stateside connections himself.

Every call was charged with emotion. If the returning POWs or the call recipients Stateside became speechless, doing little more than breathe, cry, or mutter "Oh" and the like, the radio operator had to ad-lib. "Your family is looking forward to your coming home, Lt. Owen. Mrs. Owen, you will receive further information as Lt. Owen clears quarantine. If you have any questions…"

"Yes, thank you, Sergeant."

A few calls uncovered soldiers given up for dead—others where spouses had remarried. Even in such cases, a connection could be sensed. Other callers showed quiet strength in a trying time. "Son! You call me just as soon as you get an ETA Motown. Man! We'll have a dinner waiting for you here that will not stop. God bless 'em all! You made it. Ben, you're coming home. Amen."

Time and again, all through the call list, Paul saw countless examples of how the closed culture of the military normalized demanding situations.

"What do you think?" SSgt. Morrie asked after the last call was placed.

"I'd say there are a few hundred very happy soldiers going home," Paul said. "Thank you for suggesting I sit in with you."

"Now you know there's more to it than that," SSgt. Morrie said. "Sure, you could sit out the remaining three months of your duty counting Ka-Bar knives or whatever you do for entertainment over there at Commisary, but if I was you, I'd walk over to Major Dawes right now, tell him you assisted with the Stateside patch detail, and request service as an escort for one of the returnees. Get real specific, if you like. Major, who do you have on the list for my hometown, Saint Louis?"

Another night, another skimpy catnap before dawn, and Lt. Paul waited. He was out with the crowd of GIs, dependents, and civilian workers on the Clark Air Base tarmac, waiting and watching for the three C-141 Starlifters and the lone C-9a that were bringing the POW returnees home.

Then, there.

Over the shoulder of volcanic Mt. Arayat, swooping down to glide over the cogon grass and touch down on American pavement, the planes carrying the soldiers coming home came in.

This day, February 12, 1972, Lincoln's birthday, marked for Lt. Paul the day the American war in Vietnam ended.

The Starlifters rolled to a stop, the brass band struck up a medley of "Grand Old Flag," "Yankee Doodle Dandy" and the army and marine anthems. The boarding stairs rolled into place, the plane hatch opened, and the returnees deplaned. The crowd applauded and cheered as the men descended, dressed in navy slacks and long-sleeved blue dress shirts that their North Vietnamese captors had issued to them on their release.

Dan Rather, Tom Brokaw, and other TV news correspondents were there, adding a "day at the fair" commentary to the occasion.

The man Lt. Paul would escort back to Cape Girardeau, Missouri, SSgt. Sidney Wentworth, came in the last plane, a C9A, from South Vietnam. He and those with him still wore orange prisoner pajamas, unwashed, emaciated, bruised but unbroken. SSgt. Wentworth stunk, his eyes were sunken back in their sockets, and he came down from the plane on a litter. But once the welcome ceremonies were over, he grabbed Lt. Paul's arm. "Get me a wheelchair. Please, no ambulance. I have got to clamp these tired jaws of mine around the fattest, juiciest, bloodiest hamburger this base ever pulled off the grill."

Paul couldn't find a wheelchair, but SSgt. Sidney looked vigorous enough to stand up to a short jeep ride, so that's what Lt. Paul grabbed. He reasoned if SSgt. Sidney wanted a hamburger, then by God, he'd jump by the CABOOM and grab the man a burger. He knew how to reply a soldier who had endured what SSgt. Sidney endured: "You got it, soldier,"

Once they arrived at Clark Air Base Officers' Open Mess, the chef himself personally came out to serve SSgt. Sidney a chocolate malt, a hamburger, and French fries while he sat in the jeep under the shade of the mimosa tree in the dooryard.

Most everyone inside also came out. "Welcome home, SSgt. Sidney. How do you like that hamburger?"

Several soldiers shook SSgt. Sidney's hand and asked him the name of his hometown.

"How glad are you to be goin' home?" one gushed.

Another said, "It's going to take more than one of Arnie's hamburgers to put some meat back on your bones."

SSgt. Sidney asked for all the fixin's, including pepperoncini, but after each bite, fewer fixin's remained on the burger until, after about the sixth bite, Paul put a wrap on it. As a result of his captivity, SSgt Sidney's stomach had shrunk horribly—he could hold no more. Plus, his taste buds were on fire, dormant as they were for so long. Lt Paul said "It would be good for SSgt. Sidney to break away from here, guys." He fired the jeep up and pulled away. "He's got a med-check…and he's going home."

# 16

## BUSTED

*Randy*
*April 16, 1972*

"Hi, Father, sorry to call. Hey, I've screwed up big time. You've got to help me. God, this is so fucked up like I *cannot* believe."

"Randy, is that you?" It was a tinny, lousy connection between New York and Saint Louis at 1:00 a.m. Henry Allen had been sound asleep in Saint Louis.

"Yeah, Dad. It's me, Randy." He hardly ever called his father "Dad." It seemed so unlike the man. "Father" came on humorless, demanding, full of himself. Randy caught his breath and then he unloaded, words bursting from his gut. "I'm stuck in a police station. The pigs arrested me. They handcuffed me and they're gonna throw me in jail. I don't know what to tell you, Father. I was with my friends, and these weird goons pounced on us. Threw some drugs in my pocket, I don't know how they got there. They're going to lock me up, and shit, I've got a test I need to study for Monday morning at ten! What the hell am I supposed to do? You're a lawyer, the only one I know. Please get me out of here."

When Father remained silent, Randy kept talking. "I coulda called Mum, but I called you. They're only allowing me this one phone call. So if you can't help me," Randy's voice became louder in his panic, "please call someone who can. Someone who really cares about me. Maybe the university operator can give you the number for the dean of students—if you don't want to tell Mum. Oh hell!"

Out of breath, Randy stopped talking. Dizzy, crying would be a relief, but instead he cringed. He cramped. He dried up.

Just before he began to rant again, Father asked, "Are you in trouble, Randy? Where are you?"

"Haven't you been fucking listening? I'm in deep shit! I'm about to be locked up with murderers, robbers, and rapists. I feel like puke."

"Stay put," Henry Allen said. "Hold on. Calm down. You've put me in a horrible spot, Randy, but I'll see what I can do. You won't believe this. I met an attorney at the bar association luncheon just last Wednesday. He relocated here to Saint Louis from New York, so we may be in luck. In the meantime, cope as best you can. Got it? I'll do what I can as soon as I can."

"Soon? What are you talking about? What can you do right now? Don't you have any pull with these turkeys? I don't want to spend the night in jail! There's muggers, murderers, sick people…Here, let me get someone on the phone you can talk to—set them straight!"

"Ah, Randall. It doesn't work that way. Now, settle down." Henry appeared to be getting a clue as to what had happened. He turned it up a notch. "You've squeezed yourself into a damn pickle all on your own, so don't go pointing any fingers at me!" He caught himself. A touch more kindly, he added, "I'll do what I can to be there Monday, okay? You, ah, take care, hear?"

How could this happen to him? Randy hung up the phone without answering his father. When the arresting office came to take Randy to the Manhattan Detention Complex, he received a dose of Randy's rage: "We weren't hurting anybody…Don't you cops have anything better to do, like go after bad guys?"

"Come with me," the cop said with a sharp jerk of the handcuffs and a gruff "Do yourself a favor, save it for the judge." Randy reduced his comments to a prattling soliloquy of "I don't believe this shit" and "This is fucking unreal."

As Randy was driven to lower Manhattan, he hated the complete loss of control. He should be free to do what he pleased. He, a college student, should be home in his apartment. He'd planned to study a bit on Sunday afternoon and most of Sunday night. He had an exam on Monday. He hoped to hell it didn't count for too much of his grade.

The cop parked at the curb and led Randy in handcuffs to the Manhattan Detention Complex, also known as the Tombs, in Lower Manhattan. There, Randy descended countless stairways, was stripped of his belt, wallet, watch, and shoelaces, and thrown into a cell with five other inmates. *This must be what zombie life is like*, Randy thought. *What a dark, dank swirling toilet bowl of filth. The people who are locked up here must have really done some bad things to deserve this.* Only shock kept him for going stark raving mad.

Once the corrections officer was gone, Randy counted the other inmates locked up in the cell with him. A Puerto Rican cocaine dealer squatting in the corner kept swallowing air in an effort to eject the drugs he'd swallowed from his rear end. A pair of swarthy blacks coaxed him on.

"Don't poke me, man," the Puerto Rican said. "I don't want the condom to tear." Was the guy trying to push a condom full of cocaine through his intestinal track? Sick, Randy thought. The pair of blacks fondled each other, assuring the Puerto Rican they would help him "get rid of the evidence" once it emerged from his asshole.

Time had been forgotten down in the Tombs. Sleep? Out of the question. Randy dare not even lie down. What would the other inmates do to him if did? He did not want to find out.

The other inmates in his cell included a homeless man whose clothes smelled of stale beer at ten feet. He had few teeth, and Randy swore he saw bedbugs or lice crawling all over the scaly skin of his face and hands. The homeless man muttered to himself, calling Randy "one of the lucky ones." Randy did not want any of them within five feet of him, if he had anything to say about it. The fifth inmate was absolutely hairless. Arabesque tattoos in blue, green, and red flowed over his exposed arms and neck. He wore a sleeveless black T-shirt. He glared at Randy. "Don't piss off the COs," the man said. "They'll take it out on us all." The man looked like he might enjoy finding an excuse to rough Randy up.

There were no clocks or windows; the florescent tubes gave the place a jaundiced look. Some effort had been made to disinfect the place—if that camphor smell of rotten mothballs could be believed. The stench of sweat, feces, and vomit was too far established.

Randy would not even want to visit a jail, much less be locked up in one. Randy had always seen the law, the government, as a beacon of light, the bedrock, the foundation of order. But that was when he was on top of the so-called bedrock. Now he had been buried underneath it—on the other side of life.

On Sunday morning, Randy and his cellmates were led to a mess hall where they were given cornflakes in individual boxes and milk served at room temperature. Unsure of whether the milk was spoiled or not, Randy tried eating his cornflakes piece by piece. He decided he was not hungry. Lunch didn't go much better—baloney on white bread that tasted like rubber on cotton but more digestible…if one could even work up an appetite.

Another morning and then in front of the judge. By two o'clock Monday afternoon, Randy was processed through the court and released "on his own recognizance." Other than waiting for their ride out to the airport, his father and his lawyer had no time for New York City. The lawyer, Dirk Halbers, knew a man who owned a limousine, so he took the three of them out to the airport. As they crossed the Williamsburg Bridge into Brooklyn, the whole experience weighed on Randy. Sure, he was free now, but huh? Why didn't they put up more of a fight? Why couldn't Randy deny being a pothead? He claimed he didn't know it was marijuana. It was only an ounce, a dime bag. The newspaper said the legislature planned to reduce doping to a misdemeanor with a measly $500 fine and let it go at that. Wow. The attorneys, this Halbers guy and Father, had cut a deal for him that included him being a stool pigeon— he had to fink on his supplier. Joel Scroggins was not going to go for that. But Randy tucked that thought away; the relief he felt to be back "among the living" justified anything.

How exciting it had been to know Joel. Carefree, easygoing Joel, the spirit of the Woodstock nation, convinced "everybody" could come together, collaborating and making the world a better, healthier place for everyone. Better living through chemistry. Ha ha ha. Forget all that. The world is what it is. Talk about the spirit of the Woodstock Nation, drugs, sex and rock 'n' roll…The Feds were even trying to deport John Lennon as what? *A menace to society?* C'mon.

The wind blew chill at the curb in front of the airport ticket lobby where he and Father parted. The old man wore a charcoal gray overcoat and wool-brimmed hat. There was no humor in his eyes as he dressed Randy down. He looked tired, jaded. Lawyer Dirk Halbers had a more business-like impatience to be flying. He stood silently in his khaki trench coat. After pulling his Irish sporting cap down around his ears, Randy wrapped his pea coat closer to his body to keep out the chill.

Father said, "So you're going to tough it out here in New York, *if you can*, completing your studies?

"Yes, sir."

"I have my doubts, Randy. For starters, you need to find better friends. Get with an AA program. I've heard they have drug groups as well as groups for drinkers. All that aside, I consider your arrest a personal failure on your part and an embarrassment to me. Let me make one thing perfectly clear: you are on probation. Your grades slip; you are out of here. I won't be there to pick you up next time. Are we clear?" Then Father put his hand on Randy's arm. Assuming a kinder tone, he said, "We owe many thanks to Dirk Halbers. Without him navigating us through the New York courts, you could have been held days longer and sentenced far more severely."

The closeness of Father's departure stirred hopes for Randy to climb up out of zombie mode, but Father's words thrust him back down into the pits. Mustering as much courage as he could, Randy replied, "Yes, sir. I'm sorry I let you down. It won't happen again. Mr. Halbers, thank you for your assistance."

How strange the world looked to him on being released from jail. On these words he used with these men, glossing over the compromise in his values, his associates. He maintained a strong B average. Joel was a hoot. They had a good thing going.

His father said, "Don't take it so hard, son. We all make missteps from time to time. The challenge is picking yourself back up, dusting yourself off, and carrying on. See you back home in Saint Louis. Now, the limousine driver has been instructed to take you back to your apartment. Dirk knows him, so we got a deal on it. He's a good man to know, right?" "Good to meet you," Dirk Halbers said, extending his hand. "Keep your nose clean." He winked as Randy shook his extended hand.

# 17

# THE NEW NORMAL

*Randy*
*April 17, 1972*

Once back in his apartment, Randy tried to shake off the nightmare of jail time and standing before the judge with the lawyers. Would this zombie numbness ever blow off? The assistant district attorney had been a thin humorless man whose suit smelled of tobacco. He had said, "After consulting with your lawyers, Mr. Allen, we will consider dropping the charges if you help us arrest your supplier. We may even drop charges against your supplier if he is willing to help us prosecute his supplier."

The assistant DA adjusted his tie and, with a flourish of his hand, implied he thought himself God-awful generous. He added, "We've got enough small time hoods locked up, housed at the taxpayers' expense. I'm assuming you're a decent kid who just got caught up in all the insanity infesting our college campuses these days."

Randy stared ahead vacantly.

The prosecutor continued, "The DA wants to work up the food chain, to take the largest bite possible in the illegal drug trade by nailing the bigger players."

According to the assistant DA, Randy had "no time" to think about the deal. In his shock, he let himself get rolled. He didn't ask if there were options. He didn't ask how strong "the state's" case was. The offer wouldn't be repeated. If his current offence was placed on his record, a second offense would trigger severe consequences for him. "This is a federal offense; your record will follow you wherever you go within the country." That's the way the assistant district attorney said it. But he even backpedaled a bit: "Either way, accept the deal or not, you still better be committed to cleaning up your act."

What was the offer?

Randy dared think about it again.

Simply put, the offer meant he, Randy, would toss Joel overboard to feed the pig/sharks. Oh, it was presented oh-so-much-more righteous than that. Randy would turn Joel in and then Joel would turn in his supplier.

The advantages of the offer as presented: neither Randy nor Joel would be charged with a crime. Plus the state would be working their way "up the food chain," nailing marijuana, hashish, and cocaine distributors.

But Randy knew there would be no Get Out of Jail Free card for Joel Scroggins. Joel was the one and only one responsible for turning legitimate pharmaceuticals—uppers and downers—into illicit drugs. He stole the drugs from the pharmacy where he worked as a pharm tech. The drugs had been scheduled for destruction, but Joel diverted them to the street to pay his college expenses. No fault could be pinned on anyone beyond him. He would be nailed. Once Joel got arrested, surely they would search his apartment. Maybe they already even knew about Joel; they just needed an excuse that justified a search warrant.

Once his stash of uppers and downers was discovered, Joel would be in deep shit.

Randy looked at the phone on the table by his chair. Should he call Joel?

Now hold on. He had think that one through.

If Randy placed the call, he would say, "Hello, Joel. Guess what? I got nailed. Spent two nights in jail. But I'll cruise on all charges if, the next time I buy drugs from you, I wear a wire. Then they'll nail you, too. Isn't that a sweet deal? No one gets hurt but the big boys. Because they'll offer you the same deal they offered me. Feed them names up the food chain and you'll go free. Except I know that won't work for the pills. So just ditch the pills for a couple of days, play along with the sting, okay? We knew the gig would be up someday, right? Well...someday has come!"

Only two things wrong with that scene. First, only a fool would agree to a cockeyed offer like that. Randy knew that much. And then, more importantly, if Randy could get such a message to Joel and Joel agreed to it—what if Randy's phone had been tapped? There'd probably be justification for a search warrant for Joel, and Randy would be charged as an accomplice. He'd probably be charged with interfering with an investigation or some such bullshit. Furthermore, and Randy shuddered at this, the people Joel bought marijuana, hashish, and cocaine from were probably mean motherfuckers. The kind you didn't want to mess with. People with brass knuckles, tire jacks, and guns.

If Randy was lucky, the narcs wouldn't even go after the marijuana and cocaine dealers…

Randy felt like an onlooker at his own funeral.

How bizarre the memory of the deal in the district attorney's office now felt. Father and Dirk Halbers were both nodding, rubbing their chins and cooing as if in admiration of this great civic duty Randy was about to perform "for the sake of public health." But now Randy saw the raw edge of the deal. He could stand it no more. He almost stepped out to a bar in hopes of meeting some friends, brushing the whole thing off.

Instead, he went to the liquor store, got a fifth of vodka, and drank a goodly portion of it before sleeping that night. He mixed it with orange juice. He didn't want to see anyone.

# 18

## TWO MEETINGS

*Randy*
*Spring & Summer, 1972*

Randy wore a wire when he met Joel in the Sheep Meadow in Central Park later that spring. The pigs recorded the purchase and every word Randy and Joel said. Oh, how Joel zinged everyone that day, from the Easter Bunny to Tax Freedom Day. High-spirited Joking Joel, ha ha ha. Randy purchased a half-kilo of marijuana and three grams of hashish. To ease his conscience, when he called to arrange the meeting, Randy specifically said, "I won't be needing any bennies, Quaaludes, or pills… not that you even sell those things. Everybody wants a natural high right now. Because it's spring, I guess."

Joel's high-stepping over the verdant grass was punctuated with bright yellow dandelions. Skies of blue, scattered cumulus clouds, white and puffy. Headed toward the Mall with marked bills in his pocket to pay his tuition. Two plainclothesmen emerging from the tree line and apprehending Joel as the sun went behind a cloud. Randy watching from afar.

Meeting once again with the assistant DA, who busied himself thumbing his way through a file. "We won't be cutting a deal with Joel Scroggins," he said. "Some irregularities cropped up on a search of his apartment."

Father's words echoing in his mind: "You don't have to like the deal, son. You just have to live with it."

Randy did not return to Saint Louis until summer. He moved into the spare bedroom of his apartment so he could take in two boarders in the master bedroom. A pair of undergraduates moved in with their twin beds.

Keeping busy with schoolwork helped Randy forget the deal he worked out with the prosecutors. The deal that fell so hard on Joel. Randy heard Joel got three years at Rikers Island. He could jolly well scratch that "pharm D" out of his future plans, too.

But didn't Randy luck out? Wouldn't the charges of dealing drugs alone (even without a conviction) have expelled him from med school? He could thank his lucky stars he was still on board that train, man.

The rationalizations grew stronger. Joel and he were two different people. Joel played the more dangerous game in the drug scene, traipsing much closer to the edge. Actually, Randy thought, if he'd never met Joel, would he even have tried drugs? No, of course not.

*No*, Randy thought, *give me gin and orange juice. Give me beer. In fact, I'll have another of each thank you.*

Joel knew the risks. He got caught.

Of course, Randy wanted none of his friends at Columbia to know about his hand in bringing Joel down. Since Joel had studied at St. Johns, the risk of that social faux pas being exposed was minimized.

After Randy's arrest and release, he began steering clear of drugs and dope (other than the occasional bennie as a study aid). He regretted giving up marijuana, but why bother with dope, he reasoned, when liquor was legal and the consequences of use far less complicated?

Having a whisky with Ed Jones at the NYAC, Randy reassured himself that *he did a fucking public service by turning Joel Scroggins in.*

Plus…don't kid yourself. Joel would have cut the same deal were the shoe on the other foot. No question there.

In darker moments, Randy thought, it was sad saying *Good-bye, hippie America, good-bye, Summer of Love. I've tuned in, turned on, and I got dropkicked into the hoosegow. No thanks to all that…*

But as he refocused and got on with his life, his thinking went more like, *Hey, hippie America, Summer of Love, we've changed the world, eliminated the draft, slapped the president's hand for his escapades in foreign interventions…so welcome to the new normal, it's the same as the old normal, democracy in action. Power to the people. Right on!*

Yes, Randy had succeeded. He'd neatly plastered over and forgotten his once-upon-a-time belief that selling piddly amounts of marijuana, hashish, and rec drugs to his friends should be no crime. He buried the fact that he jolly well could have challenged the case against him. Would his life truly have been destroyed if he had stood his ground? Joel got prison time. God only knew what legitimate business opportunities would be open to Joel on his release from prison. With that pharm D under his arm, Joel could have made the big bucks. But that wouldn't happen now. Randy chalked it up to lessons learned, that's life, time to move on.

That summer, Randy met with Grand-pere, the Colonel, in Margaret's office at the Sunny Day Beverage Company.

A somber experience. The room was dark and cool. The drapes shut. The dark wood paneling, a smell like baking soda in the air. Grandpere's steely gaze, his measured words. "Hello, Randall, come in, take a seat. Why didn't you come to me when you needed money?"

Randy was speechless, taking a seat before the massive desk. He barely could form the words. "I had no idea…"

His mind reeled. What if, in his hour of need, when Father let him down, what if he did call Grand-pere? Why did Mum not suggest it?

Randy had no idea that option was even open.

Damn, if only he'd thought of that. His life would have been so much simpler. No drug trial, no Joel betrayal. No ragged edges to complicate things…

Before Randy could even form a response, Grand-pere continued the "interview."

"Everyone in the family comes to me in their hour of need. I have grown to expect this," the family elder said. "I am the calm in the eye of the storm. You, your mum, and with Allen gone these many years, your father and your Uncle Stuart are continuing concerns of mine." Randy knew all about Allen, his now deceased other grandfather, Henry's dad… and grand-pere's friend since childhood. "It's your mum's doing, I know. She's set you against me." Grand-pere tapped his fingertips together as if manipulating a crystal ball. Then looking into the distance as if lost in thought. "She's made end-runs around me, her colored man shifting so much of the business north, buying their own fleet of trucks when the Saint Louis truckers raised their rates, when the Saint Louis buyers cancelled their orders. Oh, Randall, your mum is a mover and a shaker, hell-bent on her own way and a slow learner. Your father…" Grand-pere cleared his throat. "No help. But…I digress."

In the silence following his words, Randy turned to see what Grandpere had been looking at. All that Randy could see was the model of the old horse-drawn delivery wagon. Indeed, the mahogany-paneled room had little else of interest in it other than file cabinets, pictures of the old factory, and a display case of old Sunny Day pop bottles. Machinery could faintly be heard in the background.

Grand-pere resumed his monologue, as if justifying himself to Randy. He said, "I've supported your calling all along. We've many physicians in our family. That's a good thing. As for me, I followed in my father's shoes. It seemed the easy choice at the time. The business practically ran itself, for a while. People just love their sweet bubbly water." Grand-pere laughed. "It may be a fallback plan for you after you get cycled through the medical ringer a few times. People expect so damned much from their doctors and don't the insurance companies know it, malpractice rates…" Grand-pere smiled at this, expecting Randy to connect the dots.

Randy did not see this as an appropriate time to ask Grand-pere what the hell he meant by that crack.

Then Grand-pere cut to the chase. "Randy, you are my only grand-child. If the family is to cut any kind of swath in the world, it is up to you. Last year, I began gifting you shares in my company, Sunny Day Beverage. Can you give me one reason why I should continue this practice given your recent and regrettable episode with the police?"

"No, sir. It is your money to do with as you wish."

"That's a good answer. I'll take it. It is my money, but as you know, they don't put trailers on hearses. I will continue to gift you ten shares each year—provided you merit such consideration."

Randy coughed. "I won't fail you, sir," he said.

"I surely hope not, Randy, for my sake and yours. You've got so many things going for you. Your whole life. Ten shares may not mean much to you now. It pays nothing. As majority shareholder, I have voted down issuance of dividends and I charge your mum franchise fees on the formulas and rents on the building providing me with my income. In time, however, as you receive an additional ten shares every year, by the time you complete your schooling, or shortly thereafter, or surely by the time I am gone…well, then the business will be in your hands. At that time, I am counting on you to conduct yourself with better judgment than you have exercised this past year. Do you read me, Randall?"

"Yes, sir." Jesus, the man was really pounding this point home, wasn't he?

"You're the end of the line, Randall. My expectation for you as you complete your studies is for you to develop a strong sense of duty to the duties of your profession and of your class. Try to make the world a better place in whatever small way you can. Be a contributor, Randy, not a leech."

"Grand-pere, I appreciate you giving me…ownership…in Sunny Day. But I'm no businessman. I'm a doctor. What do I know of the business world?"

"Business, like anything else, Randy, is all about making choices. It's about pacing yourself and priorities. We're all either learners or we fall behind. When the time comes, you can hire managers, you can sell the company. You can step in and run things yourself. It's up to you. You were very young at the time, but your other grandfather, Allan Allen, my dear friend, went partners with me back in 1953. He bought some shares when I ran into difficulties. Then he died in a car accident. Drinking. I carried on as best I could without him."

"What happened to his shares?"

"They reverted to me. I was able to save his family through the partnership insurance policy we'd taken out to cover just such a possibility, Randy."

Randy stood up straighter. "Smart move," he said, brushing off his shirt. "Thank you for the trust you've shown me. You won't be disappointed. Eh, is there anything else we ought to talk about?"

The room fell strangely silent. A silence that Grand-pere appeared to be much more accustomed to than did Randy. How the thoughts raced through Randy's head: Grand-pere was filthy, stinking rich. Even Father was also rich—riding to his rescue in New York in a limousine no less (or was it, as Mum had it, Father, the gambling leech?)

"What did you want to talk about?" Grand-pere hunched forward. His eyes seemed to twinkle, his voice softer, more personable.

"About funding for college," Randy said. "Dad isn't able to continue, and Mum is only able to come up with little more than half of Dad's funding."

"Oh, nuts to that!" Grand-pere said, banging the palm of his hand on the desk. "Tell her to save herself the trouble. Let me be your advisor from now on. Hear me?"

Grand-pere's eyes now glinted, eagle sharp and looking right at him, eye-to-eye combat. No blinking.

Randy mustered all the strength he could to match the steely gaze.

Then, Grand-pere, the Colonel, leaned back in his chair. "When will your schooling be complete?" he asked.

"In two years. Then I plan to do my residency here."

"And when that's completed, where will you live?"

"Where else?" Randy said. "Right here in Saint Louis."

Grand-pere leaned forward. "That's good. You'll be close to your family then, and we can keep an eye on you. You know, the Bouchards helped build this town. So long as you plan to return, I'm not against funding your education at the level Henry established for you, before he, ah, ran into his problems." Grand-pere laughed. He stood up, clapped his hands, and stepped out from behind his desk. "I don't want to see any more of your tomfooleries in the police blotter. Understood?" He was all joviality, Grand-pere indeed!

Randy stiffened. "Yes, sir. It won't happen again."

"Very well then," Grand-pere said. "We'll embrace on it."

Randy and Grand-pere did embrace. To Randy, this meeting took a huge weight off his shoulders. It was back to the business of getting an education, a bit sadder, but wiser now—and much better equipped, on every level.

# 19

## MY BROTHER'S KEEPER

### *Saturday, May 7, 1976*

When Paul asked his question, Randy sat in an Adirondack chair on the rear deck. He was admiring the gingerbread trim on the old Victorian home. It was so good, Randy thought, to be back home in Saint Louis. The Bouchard house hadn't looked this clean in a long time. Paul and Linda had moved in only a few months after Bruce Jr., now two, was born. They'd really gone to work, updating and catching up on all the "deferred maintenance."

Randy and Paul had just returned from Riverfront Stadium, where they'd watched the Astros beat the Cardinals 3-1.

"So what can you tell me about the Colonel?" That's the question Paul had asked as he turned the ribs over on his stainless steel barbecue grill.

Randy took a slug of root beer before answering. "I don't know. What do you want to know?"

"What kind of man is he?" Paul said. He closed the lid of the barbecue and sat down in the other Adirondack chair near Randy's.

"Well," Randy said. "He's got his way of doing things. No question about that. Look how hard he's made it for Margaret and Daddy Bruce, threatening to sell the business, raising her franchise fees, saying the earlier pay schedules had been too lenient...I try to reach him, to talk with him, but he's usually off on some cruise or playing bridge at his club. Truth is, seems like whenever I call, it's his accountant—Bernard Jeams—who returns the call."

"Oh?" Paul said, shutting the hood on the grill. "So have you ever talked to him about something other than money?"

Randy clenched his hands together. He'd just about made his peace with the Joel Scroggins screw-up. The only real "encounter" he'd had with Grand-pere since Father and Mum's divorce had been in the after-math of that fiasco.

Randy had a nice groove going with Paul, talking and acting like he, Randy Allen, lived the good life.

If Paul was going to hear any dirt on Randy, he wouldn't be hearing any from him. "Oh, not too many personal visits with Grand-pere," Randy said. "I send him a couple letters each year, and he writes me. That's about it."

"Interesting," Paul said. He sat in the other chair. "I started writing him in Vietnam. I've continued the practice, even if I don't receive many letters in return."

"Really?" Randy offered Paul the bowl of potato chips. "Why are you writing him?"

"Just to wish him a happy birthday."

Randy laughed. "Do people still do that kind of thing? What's the point?"

"Just to let him know I'm thinking about him," Paul said. "Margaret and Daddy Bruce are getting closer to retirement every day and I want the coach to know my name when it's time for the next batter to step up to the plate."

"Oh man!" Randy about choked on his root beer. "Are you still banking on that? What makes you think the Colonel will cut a deal with you? Forget it. You've done okay for yourself. When the biz gets sold, you'll make like the cat. You'll land on your feet."

Paul stomped his foot. Then he brushed his knees. "Done okay? That's no life goal. Done okay. Boring." He laughed heartily.

Randy wished he'd been more diplomatic. "You've launched Lindy's Snacks," he said. "That's going great, isn't it?"

"Sure," Paul said, sounding quite resilient. "And were Sunny Day sold, Lindy's Snacks might stand on its own. Maybe not great, just okay. But why lose the power the two products have when combined and marketed together? Surely, the Colonel, your grand-pere, takes enough pride in Sunny Day that he would like to see it survive, to see it grow with the times?"

"Well…" Randy recalled how, years ago, Paul had expressed an interest in being the CEO of the family business. Was that what he meant now about being "the next batter up"? Not a very realistic ambition so far as Randy could see. He chose his words carefully to sound out how far Paul had progressed down this line. "Maybe when it comes to buying in to the biz, you do have an ace up your sleeve I don't know about. My understanding is that when it comes to tradition and the Colonel, all that went out the window when Mum divorced Henry."

"He's still not over that?"

"No. The Allens and the Bouchards go way back, to the Colonel's parents. Grand-mere talked Mum into marrying Henry. And another blow to tradition, I went into medicine. I'm no businessman. So tradition is shot several ways, not the least of which is, ahem, the color line—there, I said it. Besides, you're not blood. So I'm sorry. What else is there to say?" Randy stopped. He regretted his rash response. It sounded cold.

Paul stood up, opened the lid on the barbecue, and pulled the ribs off the grill, setting the platter down on the table in front of the chairs. "There's blood, and there's love," he said. "Help yourself." Quietly, before selecting his meat, Paul added, "You don't have to protect me from the white kin."

"Yeah," Randy said. "I hear you." Randy fidgeted as he tried to pick up his rib with a fork.

"They eat better in your hands," Paul said. "I've got plenty of wet towelettes." He pointed to a bowl under the grill.

Randy dropped his fork and grabbed the rib by its ends. "You must think I'm the wet towel, putting the damper on your dream," he said.

Paul shrugged. "No, forget it. If big biz was easy, we'd all be fat cats. I'll find a way."

"Well," Randy said, feeling like he needed to dig himself out of a hole he'd dug himself into. "All I can say is I'm so glad to be back home in Saint Louis. New York was great, but intense. The city never sleeps. Fifty stories tall, people, people everywhere. Crowded. You're never alone. Don't get me wrong. I'm glad I went, glad I lived there for six years. I got an understanding of the place. Every minute I was there, I felt like I was living next to the heartbeat of the world. Then I come here. I sense the quality of the space, the openness and the quiet. So relaxing. It's cool coming over here. Have I mentioned that you've done wonders with the Bouchard house?"

Paul acknowledged the compliment in his modest way.

"Thank you," Randy gushed on. "For remodeling and upgrading it. This house and this town mean a great deal to me. Frankly, it would be hard on me to know I wasn't welcome here in this place—if someone outside the family owned it. It will always be my house." Randy bit into his rib and continued.

"It's also hard for me to imagine a Saint Louis without Sunny Day Soda Pop. Or Sunny Day Beverage without some link to the Bouchard Family. So…I don't understand why all that is, Paul. But these facts are so hardwired into my psyche, things that I so take so for granted, that were they gone, I'd feel like a part of me became lost."

"I don't have a problem understanding that at all," Paul said. "You are fortunate you have ties that mean so much to you."

"Okay, well, I guess that clears the air on whatever it was we were just talking about." It didn't, and Randy knew it. Then he asked, "So tell me, I'm not much of a letter writer. What do you talk about in all those letters you write to Grand-pere?" Randy picked up another rib and began gnawing at it. He shouldn't have bothered with the fork in the first place.

"Well, for one thing, I don't use family names. I don't have quite that much swagger. I write 'Dear Colonel.' I tell him how much I admire the company, how I would appreciate meeting him the next time he's in town. I send him samples of Lindy snacks for just about any occasion I can think of. I put my business card in. When I was in Vietnam, he wrote me back about his experiences in the twenties in China."

"Grand…the Colonel served in China? I didn't know that." Randy reached for one of the towelettes, even if he did plan on eating another rib.

"Yeah, he served with Butler and the Thirteenth Marines. So he gave me a jab about being a grunt. But I still call him 'sir.'"

"Oh, hell, there may be hope for your scheme yet. With you playing that soldier card. Grand-pere, the *Colonel*, could go for it."

Paul laughed, leaning forward in his Adirondack chair. "You're just saying that now because you feel bad about how skeptical you were before."

"Maybe so, Maybe not. You've got a good thing going, it seems, with the older generation. It amazes me, for instance, how your dad's got everyone calling him 'Daddy Bruce.'"

"Yeah, we work pretty close together at the plant, too. When it comes to business, though, I do switch off sometimes, calling him Bruce instead."

"I would no sooner call my dad Daddy or by his given name than I would fly to the moon. He is one cold fish." Randy tossed his soda can in the trash.

"Sounds like you regret that," Paul said.

Randy talked louder. "What can I do? It's always been that way."

Paul clasped his hands before him. "Something must've turned him that way. I guess life's like that for some folks. Tell me, you talked about how you like it here, this house, this city. You were talking about things. What about the people?"

"Here in Saint Louis? Yeah, Saint Louis has plenty of good people. Hardly a week goes by, I don't run into someone I knew from school, when I was young, dumb, and innocent. That's always fun."

"Young, dumb, and innocent, huh?" Paul put his plate aside. Any particular event stand out where you lost your innocence…or dumbness?"

"No," Randy said, "and I'll tell you what. I'm always ready to lose even more dumbness than I have already. It's all about leaving home, and then it's all about going back home. That's the story of my life to date. You're the one with the tales to tell, with your tour of Vietnam."

"No, nobody's going to hear one of those tonight," Paul said. He looked to be in good spirits.

"Hey, ah, you probably know this, but I'm going to tell you anyway." Randy spoke in a quieter, more confidential voice. "Do you know you aren't the first colored member of the family living here?"

"No," Paul said. "I didn't know that." He moved his chair closer.

Randy explained, "Oh, five generations ago, the Colonel's grandfather married the daughter of an Osage Indian medicine man."

"Where'd they live?"

"Right here. They were the ones who built this house in, I believe it was, 1873. Shortly after Tower Grove Park was built." Randy became excited. "Another factoid: that medicine man's herbs formed the basis of Sunny Day's first root beer. Speaking of which, I think I'll have another."

"Go ahead, you know where they're at." Paul picked up another rib.

The cicadas chirped.

Before opening the bottle, Randy held it up to the light. "I like the new drier, more adult, taste," he said.

"That's cuz we're using stevia now instead of sugar," Paul said. "Glad you like it. Hey, if you don't mind my asking, how long has it been since you…put the bottle away?"

"Don't mind at all," Randy said. "Six glorious, liquor-free, clear-thinking months. So where's Bruce Jr. and Linda? Should we save some ribs for them?"

"No, go ahead. Neither of them are rib eaters. That's why I invited you over. Anyway, it'll be a while they get home. Enjoy."

The return of warm summerlike weather made being outside a pleasure.

# 20

## CINDY

*Randy*
*Thursday, June 30, 1978*

Randy rotated the bottle of champagne in the ice bucket Cindy bought him to celebrate the opening of his new offices in the Medical Dental Building in the Barnes Hospital Complex, Saint Louis, Missouri.

Yes, Randy was home, established, set for life. Home in Saint Louis. Sure, he would visit New York, he would visit all the great cities of the world again, for medical conventions, vacations, and travel, but home would always be Saint Louis.

No more short cuts, no more playing fast and loose with the law. He was at the threshold of a lifelong career, his own private practice, all legit, and he barely out of med school. What a stroke of luck.

It was Cindy who put it all together for him.

Yes, Randy promised himself…he would not disappoint either Cindy or himself. She was the most fascinating person he had ever met.

And she would be his.

As he looked at the champagne bottle, he recalled how once he had a drinking problem. Actually, no, a better way to put it: his judgment was bad…he made mistakes, "thinking errors." Following his run-in with the law—dealing illegal drugs, betraying Joel Scroggins—he drank far too much for far too long. Forget it. A bad scene all around. He made it through med school, didn't he?

Now, here he was, his own condo within walking distance of Barnes Hospital in Saint Louis, just like he'd always imagined, living with a gorgeous woman.

Cindy had gone to so much trouble: the fine champagne, the crystal drinking flutes. Surely, he could take just one sip. She knew he had a problem with alcohol. She'd put together the perfect celebration to launch his new practice, his own office. She'd worked so hard decorating his business, his home, his life.

He wouldn't let her down. Cindy brandished a full carat diamond ring to show the world that she was his.

Icy beads of condensation slid down the side of the sterling silver champagne bucket. Cindy found it in a "juntique" store. What a bargain hunter. The urn polished up so bright and clean. "This really is first class," Randy said as he turned the bottle of 1970 Rothschild to further chill it. The champagne came from a friend of the interior decorator who'd been to France. "The bubbly is much cheaper there," Cindy said. "I love Paris, don't you?" She rubbed his shoulder and blew into his ear. The rim of the bucket flared like a trumpet, its braided edge making such a baroque statement.

He would only have a sip. Wouldn't even finish one glass.

It will be all right. Cindy. Her presence in his life just made everything click into place. He would work. He would work and work and he would share delicious sex-love with Cindy—every day for the rest of his life. What a woman. He admired her now as she stood looking out the window in his apartment. He walked up behind her. In heels, the crown of her head rested below his cheekbone. Her hair was finer, softer, more radiant, more perfectly scented than any other woman Randy had ever known. A size four, Cindy wore, as she called it, an impatiens red dress with sandals to match; he'd shopped with her at Neiman Marcus for just this occasion. Yes, she was far sexier than Anna could ever even imagine—with much less baggage about social conscience and the like, too. Interesting, wasn't it, how protests and drugs were part of the same culture? No, life was all about the good life, wasn't it? Ah. Yes to wine, woman, and song.

After med school and residency, Randy had discovered a universal truth: fun is good. God knows there was enough drudgery and difficulties to go around, right? Wherever you go, whoever you see, happiness reigned supreme. Whether it was in the examination room with patients, the conference room with colleagues, or the dining room with friends and family, a kind word, a cheery outlook, did much to smooth out the wrinkles in life. For Cindy and him, the "doctor's orders" were to let the good times roll.

He had no complaints.

He drew her to him and looked about his apartment. "You're so good for me," he said. No longer bachelor digs, Cindy had a knack for putting a room together. From the scroll legs on his new chairs to the wallpaper wainscoting below the chair rail and the soft watermelon velour of his couches and upholstered armchairs, she turned the room into a very cozy cocoon. She'd arranged for similar upgrades in furnishings to happen at his new offices, too.

Yes, his new offices, Randy thought with glee. Here he was, his residency newly completed. He'd spent only a few months as an associate physician in a five-partner practice, serving more as a physician's assistant than a doctor in his own right. He'd be there still, were it not for Cindy.

She was the one who made so much of his good fortune happen. Graduating without student loans helped, as did a fresh inflow of cash from Father, a $50,000 loan mind you, at low, low, low interest rates—Father wanted to make up for that sad episode when he stopped paying Randy's way through school and Mum couldn't match Father's generous monthly allowance.

Who did Father think he was, pulling a stunt like that? Mum's story to the contrary—about gambling losses—didn't Father just always roll in the long green? Always had, always will.

And now Randy was headed in that same direction. Damn straight!

See how magical Cindy's touch was? She even had Dad eating out of her hand.

Randy recalled how he'd only met her, what, just three months ago? It was the end of the day shift. She was coming toward him down a long hospital corridor right here in Saint Louis, at Barnes Hospital. Looking him in the eye, she called out his name, opening her arms.

"You have me at a disadvantage" Randy said, somewhat startled. She stood within an arm's length, giving him a good up-and-down look.

"I forgot your name," Randy stammered.

"We haven't met," she gushed. She extended her hand. "I'm Cindy Arntsen."

"Pleased to meet you," Randy said as he continued to hold her hand.

"Shelby Reynolds asked me to look you up, Randy. When I got transferred to Saint Louis. I'd called your office, but well…here we are! You are Dr. Allen, aren't you? You studied at Columbia?"

"Yes," Randy said, certain that if she were in one of his classes, he'd remember. A bit flustered, Randy had no idea the class president knew him so well, but so far as he was concerned, a beautiful woman needed no formal introduction, no chain of recommendation—especially if she had called his office and somehow the receptionist had misplaced the message.

She handed him her card. She represented some kind of pharmaceutical company Randy had never heard of.

Anyway, it being 5:30, he invited her to have a drink with him to talk about…it didn't matter.

"How do you like Saint Louis?" Randy asked.

"I love it, so far," Cindy said. "When the company transferred me here, I had no idea what a friendly and wonderful place it is. I really would like someone to show me around." Her warmth was as intense as it was immediate. After a sip of white wine, she gladly accepted Randy's invitation to dinner. After dinner, she gave him another card, this time writing her home phone number beside her name. "Call me," she had said as she clasped his hand by the cashier's stand at the restaurant. When they said good-bye, they even did cheek-to-cheek air-kisses, continental style.

Because of that second card and the urgency in her voice, Randy saw Cindy as a lovely lonely girl who needed a friend in a strange city. But when she didn't return his evening calls to her home phone, he began to worry. By Wednesday of the following week, he decided to call her at work. She did, after all, originally give him her number on her business card.

After catching her breath, she agreed to meet him in a coffee shop at 4:00 p.m. Her formal business manner there stood in stark contrast to the coquette he'd experienced only days ago. She explained in a clipped voice how her company "made prescriptions cheap and convenient for patients through mail order fulfillment." Later, after a lull in conversation, she apologized for coming on too strong when they met the previous week! "I hope I didn't give you the wrong impression," she said, again with that vulnerable, tender look in her eyes.

Randy's heart sank. He had visions of getting very cozy with her immediately—if not sooner.

Toward the end of their coffee, she did notch it down into a more personable tone when she asked him if he recommended "preferred pharmacies" or just handed out "cart blanche" prescriptions that could be filled anywhere. Randy hemmed and hawed, thinking that "preferred pharmacies" were almost unethical. He was at a loss as to how to frame his concern to her. She made the offer sound like a true bargain for patients. All the same, Randy had his concerns when it came to playing it fast and loose with drugs and ethics. Look how badly it had gone for him in college—the worst thirty hours of his life—in the custody of the state, an experience he had no desire to repeat.

Looking into Cindy's eyes, as she ran her fingers over his cheek and then with a feathery fingertip touch over his knuckles, she said, "There is a tremendous need in this country for more serotonin to be traipsing across the synapses, don't you agree, Doctor?"

Who wouldn't agree to that? Randy nodded like a bobblehead. No question. He offered to talk with the managing partner about establishing a preferred pharmacy at Sherman, Sycamore, and Smith, the medical practice where he then worked.

Cindy said, "Great, but it's getting late. We can strategize that next time we meet." She appeared ready to go.

Randy asked if he could see her again.

She said, "Yes, but please, nothing heavy, if you know what I mean. I like you, but I don't want to date anyone right away. I'm just getting over a relationship that didn't work out. I feel…so vulnerable."

If Randy felt miffed then, it wasn't long after that before the love affair burst into full flower. One evening she called him at home. "Meet me," she said "at 4:00 p.m. in the coffee shop at the Medical-Dental Building in the Barnes Hospital Complex." It seemed as cold and clinical a place in Saint Louis for a rendezvous, but Randy arrived at the spot ten minutes early.

She flounced back on the couch in his apartment. "When are you going to open the champagne?" she asked, hiking her skirt up. He opened the bottle, popping the cork with a flourish. They raised their glasses and sipped. When the right one comes along, Randy thought, you know it. It was three months from the time Randy first laid eyes on her until she accepted his engagement ring.

"So tell me," Cindy said, "what was going through your head when you met me at the Medical-Dental Building."

"Only that I'd always wanted to have a practice there ever since the world began," Randy said. He set his glass down and took hers from her, placing both glasses on the table. He sat down next to her and ran his finger slowly up and down her stockings from behind her knee along to the outside of her thigh. "That particular coffee shop seemed such an odd place for a rendezvous. But then the leasing agent came by. I knew him from high school. Do you believe it? You couldn't have known that when you made the appointment for him to show us Dr. Norton's office. A little cheeky of you Ms. Cindy, to arrange a real estate viewing for me without letting me know beforehand."

"It was a surprise," Cindy gushed.

"Anyway, my God, Dr. Norton must have been dead, what two weeks? I half expected to find him keeled over at his desk, the place had such a smell. I guess the switchboard toggled his calls over to his emergency standby, Dr.—?"

"Evans," Cindy said.

"Yeah, Dr. Evans. Good memory. We were lucky Dr. Norton's widow didn't care for Evans. She wouldn't return his calls. Evidently, there was some history there. He would have been the natural one to take on Dr. Norton's patients."

Cindy leaned forward. Nice cleavage. "That's why it's so good you showed up when you did," Cindy said. "Now everybody's happy: you, me, and Dr. Norton's widow."

"Ah, but poor Evans," Randy said.

Cindy raised her glass in a playful toast. "Here's to you, Dr. Evans, thanks for giving us the business."

They both laughed, sipping the champagne.

"So," Randy said. "You saw the practice might possibly become available and thought of me." Randy eyed his champagne but left the glass where it was. "I still don't know how you found out about the situation."

"What can I say? I've got friends in low places." She kissed him.

"Meaning?"

"Honey love, if you're looking for changes in a building's tenants, who better to talk to than the night custodian? A business card here and there, with a small gift, a fine chocolate or a bottle of bourbon, tends to be a great conversation opener."

"Well, I'm not buying your story for one minute, but the results speak for themselves. It didn't hurt our cause any either that Benton and Allen just happened to be Dr. Norton's attorneys."

"See?" Cindy offered Randy his champagne glass. "It had to be."

He received the glass but set it back down on the table.

"If I hadn't had turned you on to the opportunity," Cindy said, raising her glass and asking Randy to pick up his. She clinked her glass against his. "Chances are, Henry would have."

"Oh no. No, Father doesn't look out for me like you have." Randy put the champagne to his lips but did not sip. Setting the both glasses down, he embraced her. After some hugging and kissing, they withdrew to the bedroom for some loving.

# 21

## FROM THIS DAY FORTH

*Randy*
*Thursday June 30, 1978*

With proceeds from Henry's loan, Cindy mailed out letters to Dr. Norton's existing clientele. She put together office-warming parties at the Saint Louis Art Museum, complete with a jazz band and a nice buffet. Health questionnaires, including a discount coupon for a physical, were passed out. She had other ideas on how to market Randy's practice.

Randy resisted at first. He said, "Doctors don't market."

"Honey love, doctors may not call it marketing, but they market. If you're not marketing, you're not growing. Don't kid yourself. The only doctors who aren't blatant about marketing are so established that their patients are their sales force. As I've been telling you all along, dieters and athletes are just like *Alice in Wonderland*. What's her theme song? One pill makes you faster, and one pill makes you thinner…"

"I don't think it goes like that."

"Oh honey love, it does when I sing it."

Dr. Norton's furnishings were a bit dated…an easy fix. Some got refinished, some replaced. New carpeting here and there and a buff job on the linoleum and they were open for business. Father extended another $12,000 loan with generous terms.

Cindy's redo of the waiting room was a bling bonanza. Velour cushions, brass chandeliers with flicker lights, indirect lighting set back in molding that ran around in a frieze at the top of the wall. Candles in crystal dishes, a Bose sound system. Very elegant, no place to slouch.

Randy refereed sports events and visited garden clubs to gain further visibility in the community. Everyone he met soon had a handful of his business cards.

Besides her skills in marketing, Cindy oversaw the books. Indeed, she was the first bookkeeper until the practice developed some momentum. She had a knack with claims adjusters, bill collecting, and insurance claims. She had an uncanny ability to combine symptomology with billing codes for prompt payment, even in Medicare. She suggested treatments patients were eligible for but had not yet received treatment (or billing) for. She had signing privileges with the banks. "We're a great team," Randy beamed.

Between his extracurricular visibility tours in the greater St. Louis community, keeping his chart notes up to date, and tracking the efficacy of new drugs, Randy had little time for the accounting side of his practice. The quick glances he did make to his books and bank account balances convinced him that he could trust Cindy implicitly.

Yes, it was a beautiful day. The sun shone brightly through the stylishly draped windows of Randy's condo on Lindell Avenue in downtown Saint Louis, just a ten-minute walk down shaded neighborhood streets to Barnes Hospital.

# 22

# A GIFT FOR CINDY

*Randy*
*Monday, July 23, 1979*

Two charcoal-gray sedans were pulled into the taxi stand in front of Randy's building when he arrived home that evening. With only passing interest, Randy noted the cars bore state license plates and mounted inside the cars' grills and rear windows were red and blue flasher-lights.

*Odd to see them here*, Randy thought. Cindy and he had been married a year now and had just returned from an anniversary trip to the Bahamas—a very strange trip, Randy recalled, as he rounded a landing in the stairwell. He winced. What had gone wrong? Sure, you can't do much when a storm rages and the beach is closed. Weren't blue skies, white sands, and sunshine what the Bahamas was all about? No one goes to the Caribbean in hopes of being trapped inside while a storm rages outside. Then along comes Hurricane…or Tropical Storm…or whatever…Claudette. The picture windows were boarded over with sheet metal shutters. The sun vanished from the storm-clouded skies. The ocean raged. For two days, they remained barricaded, restricted, and confined in the hotel against the high winds. Rain pelted the hotel at a near horizontal angle. No ordinary storm that Claudette. Once the big blow was over, going outside. Devastation everywhere. Georgetown, the Bahamas, was no longer clean and whitewashed. Downed trees, downed power lines. Palm fronds, tipped over trash cans, litter, scattered all over the lawn. The place was a mess. Booking a flight out…impossible. As bad as it was, Randy could deal with it. The hotel had lovely rooms and a beautiful lobby with pillars and a tall ceiling with marble floors. The backup generator worked fine when the power went out. Happy hour was extended. The restaurant fare...par excellence. As for Cindy and him—they had each other, right?

None of that softened the blow for Cindy. She blew up, furious. She took it hard. She got mad. She stewed. She asked Randy repeatedly, "Why didn't we go to Arizona or Acapulco?" Could Randy help it if it just so happened that Hurricane Claudette chose the same time to visit the Caribbean that they did?

She sulked and spent much of her time in the casino. "Small stakes," she said. "I'm no gambler." She just needed to "pass the time."

Anyway, whoever's fault the tiff was, now came the time to kiss and make up, right? Randy had bought Cindy a cashmere scarf. While winter was months away, he felt sure she'd just gush over it. She always did.

Oddly, the slamming of a door reminded Randy of the police cars down at the curb in front of his apartment house. *Could they be here on official business? Had an apartment been broken into? Could his own apartment have been the target of...burglars? What about Cindy?* She hadn't felt well that morning. She stayed home in bed. Highly unusual for her. That's what Randy loved about her, so god-beautiful healthy.

Randy hurried up the last stairwell home.

Turning the corner, Randy saw the door to his apartment hung wide open. "Cindy!" he called out. He stood in the entryway, stopped cold.

A line of police tape blocked his entry. Randy untaped it from the doorframe and entered his apartment. A uniformed policeman saw Randy approach. He said, "Sir, please stop. We're investigating a crime here. Please don't incriminate yourself by touching or moving anything." He tapped the badge on his uniform by way of introducing himself. "May I ask who you are?"

Randy set the gift box down on the desk by the front door. He gave the man his name. He had a very uneasy feeling. "I live here," he said. "This is my home. What happened?"

A detective, wearing a suit, stepped forward. He said, "I'll handle it from here, officer."

The detective, a Lt. Munger, spoke to Randy. "We received a call about a fight having taken place here. When we arrived to investigate, the door was thrown wide open, the jamb, as you can see, busted."

"What?" Randy said. "My wife and I live here. Where is she? Is she all right? Have you seen her?"

"No," Detective Munger said. "When we got here, the door had been left wide open. No one was here then. No one has been here since, except yourself."

"Oh," Randy said. He felt like an invader in his own home. "You haven't seen Cindy then. I've got to find her. May I use the phone?"

Detective Munger nodded, directing Randy to the phone at the small writing desk near the front door. "Careful," he said. "Use a tissue to hold the phone. That fingerprint dust is nasty stuff."

"Right." Randy called Paul. He called Mum. Neither knew anything about Cindy's whereabouts that day. He even called Cindy's mom in Chicago. No answer. He looked around the room. Things were thrown about, drawers open, the place was in an uproar.

There was another tenant in the building Randy and Cindy knew, a Mrs. Devons. When Randy called her, the elderly woman said she "saw Cindy leaving the apartment in the company of some men earlier in the afternoon." She had more to say, but Randy, just relieved to know Cindy was 'all right,' had no time for social chit-chat. He thanked her, closing the call.

Detective Munger then asked Dr. Randy some questions.

Where had he been today? Did he and his wife get along well? Did they have any houseguests?

Randy answered all the questions as in a daze. He'd been working at his office all day. Yes, he and Cindy got along perfectly. No, there were no houseguests. All the while, the question that kept pounding in Randy's his head was, "Where's Cindy?" Surely, she must have calmed down since the tropical storm upset her. Was she feeling any better? What was that about a 911 call? What had been reported? Had Cindy been kidnapped? A fight? Who, how, why? It looked to Randy like a break-in. The doorjamb had been split open, and at least two of Cindy's paintings had been taken off the wall. He asked the detective, "How long have you been here?"

Detective Munger said he'd only been there a half-hour or so. Besides Munger and the uniformed cop, another detective and a woman in white coveralls had taken control of his rooms, inspecting things, sprinkling fingerprint powder on counters, papers, the phone, and light switches.

The other detective stood watching Munger interview Randy. He'd mentioned his name, but Randy couldn't remember it. The woman in coveralls came out of the bedroom, closing the door behind her.

What had happened? Someone had broken into his apartment, that much he'd picked up. The framed Kandinsky and Gauguin, prints Cindy had bought, were missing from the walls where they ordinarily hung. At the time Randy bought the artwork, he did not know frames for such things could cost $600. He didn't have a special flair for art, but Cindy loved these artists especially. She gushed over them. What else had been stolen?

The woman in white coveralls had gone back in the bedroom. Now she came out with what? Nothing?

Randy's mind raced through some alternatives…Cindy may have picked up a stalker somewhere along the way…had Cindy been kidnapped? Or maybe it was a disgruntled patient. Randy reported the missing paintings to Detective Munger. Munger then asked Randy to provide him a list of all other things he could identify as missing.

Randy said he wanted to file a missing persons report on Cindy, but Munger said that was premature. Randy asked the police how long they planned to have the place tied up in their investigation. Munger said they would be finished soon, but Randy couldn't stay in his apartment with all the disarray, the fingerprint dust, and the doorjamb busted. The third locksmith he called said he also did carpentry work and could come out right away to secure the door.

As Randy waited for the locksmith, looking at his thrust-open door, he regretted putting "MD" after his name in the local phone book, along with his address.

Drug fiends had broken in. That's what happened. Drug dealers had fingered a doctor's listing in the phone book and decided it would be a nice private place for them to loot narcotics. His TV, stereo equipment, financial records—all these were missing too. He would have to report that to the police, too.

If Cindy been home when such an invasion happened, they may have roughed her up. Had she been hurt? Had she been kidnapped? Held for ransom? If they contacted him, should he call the police or cooperate with the thugs?

Detective Munger said a report of a fight had prompted their visit. Crazed drug fiends came in and disrupted their lives! Nuts to that. They'd have to move. Randy wondered if he should call the hospital to see if Cindy had been admitted to the emergency room.

Who made the bizarre 911 call anyway? What was this all about?

No! He shouldn't dwell on such strange thoughts. He needed a clear head to find Cindy. She would explain everything. He tried to think of places to go, people to call, to find Cindy. He wondered what else might be missing around the apartment. He wondered what other clues, what other information could be found around the apartment. Anything to help explain what had happened.

He hated how the horrible thoughts raged within him. His concentration had gone entirely limp. His mind raced out of control, so unlike himself.

Randy did not do well with chaos. He knew he far preferred his life to be orderly, pleasant, and predictable.

As for the police who came to snoop, to inspect his apartment, they *embraced* chaos. It was oxygen to them. They fed on it. It's how they supported themselves. The dark side of humanity was their bread and butter.

Even so, had they reached any conclusions? No, probably not. Did they even have any gut-level hunches? Any explanations? Whatever they did know, Randy sensed they made no plans to share that information with him. Liability issues…or perhaps they simply were as buffaloed as he.

Then again, whose apartment was it? His. Who had to live with this problem? Him, Randy. Who went home that night, totally forgetting every strange thing that happened in the apartment on Lindell Avenue? The police, the detectives, and the crime technicians. It wasn't their problem. The crime technician even wore latex gloves to distance herself from her examinations, to handle the chaos in her clinical way.

Randy did not want to linger another second in his apartment. He did not know where to go. His stomach had twisted into a knot.

He shuddered. He waited for the locksmith.

In college, especially med school, he had gone on the occasional drinking binge. It helped to ease the pain.

Pain like he felt now. Why did the crooks choose this day to break in? A day when Cindy stayed home? She hadn't been feeling well. No question but she had to have been here when the break-in, the fight, occurred.

He prayed for her safety.

Randy sat down on the floor and covered his face with his hands. It had been a strange day all around. Where was that locksmith? First, Cindy stayed home sick. She never got sick. Then the phone message left with the answering service. A Mr. Tobias of Trexler Commodities had called. That's how he identified himself, a commodities trader who called at the suggestion of his colleague, Mr. Berber. Tobias claimed that Berber "got a prescription over the phone for secobarbital." Tobias had a sleep disorder too. So he wanted "the Makofarmica Mail Order to send him some pills too."

*Randy had no recollection of a patient named Berber.*

Tobias sounded highly presumptuous. Had the man just dialed the wrong number? How many Dr. Allens could there be in Saint Louis?

Then the locksmith arrived. He put a temporary plate on Randy's front door, promising to "fix it up right" later in the week.

Before Randy left his apartment, he studied the secretary desk in his front hall. He noticed the piece of furniture wasn't real wood, like he thought when Cindy bought it home. No, it was contact paper on chipboard, and now the contact paper was peeling off.

The apartment, once his castle, the center of his universe, now seemed oddly barren, violated, filled with chintzy furniture, a quick stop on the way to someplace else. He had to go out, get some fresh air. The graphite powder stunk and burned when he breathed it. The disarray got to him.

As he turned to go, he even reached to pick up the box with the scarf in it he had bought for Cindy. Then, before replacing it, he saw underneath the gift box was an envelope addressed to him, marked "Personal and Confidential." It appeared to be Cindy's handwriting. The envelope was thick. It could have contained two or three pages. He had to get out of there. He took the letter with him. As Randy swung the door shut, it swung stiffly, as if the hinges had been bent.

# 23

## DEAR RANDY

Out on the street, Randy looked for a place to go, a place to sort things out. Given the events of the late afternoon, and the thickness of the letter, an uneasy feeling grew within him. He couldn't very well read such a letter in his car. Given the fingerprint dust and the disarray of his apartment, it was uninhabitable. No way would he be going back there until it was cleaned up. It actually felt good to get out of there.

As Randy looked down the street, it occurred to him that he and Cindy often stopped at the nearby Olive Grove Hotel after work. She may even be there now, totally unaware that their apartment had been broken into. Given his circumstances, the Olive Grove was the closest thing to normal Randy could think of. What could be safer than sitting down in a booth in the dimly lit place and ordering a small Cabernet like he and Cindy often did? As for his heavy drinking days…they were history now.

He would open the envelope. Yes, he and Cindy often stopped there to have a small Cabernet before dinner. Once or twice a month, they even stayed to eat dinner right there in the hotel dining room. Who knows, she may even be there now, sitting all cozy, waiting for him.

Once seated in a booth, Randy hesitated before opening the envelope. He became concerned. Could it be a ransom note? It was awfully thick.

> Dear Randy,
>
> As a decent, honest, and responsible person, I feel it is my duty to reveal the heartbreak our marriage has been to me as civilly and directly as is possible under such trying circumstances. No one gets married only to arrive where we are now—in less than a year. But that is where our relationship now stands—gone.

Randy put the letter down. He could not read any more. He flagged the waiter down. Soon a scotch with a water chaser stood on the table before him. Before he continued reading the typed letter, Randy gulped down the scotch and drank the water and asked for another. When did Cindy write this letter? Why was he finding it only now? *What was he doing in a bar with empty wine glass and now a second glass of scotch on the table before him?*

He tried to understand what he was reading. Surely, it was not the work of one day. It looked too thought-out, too detailed, to be a rush job. It had to be something on her mind for a long time, long before they went to the Caribbean. Wow. He had no idea. What was it about their marriage that so offended her? Doubtless, the answer lay in the rest of her letter, but already Randy felt jolted, shocked, and overwhelmed. He couldn't possibly absorb any more bad news. Already his pulse raced. What could he do?

He needed a confidant.

He recalled all the stories he'd heard in the AA meetings he used to attend in New York as he had struggled with his drinking problem.

No, Randy liked his privacy. You can't bring news like this to an AA meeting. He hadn't even been to a meeting since he met Cindy. Maybe he could check into the hotel, take a hot shower, a cold shower, have a drink, turn the TV on, and the distraction would take some of the bite out of whatever other surprises the letter contained. Or he could get drunk, go for a run in the park…

No, all those alternatives sounded so beside the point. He would confront this head on, as sober as he could.

He called Paul. Wasn't Paul the bastion of reason, of common sense? He asked Paul if he might come over for a visit. He had something urgent he'd like Paul's opinion on.

As this was Randy's second call of the day, Paul asked, "Are you all right, Randy? Have you heard from Cindy yet? I can come get you if you need me to."

"No, that's okay. I'll be there…within the hour."

He was touched that Paul expressed such concern that he, Randy, might be so grief-stricken as to be incapable of driving himself a mere five miles or so over familiar roads. What did that say about Paul's loyalty as well as his level of—how to say this?—empathic fellow feeling. Randy didn't think he sounded that distraught, but Paul picked right up on it. Another scotch appeared on the table before him, a scotch rocks. Randy didn't remember ordering it. Oh, well.

As he stared blankly at the letter, Randy realized the thing frightened him. When he called Paul, he even thought of having Paul be the first one to read the full letter—but now that he knew he would be seeing Paul soon, Randy decided going down that route would be childish, ridiculous. He'd best brace himself, face the music, and read the whole letter himself, privately, here in the bar.

He glared at the scotch. You really do need to make a point with these bartenders. Neat. They put so much ice in scotch on the Rocks that the taste was gone, and by the time you took a sip, the liquor's gone to. You have no idea if they put in just a half a cap or 1.5 oz like they're supposed to. Anyway, Randy read the rest of Cindy's letter:

> Go ahead, once you read this, cancel our
> Caribbean anniversary celebration.

Hmmm. So, Cindy had originally planned to present this letter to him before the Caribbean trip. Maybe that's why she was so beside herself in the Bahamas. She had already decided the marriage was over.

> I've had my fill of our so-called marriage.
> Call me old fashioned, but I expect a certain staidness, a certain stability in a husband. I tolerated your gambling problem as best I could, holding your money for you, and fending off your sporting event bookie buddies as best I could. I asked you to get help for gambling and counseling for our marriage, but you wouldn't listen to me. Then, on top of that, when for the past weeks, you became so heartless, so hem-haw about the sanctity of life, I knew the time had come for me to take my stand. We had agreed "no children" on many occasions before we got married and for months after. Then you

claimed Bruce Jr. changed your mind. You wanted children. When I expressed my reservations, you did nothing to work with me to resolve such an important issue. Instead, you replaced my birth control pills with placebos. How sick can you get? What if I became pregnant? Randy, children are forever. They're not your little kiddie dolls. They have feelings. They have dreams and need time, love, and respect. I shudder to think of the life you and I would have brought into the world had your plan succeeded. You know full well all the many reasons we both agreed to have no children. Way beyond our original "no children" agreement, the arguments against children for you and I are clear: your gambler genes and our dedication to career. These were both major reasons we both had discussed, understood, and had agreed to on more than one occasion.

Then there was an even higher reason, one which you had obviously forgotten: the love we had for each other, the time we loved spending together, every waking hour, at work, at leisure.

I can only thank my guiding angel that I did not become pregnant. Randy, before you drag me into the gutter with your wasteful gambling, and your child/ no child schizophrenia, I must get away while my sanity remains whole. It's over, you've broken my heart, you louse. Goodbye. No woman should suffer as I have suffered under your whimsical thumb.

Wow. Randy folded the letter up. He tried to figure out the timing of the letter. Evidently, the original letter was supposed to be delivered a week ago, but for whatever reason, she didn't do it. Birth control? Placebos? What? Randy didn't even know where Cindy kept her birth control pills. In fact, he was scheduled to have a vasectomy.

Randy had never wanted children. Neither had Cindy. Why'd that appear in the letter? Gambling problem? Until they went to Georgetown, the Bahamas, Randy had never even been in a casino. Why was that in the letter?

Bookie buddies? Possibly five times in his life, Randy may put five dollars in a Super Bowl pool at the insistence of friends…but where's the problem there? Why did she want to call off the marriage? None of what she said in her letter was true. Randy never wanted children, and neither did Cindy. No argument there.

When would he hear from her again? He almost ordered another drink but knew that would only lead to trouble. He should have stuck with his original plan to just have that one small glass of wine.

Quickly, he got up and left the Olive Grove Restaurant. Dee Dee, a waitress he and Cindy knew, scurried up to catch him in midstride. She wore a short blue skirt, a linen bonnet, and a flouncy embroidered blouse. "Dr. Allen," she said. "Good evening. Will Mrs. Allen be joining you?" He'd never been there before without her.

"No," Randy said. "Not tonight, Dee Dee. Thank you. I'll let her know you said hi. I just remembered, it was tomorrow night we'd talked about dining here. See you then."

As Dr. Randy stepped outside, he buttoned up his sport coat against the chill. As he adjusted himself to walking instead of sitting, he discovered at least one thing about himself this evening. Liquor still had a bad hold on him. He made a note to remind himself to avoid the stuff in the future. It was hard to just satisfy himself with just a sip.

He'd best get over to Paul's house before he did something crazy, like buying a bottle to take back to his apartment.

# 24

## GETTING WITH PAUL

*Randy*
*Monday, July 23, 1979*

"C'mon in Randy. Man, you look tired. What's going on?"

Randy smiled tentatively. He muttered some kind of greeting as he stepped into the Bouchard house on Fern Street.

Paul sniffed. "Phew, you've been drinking. Don't deny it. I can smell it on your breath." As Paul shut and locked the solid wood front door, Randy felt an abrupt change in things. The place was familiar to him, of course, his childhood home. The furniture was even in the same places…a couch in the front bay window, but a newer, brighter one than Mum's. The two armchairs on either side of the fireplace were the same ones Paul and he had bought as a present for Mum and Bruce's wedding. Still and all, there was a newness to things, as if the old house had been torn down and a new one rebuilt in its place. Randy opened and closed his hands; he swung his arms about then put them in his pockets. He was damp with sweat, feeling agitated.

"Hey," Paul said. "Relax. Take a load off, man. Come sit down. You okay? What happened, exactly? We haven't seen you in a while. Then two phone calls in one night…"

"Yeah, well, you know how it is. We all get so busy," Randy said. Standing there in the wood-paneled front hall, Randy took a passing glance into his father's old office on the right before entering the living room on the left. Linda sat in one of the armchairs by the fireplace doing some sewing, a bright floor lamp beside her. She wore a royal blue corduroy jacket with pants that matched, her hair tied in a short ponytail. The place looked a picture of domestic bliss. God, Randy felt so agitated. He fidgeted. Would he ever find relief? "I hate to intrude," he said. "It's not your problem."

"Forget that, man," Paul said. "You go ahead, come on in here. Sit back on the couch, if you like. Kick your shoes off, too, if you like. Relax." He exchanged a glance with Linda. "We can tell you're hurting, man. Take a load off. Can I get you something to drink? Coffee? Tea? A glass of ice water?"

"Yeah," Randy said. "A tall glass of ice water would work. Easy on the ice." He coughed out something of a laugh, as if too much ice would be a problem. "Yes, I've had a drink this evening. I received some bad news. Oh man, this is awful." Randy fell uneasily down on the couch while Paul went to get the water.

In the short time he was away, Linda and Randy visited some on her sewing project—shortening the pant-legs on some new pants for Bruce Jr. "so he can grow into them."

Once Paul returned, Linda said, "So—don't keep us in suspense. What's going on?"

Randy blurted it out. "Cindy left me. She not only left me—she's mad as hell. Claiming I did all kinds of weird stuff. When I came home…"

"Hold on," Paul said. "Is this just your first fight?" He had retaken his seat in the other armchair.

"No, nothing like that. I mean, I can appreciate that married people fight…" Randy recalled how Mum and his father fought and divorced. Randy took a large gulp of the water.

Paul said, "We got plenty of water. Drink all you want."

Linda turned her chair around to more directly face Randy. "I'm so sorry to hear that," she said. "What makes you so sure she's leaving? The two of you were such lovebirds."

Randy thought he detected some tongue-in-cheek in her tone, but he made no comment on it.

"That's the part I can't understand," Randy said, checking to make sure the letter still rested in his inside coat pocket. "She wrote me this crazy letter. She accused me of…" Randy shook his head. "The way she described me, it's like I'm this big fat monster. None of it is true." Randy pulled the letter out of his inside coat pocket.

"I know the girl meant a lot to you. What happened?" Linda set her sewing down.

"Why don't you read the letter for yourselves? See if you can make any sense of it. None of what she says is true. I don't know why she's doing this to me." He got up and handed the letter to Paul.

Once he'd handed off the letter, Randy continued on into the kitchen to refill his glass of water. When he returned, he saw Paul stood crouched over the back of Linda's chair. They were both reading the letter together.

Linda harrumphed a few times, and Paul shook his head and scowled. "I don't believe this," he said.

Linda said, "The man in this letter does not sound like you. How well do…did you know this woman?"

"Up until now," Randy said, "I thought I knew her very well. She was warm, friendly, smart…a great lover and a hard worker."

"Did you know her people?" Linda asked quite simply.

This threw Randy off. "I met her mother once. She lived in Chicago. Cindy would go visit her sometimes, maybe every six weeks or so."

"That says something about her, I guess. That she's so devoted to her mother. Why'd she go so often?" Linda asked.

"The woman wasn't well," Randy said. "A smoker and not very mobile."

"Was she in a wheelchair?"

"No, but when she walked, she got up with effort and walked in a slow, measured way, with a cane. What's that got to do with anything?"

Paul said, "Probably nothing. I think Linda's just trying to get a better picture of who Cindy was. You see, neither of us really got much of a chance to get to know her."

"Yeah. There was *that* about her," Randy admitted. "She really didn't want to get to know my side of the family and so far as I knew, it was just her and her mom."

"Did you go with her to Chicago?"

"No. Only once. There wasn't a whole lot I could do. We never went anywhere. When Cindy visited alone, she'd go on a Monday, coming back by Thursday, so we had our weekends together."

"Who else did she know here in Saint Louis?" Linda asked. "Did she leave you for another man? That's often the case, from what I've heard."

"I don't know. All I know is I love her, and when I came home tonight, not only did I get this letter, but our house had been broken into."

"That does sound strange," Linda said. "Do you think the two things are related?"

Randy shook his head. "I'm at a loss. Can't even think about it. I mean, everything was going perfect, and then all of the sudden, the floor just gives way, and this letter. She makes our entire marriage sound like some kind of sham. I can't figure it out."

"Well," Linda said. "Neither can I. It did amaze me at the time, how quickly it all happened. She appears out of the blue."

"She latched on to you from the start," Paul added.

"Interesting now to learn she had no other friends in town."

"Slow down, you two," Randy said, holding up his hands. "She's not here to defend herself." Randy caught himself. What was he saying? Here he was, despite the letter, despite the situation at the apartment, defending her. To hear the others analyze her alarmed him. The letter was typed. Maybe someone wanted to make it *appear* as if Cindy had turned on him. They just wanted to get him all worked up, then they would spring some kind of ransom demand on him. Whatever the case, things obviously weren't what they appeared to be. Still, his pride would not let him believe she no longer cared for him. That she somehow got her jollies by surprising…no, hurting others.

Now Linda was talking again. "So okay. Let's back up. If I understand all this, so far as children are concerned," Linda said. "So far as you know, you never wanted children and neither did Cindy."

"Right," Randy said. "What's so hard to understand about that?"

"Do you know if she was pregnant?" she asked.

"If she was…" Randy started. "No, she said in the letter that she was not pregnant."

"That she knows of," Linda said.

"That gambling thing could also be important," Paul said.

"But you don't gamble either."

"No, of course not. I don't even bet on the Cards-Cubs game."

"Well, we all know what a shoe-in that is," Paul said.

"Especially if the game is in Saint Louis," Randy added. Then he sighed. "Hey, you guys are golden," Randy said. "Here I am at a complete loss to deal with this thing and you've opened your home and your hearts to me. I don't know. I just don't understand anything that letter says. Cindy could never have written it. The facts in the letter don't match what we had going."

The two of them were looking at him now, a hard, scrutinizing look.

Randy caught the seriousness, the immobility of their expression. He said, "Ah, look, if you've got something you want to tell me…Just go ahead and say it. I'm not sure I know what to think."

Paul exchanged a look with Linda. "Neither do I," he said. "But maybe a good place to start is by washing some of that alcohol out of your system. Let me get you a tall glass of iced tea. Then I'd like you to do me, do yourself, a big favor, okay? Stay here tonight. With us. We've got a spare bedroom. This may sound like something you'd read in a sob sister column, but I'm serious. You've had quite a blow today. And the first thing you did to cope with it was have a drink. In fact, my hunch is you had quite a few drinks. I'm thinking the best thing you can do right now is take a deep breath, try to screw your head on straight. Think about your situation. This is going to sound hard. It's going to sound unsympathetic. I'm going to say it anyway. Forget all about Cindy." Paul held up his hand when Randy made to speak. "Forget about seeing her the way you saw her up until now. I don't know what it is, but I'm thinking there's plenty more trouble hiding underneath this letter than what we see right now. Will you stay here tonight?"

Randy looked at Paul. He looked at Linda.

"That girl really wanted to knock you off your feet, in the worst way," Linda added. "For whatever reason. I'll go see if that bedroom is ready. Maybe you and Paul can talk over old times."

Randy fell back on the couch. "I'm not looking forward to tomorrow," he said. His gaze fell on the Chunky Sam bird logo for Sunny Day soda. Ordinarily a fat, anthropomorphic chicken, a klutzy looking thing, this Chunky Sam was done in an upscale Coq de Gaulois style wearing a Cardinal's ball cap.

"So," Randy asked. "What's new at Sunny Day Beverage?"

# 25

## RANDY GETS THE PICTURE

*Tuesday, July 24, 1979*

"No, this is not a sales call," the caller on the other end of the phone barked. The thin edge of civility in his voice vanished. Abruptly, he said, "My company, MCS, represents the $1,349.82 you owe Makofara Pharmaceuticals, Dr. Allen. How can we schedule *your* payments on this outstanding balance?"

This was not the kind of call Randy needed just then. It had come through when Randy had picked up the phone to call the bank. How'd the caller even get his back line?

The blunt edge of the caller's voice…

His intensity…

The rudeness of the thing…

This must be the kind of treatment deadbeats get. Randy ran a respectable and robust medical practice. Already the man had threatened to call daily until he got an answer. If the money was not forthcoming within the week, every credit bureau in the country would lower Dr. Allen's credit rating to where it would hurt. Dr. Randy took down the man's phone number. He said, "I'm hanging up now. I'll get back to you," even as the man continued shouting expletives.

The call had come in as Randy sat in the accounting office. A patient had cancelled her appointment, giving him time to look through his filing to see where Cindy had left off on the bills. He couldn't even find the business checkbook. That's why he had wanted to call the bank.

So far as Randy was concerned, the marriage could still be on. Yes, despite the letter and the upheaval at the apartment, the way Randy saw it, women were emotional, you had to cut them some slack every now and then. The apartment? That was someone else's doing…drug addicts.

Until he heard it directly from Cindy, face to face, the marriage was still on. She would have to look him in the eye, say she wanted out, that she didn't love him. Then and only then would it be over.

He had a vision of her in his head that he just could not—would not—shake.

Didn't she have it all? Charm...beauty...enthusiasm...talent...the list went on and on. No, he didn't want to lose her.

Yes, that's exactly the way the thing stood between them when Randy came in to work that morning. But now, unable to find past bills, unable to fend off scurrilous calls from bill collectors, unable to even find so much as the large three-sheets-to-a-page big black check ledger...well, even a patient man has his limits.

At the very least, couldn't she at least walk him through where to find the checkbook, the payables file, and the bank account balance? Would she remain mad at him forever?

But then Randy's eleven o'clock was in the office and he became busy with patients again.

Wednesday brought more problems. The morning mail contained several overdraft vouchers. These made serious dents in his checking account. One overdraft in particular had to have been charged to his account by mistake. The amount was $5,000! Randy called the bank. It had been presented by a bank in Florida. Something to do with the casino in Freeport.

Hmmm. Still, Randy tried to justify the situation. Maybe Cindy thought him too demanding. She had done so much for him, for their marriage: lover, confidant, business advisor, homemaker, bookkeeper. Was it any wonder she had to take a couple days off? She didn't know how to stand up for herself. That's why she wrote the angry letter. As it was, perhaps this extravagance, this $5,000 to settle with the casino, was what sent her into hiding. She didn't want to fess up to her indulgence.

What could she have possibly bought from the casino worth $5,000? Was she gambling? Had the roulette wheel so fascinated her that she forgot it was real money? She must have been under an awful lot of stress. Some people just aren't cut out to be with the same person twenty-four hours a day. Wife, homemaker, companion, brilliant accountant—he really had come to rely on her for an awful lot. Once she did show up, Randy would see to it that they found someone else to do the books at the office. She could go for help, get treatment. Get rehabilitated.

Was he a pushover? A softie?

No, he was numb. Running on autopilot.

Randy did however have enough sense to call Robert at Sherman, Sycamore, and Smith. He was the 'go-to guy' there. Robert suggested Randy get a sub from Med Temps. When the temp came, Randy set her on a quest to reconstruct his accounts payables. "If you have to, call the utilities, the landlord, and look through patient files for any clues as to whether the insurance company filings had been made and received." Joyce, that was the temp's name, expressed some concern that the job might be too difficult for her, but she would do her best.

As it turned out, all the receivables from the insurance companies were very current, "so far as the insurance companies were concerned." The odd part was that they had paid into an account at Amalgamated Union, a bank Randy had never even heard of. A call to the bank confirmed that Randy's name was on the signature card.

"Oh?" Randy asked. "And when did I do that?"

The banker said it had been "just six weeks ago."

Randy leaned back in his office chair. He looked out the window across the Mississippi River. Amalgamated Union? Why would Cindy set up an account at that bank? For starters, it was on the other side of the river, in Illinois. Randy's office was in Saint Louis, Missouri. It was late afternoon.

Joyce, the temp, came into his consulting office. A short, heavy, dark-haired woman in a black dress, Joyce reported that, "Your phone is about to be cut off, Dr. Allen, and the landlord will be bringing by a thirty-day notice of eviction in the morning. Your accounts are a mess. Supply companies, Makofara Pharmaceuticals, among others, are seriously delinquent; I'm talking sixty, ninety days and more. You need to get a CPA in here. I'm telling you, someone with a cool head and nerves of steel." She sighed. "I'm telling you, your creditors wore me out. They are so angry. I didn't know what to tell them." Joyce looked like a cheerful person. Even other people's bad news upset her. She gulped and began talking faster. "I've written down the names and the amounts of everyone I talked to. I told them I would get back to them when I had more information. Please, Dr. Allen, I can't take another day of this. Please don't give the agency a bad report on me. It's not my fault. I really tried to do my best…Also, I found this." Joyce handed him an envelope. The return address was from his original bank, the one he actually did open with Cindy.

After Joyce left, Randy opened the envelope. It was a bank statement for his checking account, complete with cancelled checks. The last six checks were all marked NSF, non-sufficient funds. In particular, one check told a tale. It was made out for $5,000 to "Casbah Casino, Las Vegas." Randy recognized the signature. It was Cindy's.

Randy looked at the date on the check. When had Cindy the time to go to Las Vegas, what with tending to her mother? Randy pulled out his appointment book. The date on the check matched a week when Cindy was supposed to be in Chicago visiting her mother.

Goddamn! How blind can one person be! How long does it take an idiot to get a clue! He'd been taken for a goddamned ride by someone on whom he thought the sun rose and set. He'd been given cement over-shoes and tossed in the river. Cindy had no love for him. She had sucked him dry, for what? Grins? To feed a gambling habit? To bundle up a little booty for herself? Did she do it alone? Who else was in on it with her? How would he tell his friends about her betrayal? No, that was too kind a word. Treachery? Randy burned. When he rubbed his face, he could feel how tightly he'd been clenching his jaw. How wound up he was. No, sympathy on Cindy or himself was wasted. Only if there was a God in heaven and justice in the courts could Randy pray they would both devour and spit out her criminal soul. She had used him. She had embezzled money from his practice. He was about to go belly up.

Action plan: find an honest accountant. One versed in the machina-tions of the criminal class. Randy called Bernard Jeams, the Colonel's accountant. He explained the circumstances and asked for advice. His heart may be breaking and his business hemorrhaging, but now was no time to dally.

Jeams had a few suggestions: Hire a forensic accountant. Follow a course of action for a businessman/doctor when their staff embezzles. Pursuit your rights when a marriage goes south.

Next, hire a lawyer. But who? Sure, he could ask his friends for law-yer recommendations. He could very easily do that, if he didn't value his privacy. If he wanted everyone to know what an embarrassing botch he fell into, what a complete idiot he had been.

He could also have called his father. Henry was a lawyer. But Randy didn't have all that much confidence in Father's capabilities. For one, according to Mum, Father had a gambling problem. Plus, Father had gone out on Mum. No, Randy did not want to involve Henry until he at least had some inkling, some clue, as to what he should do. No sense in getting railroaded to who knows where by Henry Allen, attorney at law.

The other thing about Dad that troubled Randy was how enthusiastically he had been taken in by Cindy. Randy remembered the pleasure, the immediacy, with which Henry came forward with a gift/loan to start the office. He loaned them money, not once, but twice. He praised Cindy for her zeal, her cleverness, and how she "stood behind" Randy.

Oh shit. Randy was not ready to see how the tables would turn on that one.

Yes, eventually Randy would have to tell everyone his marriage was over. But that could wait. Right now, he needed professional help. He needed the best talent he could tap, given all his constraints in both time and money.

Sure, he'd like to locate the ultimate low-cost, high-results, divorce/embezzlement/fraud criminal lawyer. Who wouldn't? Given the circumstances he found himself in, finding a package like that would be ideal, but Randy's resources were limited.

He wracked his brain. Then, on a fluke, Randy called Dirk Halbers. Dirk was the only attorney Randy knew other than his dad, other than patients. True, Dirk Halbers had represented him during his college days in New York. But he now lived and practiced in Saint Louis. When Randy called him, Dirk offered a free forty-five-minute interview. Surely, in that time, Randy reasoned, couldn't he get some kind of glimmer of a strategy? So Randy went to see Dirk Halbers.

Granted, Randy had his reservations about how Halbers handled his case back in his college days. But when it came to legal and financial questions, especially when it came to legal and financial matters where he screwed up, Randy also believed the fewer people who knew all the bloody details, the better.

One thing for sure: he needed to report the embezzlement, lock the barn doors as it were, before more horses got away.

Then, too, the fiasco at his apartment needed attention. Randy clearly had his hands full.

# 26

## THE EXPERTS WEIGH IN

### *Randy*

Randy hired Dirk Halbers, and in no time, Halbers got surveillance camera footage of Cindy opening the account at Amalgamated Union. Indeed, why did the cosigner sitting at the banker's desk with her look so familiar? Randy looked long and hard at the image flickering across the screen. Clean-shaven and neatly barbered…could it be? Then there was that bumpy mannerism with the pen as he reached to sign the account card. It was Joel Scroggins! Joel from college days. Joel, once a pharm D candidate, until Randy stepped in to make Joel the target of a police sting. Damn! Randy had busted Joel back then. Now Joel had busted Randy. Joel had carried a grudge! Was turnabout fair play? Sow the wind, reap the whirlwind?

No, this revenge struck Randy as severe overkill.

He was going to ask Dirk Halbers if any other strategy could have been used in his old case, but ever diligent, Dirk had requested more video surveillance camera footage. This time from the Casbah Casino in Las Vegas. There they were again, Cindy and Joel Scroggins purchasing poker chips at the cashier's cage.

Evidently Joel did not forget how Randy had destroyed his budding career as a pharmacist. It appeared the two of them, Cindy and Joel, had teamed up to fuel a rambling-gambling lifestyle at Randy's expense. According to Dirk, some of the funds they tapped were contestable. Randy would not be liable for those. Randy did, however, remain on the hook for other debts. As to how much money had been exhausted on gambling and how much scurried away to bank accounts out of sight or offshore…that was anybody's guess.

Any way Randy looked at the matter, one thing became perfectly clear: he had been thrown on the rocks, hung out to dry.

Bernard Jeams, the CPA, set up new accounts, closed old accounts and reckoned "the nut" Randy had to come up with to keep his office, regain the trust of his creditors, and consolidate his outstanding credit cards balances. It was $211,500 "in round numbers" and more, depending on terms and interest.

All around, it had been a very hard summer for Randy. He went through a string of bookkeepers. The ones with technical skills snubbed Randy for the disarray of his books, and the ones who were easier to talk to didn't know the intricacies of their job. But none of that amounted to much. Where would Randy come up with $211,500 to keep his practice afloat? Even were he to secure a ten-year note, the monthly payment would be in the thousands of dollars.

# 27

## TRICK OR TREAT?

*Randy*
*Wednesday, October 31, 1979*

Eventually, Randy moved back into his apartment. The flood, fire, and emergency restoration service saw to the clean-up and repair of broken drawers, the door, and the like. The insurance policy even covered the expense, as it was considered the results of a break-in. But Randy no longer wanted to live there. He listed the apartment, a condo really, with a real estate agent.

Detective Munger said he had no further information on the break-in or altercation—he wasn't even sure what to call it. Randy knew, though. Cindy had set him up for a major sting. She had sucked him dry of money he did not even have. Mrs. Dover came to talk with Randy one evening after Randy resumed living in his apartment. She said she had asked the painters who came to repair the break-in damage to paint the wall on the second floor of the stairwell where the wallboard had been dented. Why didn't they do it?

Randy was at a loss. "Did that happen the day of the break-in?" he asked.

"Of course," Mrs. Dover said. "That morning, I met Cindy in the stairwell. Two men were with her, jockeying a large Kandinsky painting up over and around the banisters. So she knew the damage had happened that day."

"I'll take care of it," Randy said. "Since you requested it at the time they were here."

Then his father, Henry Allen, phoned Randy one evening to ask, "When can we get together?" He sounded oddly upbeat.

They met in the law library at the Benton and Allen law firm. It was Halloween. The windowless room was lit by a bank of white florescent lights that were recessed into the ceiling. The two of them were quite alone in there. Well insulated and sound-proofed, a thick carpet on the floor, the place was quiet. Thick law books crammed into the floor-to-ceiling bookshelves surrounding them on three sides of the room. The slightest whiff of copy machine toner came into the room through the air duct that blew otherwise fresh air into the room. The main piece of furniture in the room was a Formica conference table with a simulated wood grain. In the middle of the table were a plastic jack-o-lantern and a small cast iron caldron filled with chocolate in foil wrappers and candy corn in cellophane.

Such frippery stood in stark contrast to Randy's somber mood.

"So how are you, really?" Henry asked as they sat down to coffee. Father held a sheaf of papers in both hands upright like a shield before him. It concealed his coffee cup. "You've been through quite a rough patch."

"Yes," Randy said. He coughed. It sounded strange to talk about his problem as just a "rough patch." Cindy had raked him over the financial coals. He'd been buried under a mountain of debt. And beyond that, she'd flown false colors, claiming to be a lover when she really was an embezzler, a cheat, a liar.

All that nothing but "a rough patch?"

Shit.

Couldn't she please just get run over by a freight train or arrested, especially if any of his money was recoverable? But Randy had given up hope of that. She had most likely spent every last cent. Yet despite his frothy thoughts, he heard himself reply, "Yes, it has been a rough ride."

Father's face lit up. "How would you like to put all that behind you?"

This tipped the scale for Randy. Was Father really that out of touch with pain? Randy sat up straight and prepared to give Dad a piece of his mind.

"Well!"

*Thud.*

Henry dropped his sheaf of papers on the table, before Randy could even start to sound off. "There's no reason, is there?" Henry said. "I mean, just supposing, if you could, why you couldn't just pick yourself up and go on...is there?"

Now Randy could respond. Deep and loud, he said, "That's a mighty big IF. How can you even say such a thing? I'm nearly a quarter million in debt. My credit is shot."

Henry gave a toothy grin. He raised his eyebrows, his eyes opened wide. He smiled mischievously.

"What's so funny about debt?" Randy asked. "You should know. I owe you money, I owe more than one bank, two landlords, more drug companies than I care to count. I'm hoping to get a decent price for my condo. At least that will wipe out one debt. How'm I going to reestablish my credit? How'm I going to just pick myself up? You talk as if nothing had happened!"

Henry raised both his palms. He slapped his chest above his heart. "I'm not without feeling on this, Randy. Believe me, I've had some setbacks in my life, too," Henry said. "I know where that's at. Of course something tragic happened to you. Something awful. It shouldn't happen to anyone. I'm not without sympathy, son. How long shall we commiserate on this?" He looked at his watch. "Five minutes, ten minutes?" He tapped the face of his wristwatch. "Or I can present a solution to you right now, so you can get on with your life as if nothing had ever happened."

Randy almost considered his father was playing cute with him. Mocking him. Or had a bum idea. But no, the man did appear to have something up his sleeve. The bundle of papers in his hand was about an inch thick. So Randy said, "If you've got something to say, shoot."

Father continued. "I can understand you're struggling with many things, son. Maybe you've written me off; I'm out of your life, doing my own thing. I've abandoned the family. But it doesn't work that way. We're blood. Our family is much larger than most you see. Despite the setbacks and challenges that have come your way, you still have an amazing set of resources. It just so happens, Randy, that recent changes in estate taxation have prompted the Colonel to reexamine his will, to reexamine the Bouchard Trust, of which you are an interested party. The chief asset of the Trust is of course, the Bouchard Beverage Company, dba Sunny Day Soda." Henry separated out a copy of his papers and handed them to Randy.

Randy moved his coffee cup and looked through the papers before him.

Henry said, "Here's the estate plan I'm recommending to Colonel Bouchard. You stand to benefit from it immensely, so listen carefully. You know the Colonel has been wanting to sell the bottling company since forever. Now, with your mother nearing retirement age, and given your predicament, the time may be right for him to sell. The sale will fully fund his legacy and release the family of any further obligations about the bottling company."

"Okay," Randy said. "How's that?"

"It's simple," Henry said. "Stuart and I have made certain confidential inquiries with a business broker. I believe the Colonel would prefer the family got the benefit of his money instead of the feds. I think you'll agree with me that an estate tax rate of 70 percent is a heavy hit. The company could not possibly come up with the $1-2 million required in estate taxes, so liquidation really is the best alternative anyway."

Randy bonked. How could his mind straddle this? On the one hand, sell the firm. What would Saint Louis even look like without Sunny Day Beverage? On the other hand, millions of dollars in taxes—that made his $250,000 pale by comparison.

Henry continued. "Jeams tells me you got notice on your offices."

"What?" Randy said. *What business does Jeams have snitching on my business to Dad?* But he kept his anger to himself. "No, that's been resolved for now. I've got until December."

"Is it true? Did you get notice on your office?"

Randy nodded. *Where was this going?*

"If we get right on it," Father continued, his words rushing together. "You may be able to satisfy any new stipulations your landlord has placed on your office—so you can keep your private practice and all the rights and privileges thereof. What do you say to an opportunity like that? Would you like to hear more?"

Randy scowled. He felt skeptical…but minute by minute, the skepticism faded. What was Dad up to?

"Okay," Henry said. "I know the old saying. If it sounds too good to be true, it probably is. That doesn't apply in this situation. Like I said, we've known the sale would take place for a very long time now. But maybe you've forgotten all that. Maybe you aren't ready to see the sun come out after the storm." He went to pull the packet of pages away from Randy.

"No," Randy said. "Go ahead. I want to hear more. So far I haven't heard anything I object to."

Henry laughed. "Good. Think of it. Back in the good graces of your suppliers, able to overlook the fact that your insurance company payments got waylaid? You maintain patient goodwill. No need to declare bankruptcy. You can just keep on doing what you've been doing. Wow. How amazing. He studies for ten years at university, trains in residency, and builds a viable medical practice. Yes, son. That is amazing. I hate to break the news to you, Randy. Just open the phone book and see how many doctors there are in Saint Louis, each of them in private practice. It happens all the time."

"I got it," Randy said. "Enough said. All right, I'm cautious. I just don't want to get swindled again. Incidentally, whatever happens, bankruptcy is out of the question."

"I admire that about you," Henry said. "I know I can't very well afford to write off the $62,000 I loaned you." Henry tapped his papers. "Look at these numbers," he said. "You could let my loan sit in the Trust for a couple years…it can draw interest there as easily as any place else. There is a tax advantage to me for you to pay me in annual installments. You'll still have everything paid off much faster under the plan I've presented to you than any other option you'll ever run across. It really is a once-in-a-lifetime opportunity." Henry's eyes lit up. Randy could see the idea thoroughly enthused the old man.

"So okay," Randy said. "The big problem I see with your plan is you're talking millions—is this all liquid money? Last I heard, Sunny Day was brick and mortar, steel and rubber. It produces a stream of money, not a lump sum."

Henry leaned forward to whisper, "Would you believe Consolidated Cola has made an offer of $7.5 million for the company? If the stockholders approve the sale, the Colonel could then gift three million of it to the University of Missouri for their new Bouchard Ball Park. The highest tax rate for estates is 70 percent. It used to kick in at the ten million mark, but last year they lowered it to five million. Anybody's guess where it will be next year. Two million? So if we structure the sale this year…see? So the part that's going to get the big tax bite, in excess of five million, is donated to the University. You know Grand-pere and my father, Allan Allen, played on the Mizzou football team, don't you? They get their stadium renovations, and here's the kicker, Col. Elijah Bouchard gets a lifetime annuity. The balance is for the immediate benefit of you, his heir. We can structure it so you can draw on that money to promote your vocation."

"What about Mum and Bruce?" Randy asked.

"Oh, they're covered, too. Their pension plan will be funded by a lump sum settlement, as I recall."

Given Randy's dire circumstances, stumbling on such a windfall blew him away. No wonder Henry Allen had been set on fire. The old man grinned, nodded, and gestured grandly. What was going on? Was Father happy for him? Other than warm fuzzies for his son, what did Father get out of the deal? Money? Randy didn't care. Accepting the deal, going along with it, meant he would rise above his problems! Halleluiah! The old feelings lived on. Randy recalled the last time he had been charged up with so much excitement. Not all that long ago, either. The occasion: when Cindy had found Dr. Norton's old office vacated. Together, they took over Doc Norton's practice, making it the foundation for his own private practice.

Randy struggled for something to say. Caution warned, "Be skeptical," while his heart said, "Yes! On with the Dr. Randolph B. Allen show!" After mustering his emotions, Randy asked, "Who else knows about this?"

"What?" Henry said, a blank look on his face.

"What?" Randy repeated. Maintaining his skepticism was hard work. He held back a smile. "What have we been talking about for the last ten minutes? The sale of the company. I talked to Mum just this past Sunday. She didn't say boo about any sale."

Henry shrugged. "That's strange. A letter went out. I'll have to check with the staff. I admit it, though—the offer from Consolidated is very recent. So we're all racing to keep up with the latest developments. Look, I'm taken aback by all this, too. Benton and Allen have been lawyers for the Bouchards for years. Allan A. Allen, my father, used to say since 1908. And I realize, too, things are strained because Benton and Allen, my brother Stuart actually, represents Elijah, Grand-pere. Then mother and I…exes…but, well, nothing lasts forever, trees don't grow to the sky." Henry spoke in greater earnest. "So here's where you come in, Randy." He leaned hard toward Randy. He almost whispered, "The Sunny Day Beverage Company stockholders' meeting will take place next Monday afternoon right here in our conference room. All the family will be here. All you need do is support this deal, and you will receive your inheritance. Enough of it I'm sure, given your circumstances, can be released directly to your creditors to save your practice from going underwater. That's it. It's that simple. All you have to do it vote the measure in. What do you say to that?"

"Frankly," Randy said. "I'm amazed. Overwhelmed. Of course, it couldn't have happened at a more crucial time for me. But what do you get out of it?"

"Me?" Henry slapped his chest. "How thoughtful of you, Randy. Thinking of others in your time of need. What do I get out of it? I get to see my son continue on in his career serving the public, being a healer. I get to be of service to you. Believe me, it gives me no satisfaction watching you suffer as you have, son."

"Okay," Randy said. "Fair enough. I feel I need to do my due diligence. Is there any reason why this plan should not be put in place?"

Henry leaned in. "No. As I've said before, everybody in the family benefits from this deal. So there should be no opposition whatsoever. Just be here at the family meeting this Monday at two, right here in our conference room. It's as simple as that. What could be better? Mother got her shot at running the business, Elijah gets his memorial, and you get to continue your career—in the style in which I'm sure you've grown accustomed, despite your, ah, rash choice in, ah, relationships. Bless your heart."

Randy pursed his lips. "You don't have to rub it in," he said.

"It's a done deal then?" Father stood up. Randy stood up. They shook hands. Henry walked with Randy out to the elevator bank.

As the news sunk in, a giddiness came over Randy. He could hardly contain his glee. This was great news. He hated seeing himself as a victim of a gold-digger. An operator. Now he didn't have to. He felt ironclad. She couldn't touch him. Between now and Monday, he would double check everything so make sure his financial house was as tight as possible so he would staunch the flow of money from the gash Cindy had given to his finances.

Out in the elevator lobby. Randy in his overcoat, others were there too. Everyone waiting for the elevator ride down to the street. Father offering to shake hands again. He said, "I'm counting on you, Monday, two o'clock. Be here. Vote the measure in." Then Henry gave Randy a pat on the back, excused himself, and returned to his office.

Out on Market Street, all the office girls hurrying home looked especially pretty. Having someone to love him…that's what it was all about.

And so many of these girls looked so fully qualified. Cheery, eager, sexual. Maybe a little less possessive this time. No sense in rushing into anything. Have some fun. Marriage can wait. Randy felt good. A heavy burden lifted from his shoulder. He was golden. His private practice had hit a snag, but that had been taken care of, put to bed. Those testy bill-collecting piranhas could just go gnaw on someone's carcass. He was free.

As Randy pulled his Riviera out of the garage, accelerating and cutting into traffic, the old devil-may-care attitude came on strong. How'd it go? *Nothing ventured, nothing gained!*

Of course he would take Henry up on his offer! Why did the old man make it sound like skullduggery? Randy could keep his private practice. His apartment, too, for that matter. Moving was such a hassle. No, say all the bad things you wanted about Cindy. At least she did get him started on his own private practice. You could at least say that much about her.

It was after dinner, Randy was back at home, when the phone rang. It was Clay Sherman, Dr. Sherman, the head of the group practice where Randy had worked for a few months before opening his own office. "Dr. Allen," he said. "I've heard your new practice is doing quite well."

"Yes," Randy said, choking back a bit. "I can't complain."

"That's good. We were sorry to see you go. You are one of the good ones, diligent, conscientious. Not a pill-pusher like some. But you know all that. I believe some of your patients here followed you to your new offices."

"That was their choice," Randy said. "I sent no announcements to your patients."

"Oh, that's not the reason why I am calling tonight. Accept the compliment, man. You're that good." Dr. Sherman paused. "Look, we want you back. Medicine is becoming an increasingly complex field, isn't it? Keeping up the back office, insurance billings, specialties, on-call substitutions, continuing education requirements. You know all that. We'd like you to come in to discuss a partnership for you, if you're interested."

"Oh?" Dr. Randy said. "Really? Well, there is some truth to what you say about complexity. Yes, I don't see where it would hurt to talk."

They set up an appointment for the next week.

As Randy hung up the phone, he recalled the conversation with Mr. Tobias, the patient, the commodities trader who wanted a prescription for barbiturates filled—sight unseen. How many other icebergs like that were out there, floating in his patient file, sight unseen?

# 28

## CRUNCH TIME

*Monday, November 5, 1979*

Coffee, hot cereal, a bowl of canned grapefruit, sausage—it looked like an ordinary Monday morning breakfast.

Yet Paul knew full well this was anything but an ordinary day. Even the headline of the *Post-Dispatch* screamed that the world had been knocked off its axis, spinning out of control.

"Iranians seize US Embassy."

That's what the headline said. Paul scanned the story. Militants stormed the US Embassy in Tehran. Seventy-two Americans held hostage. Their release unlikely any time soon. The militants demanded the Shah be returned to Iran so he could be "tried and executed." (*Yeah, right*, Paul thought, *tried and executed fair and square*.) Fat chance President Carter would bow to a demand like that.

In a sad way, Paul welcomed the distraction offered by the foreign service officers. It set his mind to armchair quarterbacking a military-grade rescue mission. As the military had countless battle plans drawn up for every contingency, what would one look like for this?

Yet right now, Paul could use a few contingency plans of his own. Today, the Sunny Day owners would meet to decide whether the company continued or would be shut down. No, that made it far too abstract. The company was not a "person." Paul, Linda, and Bruce Jr. They were living, breathing, real-life people. Their future hinged on the decisions made today. And employees…how many employees? Who got to tell them their services were no longer needed? The place would be shut down? He couldn't believe it himself. There must be close to one hundred employees involved with the company now. The place scrapped? Consolidated? Why? Did the Colonel know what a gold mine he had on his hands?

All the effort he'd put into the company over the past several years…
gone. Yes, Lindy Snacks would survive, but the efficiency gained by co-
marketing the products? Gone.

Losing Sunny Day would definitely be a step down for Paul. As for
Margaret and Daddy Bruce…true, the sale did come with a lump sum pension. But not near enough. Not with inflation and the ever climbing cost
of living—to say nothing of the loss of their vocations. What would they
do with their time? No pension could approach the full value for the lives
they devoted making Sunny Day the flourishing company it had become.

Already, Paul shouldered much of the responsibilities for day-to-day
management. If he were to step up to become the chief operating officer, he
could rely on Margaret and Daddy Bruce on the board of directors. Their
expertise, connections, and vision would be extremely useful in strategic
planning and exploring new business options and efficiencies that hands-
on managers just didn't have the time for, vital as those tasks were.

Yes, each of them, Daddy Bruce, Margaret, he, and Linda, knew the
risk of a sale was there. A sale *might* come. But that did not soften the blow
when, as now appeared so evident, the risk of the sale had finally come.

Think about the sale in a calm, detached, matter-of-fact, that's-the-
way-it-goes kind of way? Not hardly. Not for Paul. The tension crawled
up his neck and cramped his jaw. Psychic pain, he thought. He poured
another cup of coffee. *Careful now,* he thought. *Am I sharpening my wit
or getting wired up for a ride on the Stressville Espresso?*

News of the meeting had come to Paul this way. A week ago, Margaret received notice in a letter from Stuart Allen, Col. Elijah Bouchard's
lawyer. She no sooner opened the letter than she told Daddy Bruce and
Paul the news.

As strange as it was to imagine, all three of them knew that Stuart
Allen had been working for some time to get Colonel Bouchard declared
incompetent. Stuart, the executor of the estate, held a power of attorney—most likely far more limited than Stuart led everyone to believe—
but power of attorney nonetheless. Up until now, Margaret and Randy
had easily stood him off by putting together a panel of doctors who stood
ready to testify to the Colonel's mental acuity should Stuart ever dare
press for a competency hearing. The stockholders' meeting appeared to
be Stuart's latest strategy to wrest control of the Colonel's personal fortune and inevitably control of Sunny Day away from the *paterfamilias*.

In response to this threat, Paul, Margaret and Daddy Bruce, along with Linda, Paul's wife, went to visit Col. Bouchard at his home in Ladue. Randy had been invited too but could not be persuaded to join them.

On the drive out to Ladue, Margaret explained how Meriwether Manor had been built in the late 1940s by Francois "Frank" Bouchard, Col. Elijah Bouchard's father. Colonel Bouchard had been given the family homestead, the Bouchard house, as a wedding present. Frank Bouchard had been the true driving force behind the Sunny Day Beverage Company. Under his leadership, the company had warehouses in Trenton, New Jersey, and Bakersfield, California in addition to the facility in Saint Louis. His plan was to build bottling plants there when he died of a heart attack.

Paul pointed out how the present expansion plans were, in a sense, making up for lost ground.

Meriwether Manor sat in the midst of a six-acre park accessible through a magnolia-lined driveway leading up to a classic Southern plantation house, complete with six thick white columns twenty feet high supporting the gabled roof of the massive front porch. When Arlene Bouchard died the year before of a pulmonary infection, the Colonel invited his bridge partners to "come live" with him. As the Colonel often hosted the card game anyway, according to Margaret, it wasn't hard for the others to accept the offer. The home was assessed, and the other three (two widowers and a married couple) bought in.

The upstairs was remodeled into four bedroom suites, complete with full baths and dayrooms. Downstairs, there was the great room, living room, study, reading room, grand and small dining rooms, breakfast nook, and kitchen.

The ceilings downstairs were ten feet high, done up with a brocade finish and beveled edges with indirect lighting. The furniture was quite elegant, the various tables done in a lustrous cherry with graceful lines that Margaret described as in the French Empire style. The upholstered furniture appeared quite inviting, and the views out the windows featured wide grass lawns, rhododendron bushes, and oak trees.

A grand staircase and elevator served the upstairs. The basement had a full bar and billiard room. An administrator who Margaret called Smitty showed them in. A couple lived in a cottage in back—a full-time cook married to a personal trainer/male nurse.

Margaret showed them around the place as Grand-pere's bridge partner took a little extra time choosing his cards.

When they finally did have Grand-pere's attention, he was somewhat abrupt. He said, "While I appreciate your visits, Margaret, especially today with your management team, I do not want to talk about business. My advisors assure me they have a proposal designed to maximize value *for all concerned*. Until we know what that is, what's the point of speculation? Give me the facts every time."

He appeared to be brushing them off.

Paul would have none of it. He stepped forward. "Speaking of facts, then," he said. I've prepared a report, based on your own CPA's numbers. I think you'll find the trends from 1960 to the present, 1979, are phenomenal, especially in light of all the talk these days of...stagflation." Paul handed the Colonel his copy

This plea appeared to speak to Colonel Bouchard. "All right," he said as he took hold of the copy. "I'll look at your numbers. Any step I can make toward stamping out that god-awful word Stagflation is a step in the right direction so far as I'm concerned. Good day, gentlemen, Margaret."

Stagflation, ubiquitous in the press of the day, was a word coined to describe 'an economy stymied, without growth, due to inflation.'

Paul's report charted revenue and expense year by year, dramatically showing the phenomenal growth in revenues, lower expense ratios and higher returns on investment. It emphasized as directly as it possibly could the company's expansion, especially in the past three years.

As Margaret had said on the way out to Meriwether Manor, the real mover and shaker of the Sunny Day Beverage Company had been Col. Bouchard's father Frank, not the Colonel. Not by a long shot. And now, Margaret, Daddy Bruce, and he, Paul Elser, had once again put the company back on a robust path. They had built a warehouse in Trenton, with plans for a bottling plant there as well. They had identified excellent local people who could be developed and grow with the business. Similar arrangements had been made in California, although the decision had been to locate in Irvine rather than Bakersfield. Paul had decided that Col. Bouchard may have been a great big booming extrovert and even a master bridge player, but he was no businessman.

In the 1950s, the era when the Colonel ran the show, sales had shrunk. He had sold off the Bakersfield and Trenton plants. He focused the business in Missouri and the Midwest, cultivating the distributors handed down from his father, but he did not get along well with everyone. If someone rubbed the Colonel the wrong way, that person found their deliveries were delayed and their spoiled product returns not given full credit. That was one of the challenges that both Daddy Bruce and Paul faced as they built the business. No wonder the Colonel wanted to sell when his attorney said he'd found a buyer. For all Paul knew, Col. Elijah Bouchard may not even know how Daddy Bruce, Margaret, and he had steadily built up the business in the Midwest and how they were expanding distribution back to regain both coasts, adding Toronto and Florida in the bargain.

Paul picked up a copy of the report he left with the Colonel. It had been laid out with the key points highlighted and an executive summary, as well as all the detail even a demanding auditor would expect. Under the column for every year's revenue and profit margin was confirmation that the numbers were taken directly from the Colonel's own CPA. The Colonel had even said he would run the report by his CPA for verification. The firm was growing at an annual 20 percent for the past five years. Nothing wrong with that, not by a long shot.

If only Paul could share these numbers with Randy. For once Randy saw these numbers and knew what was at stake, he could most likely be persuaded to hold onto the company. While $7.5 million was a great deal of money, if the firm was really worth $10 or $12 million, the firm would be sold at a loss. And that said nothing of the intangible issues, like the loss of jobs.

As to what Randy knew or who might be bending his ear toward selling, Paul would only know that once he had a face-to-face with the man.

This owners' meeting had been sprung on them all so fast. Once again, Paul felt that bile brewing within him. How could anyone expect a $7.5 million decision to be made on the basis of one meeting, with little more than a week's notice?

Paul and Daddy Bruce weren't even invited to the meeting except Margaret made a very heated point of placing a "report from management" on the agenda. Certainly, there must be at least an ethics, if not a legal, violation in jamming this meeting down all their throats.

Paul leaned back in his chair. He stretched his arms. Okay, what are the facts of the matter? Who are the players? Who owns stock? The Colonel, obviously. Margaret, yes. What about Randy? He'd been invited to the meeting, so he had to own something. How much? At this point, that was anybody's guess. As animated as Stuart appeared to be about the thing, Paul would definitely like to know that guy's stake, too. Maybe some commissions from the sale, maybe some commissions from handling the resulting money, but what about actual ownership? In fact, that was one of the key facts Margaret, Daddy Bruce, and he wanted to know when they visited Elijah Bouchard last Wednesday. Margaret recalled that back in 1953, shares had been sold to Allan Allen, Stuart and Henry Allen's father. Was that true? If so, what happened to those shares?

So far then, as Paul could see, the fate of the company rested on reaching Randy. But Randy had not returned his calls. If he had to, Paul would stop by Randy's office on the way into work this morning.

Linda came into the room carrying Bruce Jr., who stirred in her arms. She sat down next to Paul, pulling her chair close to him.

"Look who's awake. Good morning. How are you? Ready for another day, my little man?" Paul asked, stroking the baby's cheek and kissing him. The happy little babe smiled back at his dad. How his eyes sparkled. So innocent, so eager. *He smiles at everyone he sees*, Paul thought.

Linda sat down and resumed sipping her coffee, balancing the baby on her knee, not a care in his little world. The youngster busied himself inspecting a spoon and a saucer, seemingly amazed by all he saw.

Linda sighed. "The world isn't going to fall apart, is it? This sale isn't going to kill us, is it?"

Paul shrugged. "No. Not by a long shot. Keep the faith, girl." He kissed her.

The phone rang. It was Randy. "Yeah, good. Thank you. Let's get together for lunch. O'Connors. See you there. Bye."

"See? It's easy." Paul's relief was palpable.

They both laughed. The past week had been anything but easy on either of them.

The dining room at O'Connors was dim, smoky, and crowded. What a commotion this lunch crowd made. Trying again to distract himself from the intensity of the day, Paul thought what a challenge it would be for filmmaker to create a medley of all the bits and pieces of conversation taking place in this restaurant at noon. What did people talk about? Their personal health, marriages, last night's games, graduations, relative's health, new lines of work, closing various deals, divorces, job hunting, new golf clubs, add it all together…talking about this, talking about that. The cacophony of life. Add in the clatter of silverware and the comforting odors of tea, beer, cabbage, corned beef, and was that a peaty and piney tang placed in the ventilating system to mask the smell of tobacco smoke? Put it all together, and there you have it: the usual noontime crowd at O'Connors Bar and Restaurant.

If Paul listened carefully, he could just make out a melody played by a flute, a penny whistle, and a tambourine piped in over the ceiling speakers.

His flight of fancy didn't work. He still did not like the last-minute timing of this meeting. No one did, except maybe Stuart, who appeared to be orchestrating the whole thing. Why the pressure? As a general rule, Paul considered himself a guarded optimist. There was hope here, he thought. The Colonel could have as easily delivered his decision by fiat; he had the clout. *The business is sold, everybody clear out your desks.* That would be the hard-guy approach.

But framing the decision as a stockholder's meeting implied, at least to Paul, that discussion and voting would take place.

The other cause he had for hope was the Colonel's manner when they went to see him at Meriwether Manor last week. Something in his touch, his tone, his eyes, suggested a little more receptivity than did the *fait accompli* tone of the letter from Benton and Allen-the lawyers. Did he perceive those things accurately?

So could he put numbers on all that? That morning, Margaret said the Colonel owned 575 shares and she held 425 shares. Once Randy showed up, that would be crucial information. Anything over seventy-five shares would turn the tide if Randy sided with them. It would have been better if Randy had gone out to Meriwether Manor with them.

Margaret had invited him, but Randy said, "No, I've got no time," and that he "got the low-down from Henry."

Damn! What the hell did that mean?

Margaret had really gone to bat on this. Paul was in her office when she called Stuart on lack of management representation at the meeting. She raised a ruckus. "I want management at this meeting too, to give their report," she had demanded.

So Daddy Bruce and Paul would be there to give the owners a true picture of what a tiger they had by the tail in the Sunny Day Beverage Company.

Yes, Paul reasoned; there had to be more than that 55/45 split they all knew for sure. Somehow Randy had a voice. Estate planning, wealth management, and all kinds of other issues had to be pieced into this thing, too. That's where talking to Randy came in. Reynolds, a CPA friend of Paul's, knew about succession planning in a family business. Reynolds had said the question is, "Has a trust been set up, or is a simple gift?

As to the Colonel's philanthropy, how much money he cared to keep in the family, taxes, and all the other details of such arrangements—as well as any favorable view of the blended Elser-Bouchard family—well, all that could be seen clearly...through a pig's eye. Over the years, how much grief had the Colonel given Margaret over her choice to be a woman of business? Too much grief. And of course, in the Colonel's eyes, the divorce, the mixed marriage, and racism...none of this bode well for a decision in favor of keeping the business under present management.

One last strength Paul saw in Sunny Day Beverages centered on its place in the life of the community: the many employees, second generations in many cases, who had been with the company for years. That had to count for something more than *remains* to be liquidated in the ruthless pursuit of the almighty dollar.

No, for the sake of the people, for the sake of the profit, the Colonel could not possibly find a better place to invest his money than where it was right now...in Sunny Day Beverages. The company was a Saint Louis institution.

Paul looked up at the photo on the wall above their table. In the photo, the Card's World Series pitcher Curt Flood had his arm around Mick O'Connor, the owner of the restaurant. Behind them, slightly out of focus, but still quite easily made out, was a soda dispenser with Chunky Sam, the Sunny Day bird, visible for all the world to see. Curt had written a thank you on the photo for some banquet or another Mick had hosted for the Boys and Girls Club, which the Cardinals attended.

O'Connor's had all kinds of pictures all over the walls. Him and Joanne with this and that celebrity—but this one, in this booth, made it a favorite of Paul and Daddy Bruce's because Flood was a big hero to them both and because of…well, the Sunny Day tie-in.

Then Paul saw Randy. He carried a newspaper under his arm and a beer in his hand. As he slid into the booth, Randy said, "You're early. I was hoping to get a chance to read the paper. What do you think of that? Our embassy staff has been taken hostage." There it was again. Paul read the headline: "Iranians seize US Embassy."

Paul nodded. "I think the chickens have come home to roost. Didn't the CIA and MI5 reinstall the Shah back in 1953, defying the popular vote for democracy?"

"What?" Randy said. "The story didn't go into that, did it?"

"Read further," Paul said. "It's no secret."

Then Nola came to take their order. "Good afternoon, gentlemen," Nola said. She passed out menus and refilled Paul's coffee cup.

The aroma of corned beef and cabbage filled the room, so Paul didn't even bother looking at the menu. He ordered the corned beef. But Randy had studied the menu as if it were tea leaves. Suddenly, he dropped his menu to the table. He nodded at Nola. "Same here," he said. "That's easy."

Once the waitress left, Randy confided, "She played me for a bloody fool, that's what she did, I'm so pissed." He guzzled down his beer. His face turned red, embarrassed by his gullibility. He looked ready to hurt somebody or something.

"Hey," Paul said. "Easy now. I hear you. Don't be so hard on yourself. It's got to be tough on you. I know. I'm sorry for your loss. But you'll get through it. Just give it time."

"Yeah. Time," Randy said. "There just doesn't seem enough of it these days." Steam appeared to be boiling out of his pores.

*How*, Paul thought, *am I going to get him to concentrate on the business at hand?*

Then Nola came back with two corned beef plates. "Be careful," she said. "The plates are hot."

Randy put his arm around her. How long had Nola been waiting on them? "You're a sweetheart," he said. "Thanks for taking care of us so fast. Any chance I could get some stone ground mustard…and another beer?"

Nola pulled a bottle of mustard out of her apron pocket. "I thought you'd never ask," she said and laughed. "The beer? It will take a little longer."

"Thank you," Randy said, slathering his corned beef with the mustard before arming himself with knife and fork to pounce on his meal.

Paul ate at a much more leisurely pace. Should he call Randy on his lunch hour drinking? No, he decided to stick to business. "This stockholder's meeting has come on us fast," he said. "From what I hear, the reason for the meeting is to respond to an offer to purchase the company. Is that what you've heard, too?"

Randy nodded. His mouth was full. "You heard right," he muttered. "You make it sound tentative, though. Evidently you have some arguments against the sale?"

"Yes," Paul said. "It'd be a tough break for me if it went down. Have you talked with your mom? Where does she stand on the deal?"

"We talked on the phone. She invited me to go out to visit Grandpere, the Colonel. I would have, too, but man, I've been just running my head off lately. I don't think I've slept more than three hours a night. I am just exhausted."

"You know, then, how she feels about the company."

"Yeah. But I don't know. I'd be happy to stand with you guys on this. You want to keep it going, right? But I mean ultimately it's up to the Colonel. I understand he wants to do something for U Missouri, add some seating to the football stadium or something. Enough so they'd name the place after him."

"Impressive," Paul said. "I hadn't heard that part. A decision this big, though, it seems rash to move so fast on it. The people involved… given that its family, not just the Colonel…their perspective ought to be considered, too."

Randy pushed his plate away. "I get that. I talked with Mum. She thinks the company is worth more than what's being offered for it. It that your opinion, too?"

Paul nodded. "Yes. It's worth much more alive than dead. Please, so much as you have a voice in the decision, please consider the sale is not written in stone. Vote against it."

Randy leaned back. Paul's candor appeared to amuse him. "Okay," he said, looking around the room. "I'm sorry. I know I'm coming across like Mr. Hardass. I'm busted, man, and they're waving millions in my face. Give me some ammunition to fight that fight with. Big ammo. I don't want to get shot down when push comes to shove."

"Funny you should ask." Paul smiled carefully, amazed that this decision could take on a business school case-study air. "I just so happen to have a chart that shows just that. May I show it to you?" He moved over to sit on Randy's side of the booth to show him the numbers.

Randy looked the chart over. "Did you mail a copy of this to me?" he asked. "Because I haven't had a chance to look at what you sent a few days ago."

"Yes, this an exact copy of the report I mailed you. The Colonel got his copy Wednesday. So look. Do you have any idea of what stake you have in the ownership of the company? Think, it's important."

Randy took control of the reports. He flipped through them. As he did so, he said, "Every month I used to get reports from my broker. I had stock in GE, GM, IBM, Xerox, Polaroid, and Bouchard Bottling dba Sunny Day Beverage Company. Then when? Two months, three months ago, last summer? That goddamned bitch sold everything that was marketable! All I have left is the Sunny Day. The broker called me to verify. I brushed him off, saying, 'Cindy handles all that now.' Damn! Thankfully there was no market for Sunny Day—until now. It's valued on the reports at a par value of $.25. So how that relates to the market value, I've no idea."

"If they are full shares of common stock," Paul tried to sound as sympathetic as he could, given Randy's outburst. "All you need to know is how many you have for the vote. Par means nothing."

Randy countered with, "As far as I know, the money from the sale is going to be rolled into a trust, and that's how I'll get some cash to get my life back on track."

"That's *one way* you can get your life back on track. There are others." Paul moved to put the report back in the envelope and handed it to Randy. "Think. Do you have any idea how many shares you own?"

"Well, as I recall, every year, Grand-pere gifts me…ten shares."

"How long has that been going on?"

"I don't know…since college…1971."

"In that case, you could have eighty shares." Paul thought about that. "Unless those are new shares, that means your mother and you are now in control." Paul scrawled some numbers on a napkin. "She's got four hundred twenty-five plus your eighty gives us five hundred five to Col. Elijah's four hundred ninety-five. If you vote against the sale," Paul said, "we can resume paying dividends. See? That's another way you can get your life back on track."

"Possibly," Randy said. "You've worked hard on putting that report together. You and your father have worked hard on putting the company in the black. Fact is, you've got a better thing going on with Daddy Bruce than I have with my father. But…" Randy furrowed his brow. He bit his lip. He shook his head. He appeared troubled.

"I realize I'm leaning on you," Paul said. "And I admit my relationship to the Bouchard family is not blood." How far could he take this? Randy looked ready to bolt. Paul persisted. "My stake in all this is based on the love between my daddy and your mum. That's the family part. As for the money part? Well, the company has never been stronger, the prospects never brighter. Daddy Bruce, Margaret, and I have poured our life's blood into Sunny Day." Paul was racing now. "If you want to look at the Sunny Day Beverage Company as a cash cow, welcome to the club. All I'm saying is that this cash cow will serve you better alive than dead. As to naming rights to the Mizzou Stadium, or whatever else has been bandied about, wouldn't the Bouchard name have more punch if it were attached to a living organization like Sunny Day Beverage? Than to a tombstone that seats seventy thousand?"

Randy looked away. Had Paul lost the man's attention? On an impulse, Paul looked to see what Randy saw. It was the photo on the wall above their table. The photo of the Card's World Series pitcher Curt Flood standing with Mick O'Connor, the owner of the restaurant. In the background was the soda dispenser emblazoned with Chunky Sam.

"Okay," Randy said, looking now at Paul. "I'm getting a little pissed. Here you are. You're well situated, with or without Sunny Day. And yes, my father did make, as you put it, representations to me. Half the time, I'm not so sure that Stuart Allen is doing grand-pere any favors. But all that aside, it's like you're pulling one arm while Henry's pulling the other. Meanwhile, my life is the pits! Everybody wants a piece of me. I don't know what to do."

Paul nodded. "I'm sorry to hear you struggle, man. I understand it's your call. All I'm saying at this point is thank you for hearing me out. Anything I can do to help. You got it. There's more than one road leading to Rome. Let me buy lunch, okay?"

"Well, thank you," Randy said. Then he looked at his watch. He looked around the room. "Guess we'd better get on downtown, huh? Look, I ah…didn't tell my office that I wouldn't be coming back from lunch. I'll need to check in with my answering service and give the receptionist a heads-up on my schedule." He paused, as if waiting for acknowledgement or a counterargument from Paul. Then, with the envelope in his hand, Randy began to turn, to get up out of the booth.

"What about the meeting?" Paul asked.

"Tell them I'm on my way," Randy said.

# 29

# THE STOCKHOLDERS MEETING

*Monday, November 5, 1979*

A warm blast of air hit Paul's face as he entered the 400 Market Street building. A glass faced office tower twenty-some stories high, 400 Market had just been built a few years ago. Paul lingered to admire the tall marble pillars of the lobby and to look for Randy. Should he wait here for him? They just had lunch together.

Paul unbuttoned his overcoat and soaked up the bright light of the massive open-air lobby. It had been damp and blustery outside.

A man in a wheelchair banged his cane against the side of an elevator door that wanted to shut. "Just push it through!" the man cried to his attendant. "You've got to get it up over the threshold."

Approaching closer, Paul saw that the man in the wheelchair was Col. Elijah Bouchard.

He wore a heavy wool overcoat and a fedora, while the attendant wore a black leather car coat, possibly a hand-me-down from his employer. "Easy," Paul said as he hurried up to them. "Excuse me, the Colonel's coat seems to be caught in the wheel. Back the chair up a little. Then I will pull it loose."

The attendant did so, thanking Paul for his help. "Do I know you?" the Colonel asked.

"Yes sir. I'm Paul Elser. We all came to call on you last week at your home."

The Colonel propped himself up in his wheelchair. A head of thick white hair, bushy eyebrows, and a fire, a vibrancy in his eyes spoke of years of command and assurance. The embers now seemed to stir again. Paul had never been one-on-one with the man before. He waited to hear how the Colonel might respond to him.

"Yes, I've heard of you," the Colonel said as the three of them rode up together to the lawyers. "You've made quite an impression on my daughter. Looks like we'll both get an earful today from the lawyers too, eh?"

The Colonel pulled a vinyl pouch out of his overcoat pocket. Opening the flap, Paul could see the pouch contained vinyl tubes. Gesturing for his attendant to lean over so the man could ask something about "the air tank in place"…was all Paul could make out.

At the ninth floor, the Colonel no sooner had been wheeled out of the elevator and onto the landing area than the receptionist saw them. She stood up, removed her telephone headset, and walked over to open the glass door leading into the offices. As they closed the distance from the elevators to the office door, Paul saw she wore a stylish dress that complemented her well.

It would be hard also to miss the offices. The name "Benton and Allen, Attorneys at Law" made a powerful statement, etched in large black letters on the plate glass on both sides of the double glass doors.

These offices were smart. Even from the elevators, Paul could see beyond the entry glass wall, through the conference room glass wall, and out the window to…it had to be Illinois, across the Mississippi River. The law firm took up the entire eastern, or river side, of this floor of the office tower. The receptionist stood smiling as she held open one of the large glass doors. Paul pulled the handle on the other door, providing the Colonel a grand entrance to the law offices as his attendant pushed him through.

"Good to see you, Col. Bouchard," the receptionist said. Then, leaning very close and putting an arm around the old man's neck, she whispered in his ear, "You're all set up in the conference room."

"Thank you, Violet," the Colonel said, giving her hand a squeeze.

Just like the entry into the offices passed through glass doors set in a glass wall, so too the conference room featured sliding glass doors to separate it from the reception area. The doors were pushed aside so the three of them walked right in. Paul could now see the sweeping vista of the Mississippi River in the large floor-to-ceiling window of the conference room. Just off to the left of the building stood the Gateway Arch. The offices were possibly a fourth the way up the Arch, a mere block or two away. After admiring both the river and the Arch, Paul turned around to take in the offices. Both the conference room and the waiting room were paneled in black walnut. Currier and Ives pictures of steamboats, clipper ships, and horses hung on the walls, and the hallway leading back to the offices proper were lined with shelves of heavy law tomes.

At one end of the conference room stood a tall bookstand. Open on it rested one of those exhaustive dictionaries, a two-hands-to-carry job. The Colonel's oxygen tank had been placed next to the dictionary on a hand truck.

Violet resumed her seat at a table-like desk out in the reception area. It had a pink and grey granite top, and she smiled at Paul as she fitted her headset back on.

Many of the swivel office chairs in the conference room had been rolled to the far wall. There were only eight chairs left at the long blond wood conference table, and only Henry Allen waited there for the meeting to begin. He got up, greeted Col. Elijah, and wheeled one of the upholstered swivel office chairs aside, asking, "Would you like to get out of your wheelchair, Colonel?"

"By all means," Grand-pere said. He grabbed his cane and stood up. "I hate the damn thing. Mercury, take the wheelchair somewhere. Do you have a place where he can wait for us, after he parks the car?"

"Of course. This should hardly take twenty minutes," Henry said. "It's easy."

"Bull hockey," the Colonel said. "I never saw an easy million-dollar deal yet. It'll take as long as it takes. That's the trouble today, isn't it? Everybody wants easy. Well, give me all the details every time. It's all that keeps me on the green side of the grass." The Colonel coughed. Paul wondered *Did his doctor approve of the Colonel being out in public?*

Henry acknowledged the humor, and the attendant excused himself, taking the wheelchair with him.

Margaret and Daddy Bruce arrived. They placed their leather briefcases in front of them on the table. They were dressed business semi-formal: Margaret in a gray pinstripe pantsuit, Bruce in glen plaid that complemented the black man's complexion.

Small talk went in bursts and gaps between Margaret, Daddy Bruce, and Paul, punctuated by silence and unease from Henry. Sports, weather, the economy, the election, the hostage crisis, every topic got a shot, but nothing took hold. The mood grew tense.

"Everybody's here," Henry burst out. He looked at his watch. He fumed, and then he shifted in his chair and got up, abruptly pushing his chair back. He walked around the large table and partially closed the sliding doors leading out to the reception area.

"Everybody?" Paul said. "Aren't we expecting Randy? He should be here any minute. We had lunch together."

Henry drew the drapes, closing off the conference room from the reception area. "Let's get started," he said to the Colonel. "I'll go get Stuart."

"Yes," the Colonel said. "That would be good. I'd like to talk with Stuart. Please do have him come in now, will you, Henry? Thank you. But Randy's not here yet. We won't start the meeting proper until he's here. You invited him, didn't you?"

"Yes, of course I did." Henry sat back down, quietly fussing and fuming.

The Colonel asked, "Why did you sit back down, Henry? You said you were going to get Stuart. The meeting was scheduled for two o'clock. Doubtless I'll be billed from two o'clock on. So, please do get Stuart. If you can't get him yourself, have someone get him. Let him earn his keep."

Henry left the room on his errand, muttering "Randy? Nonsense. His presence is purely perfunctory."

"Perfunctory?" Colonel Bouchard said. "Where'd Henry get that word from? *Readers Digest?*"

The others remained silent.

Stuart stopped outside the conference room to give Violet some instruction, then darted in, adding in his general complaints against the economy. He assured Col. Bouchard he would not bill "from two o'clock," though no one laughed. He sat for a bit, moaned about the economy, and reminded Henry about cruising the Intracoastal Waterway in his "bluewater sailor…"that very weekend coming up—We may even take a tack out the Boynton Inlet." Then Violet came in to tell Stuart he had an urgent phone call. Seemingly pleased at the excuse to leave the room, Stuart bowed as he complained of "all these little fires that keep popping up, requiring my attention." He shut the sliding door behind him.

As the room again fell silent, Paul saw how the Colonel wheezed every so often. Then there was the oxygen tank. Surely, Col. Bouchard must be defying doctor's orders to be present at such a meeting. It must be hard for a man like the Colonel to let go of all the power he had accumulated during his life. He had made it so hard on Margaret and Daddy

Bruce ever since they became responsible for the daily operations of the company.

Randy then entered the boardroom. Henry scowled. "You're late," he said. "We've all been waiting here for you."

"So sorry," Randy said. He sat down and did not rise to Henry's barb. Paul saw Randy tap his chest as if to verify something in the breast pocket of his sport coat.

Henry addressed the crowd at large, no one in particular. "It must've been hard on you, Randy, having to pick up the pieces, as it were."

Elijah Bouchard cut him off. "If we can bring this meeting to order, shall we begin?"

Henry summoned Stuart, this time using the intercom. Looking preoccupied, Stuart came into room, glanced around and picked up sheaves of papers from a side table—one to each one present. "Really," he said, "the decision is, practically speaking, Elijah's. Margaret, it looks like you're just here to witness this thing."

Margaret spoke up. "That's *your* way of looking at the thing, not mine. As I instructed you, management is also present and will give their report so we can all avoid making a grave mistake."

"Yes, yes, all of that," Stuart said. "May we continue?"

"Hold on," Col. Bouchard said. "Continue what? Do you want to add anything to your concern, daughter?"

"Yes, I do. Usually when a business sells assets, it's put on the market first. Before it's put on the market, some discussion takes place. Why have all those intermediate steps been eliminated? Could you please give us all some history, Stuart, as to how this decision has even come before us and why we are only meeting on it today?"

"Management, vested management, I should clarify," Stuart said, scowling at Margaret as if she were out of order, "has their pension intact, the terms of which will be announced later. Speaking on behalf of Col. Bouchard, if I may—"

"You may not!" Elijah Bouchard thundered, taking on much the vigor of his Old Testament namesake. "Answer Margaret's question, please."

"What?" Stuart said. "Why sell? It's very simple. You gave us standing orders to sell. You've always wanted to sell. Not that we launched a campaign or anything, but certain discreet inquiries have been made.

From time to time, we've reported on expressions of interest strongly implying intentions of offers. Now an especially promising offer has come forward. So, it's our position we'd best strike while the iron is hot. Consolidated Soda has expressed some interest and now have made a very attractive offer. They may very well withdraw their offer if we equivocate, stall, or otherwise put them off. We've got to act now before the market sags or the regulators complicate things."

"Did you receive any earnest money from them?" Randy asked.

Stuart pulled his papers toward him, glaring at Randy. "Of course they're in earnest," Stuart said. "Papers were signed, pledges were made. There are also tax advantages to consider in managing the estate. That's the way these things are done. If no one else has any further delays, I'll read the motion, and then we can vote on it. 'In consideration of the contract herein described, the Seller—'"

"Stuart," Randy said, much louder this time. "Do you have selective memory loss? There was some discussion of reports from management."

"Randy," Henry said. "We have an agreement."

"No. There's no 'we.' You had an agreement," Randy said. "I have a question. In fact, I have several questions."

"I hardly expected this much discussion on a decision that appears to be so simplistic on its surface," Stuart said. "And I might add, from you, a nonvoting second-generation attendee.

"Yes!" Henry chimed in. "This is all really supposed to be pro forma. Elijah, you're the principal shareholder. What you say should go." He rattled his sheaf of papers. "These are your attorney's recommendations. May we proceed?"

Elijah Bouchard laughed uneasily. "Yes, of course. So far as I can see, we are proceeding. Randy, please present at least one of your many questions."

"Yes, thank you. I would appreciate some clarification here. Just what kind of authority has been given these attorneys that they can negotiate…this sale? Had you known they'd gone that far, Grand-pere?"

His brow lowered, his voice tentative as if thinking things over, Grand-pere said "No, I did not."

"Well," Randy said. "I'm picking up that some kind of steam rolling is going on here. In fact, I would go so far as to ask why are the attorneys running this meeting? Why, for instance, isn't my mum doing it?"

"Because," Stuart said, "Col. Bouchard is chairman and I am speaking on his behalf. In his condition, we can hardly expect him to stand up to all the *heat* this family throws on any effort to follow sound, conservative business practice. Col. Elijah has done his share. Age has its privilege. Can we all please now honor that?"

"I would suggest," Randy said, "significantly less heat would be thrown once we hear from management and they are given the attention they so rightly deserve. Have you seen Paul's report? Have you seen the trend in sales? I'd like to hear from management as to their response to this proposed sale."

"Management serves at the discretion of the board," Stuart said.

Randy became more and more animated. "All right. What's it going to take? Management suing the attorneys for malfeasance? How is management compensated? That lump sum pension? Peanuts. What about our employees and their families? You want to take their livelihood away from them? Sell out to the competition? What's with that?

"Then, beyond that," Randy glowered, "this whole football stadium thing. Maybe there's sentimental value attached to putting Grand-pere's name on it now, while he can actually see it. But I say let the Bouchard name continue on as a living company, not as a tombstone that seats seventy thousand."

Henry ruffled his papers. "You may be a decent doctor, Randy," he said, "but addle-brained touchy-feely nonsense has no place in business. The bottom line is all that counts. You'll learn sooner or later that those with the gold make the rules."

"Ha ha," Randy's face turned a livid red. "Clever twist on an old proverb. Can we apply that rule to all this talk of declaring Grand-pere incompetent? He looks sharp enough to me. All this selling scheme boils down to is you guys foisting some razzle-dazzle on the man in hopes he'll sign. I don't know where you guys come off on this deal, but I do not see it as favoring the *intact* family."

"Intact?" Henry said, his arms flailing as if he were restraining himself from a more 'physical' argument. "Why, you ingrate. No son of mine would make such an outrageous accusation."

Randy and his father stood at opposite ends of the table. The electricity between them charged the air.

Then Violet came in with a trolley of coffee and soft drinks. "Coffee anyone?" she asked. A truce thus established, Randy and his father sat down. Paul and Randy took their coffee black. Elijah requested sugar and cream with is and Henry just simmered, impatient to resume the meeting. The smell of caffeine permeated the room.

A sense of civility restored, Randy said, "Paul, have these attorneys seen your report?"

Stuart busied himself penciling notes on his agenda. He said nothing.

Paul said, "I mailed them copies and made follow-up phone calls just last Tuesday. Beyond that, I can't say, as my phone calls and messages went unreturned."

Colonel Bouchard said, "Go ahead, present your report now, Mr. Elser. We've heard so many cries for management to present their case. So go ahead. This should be good."

Paul did so.

After the presentation, Stuart, his drollness reaching new lows, said, "Impressive numbers, if they can be corroborated."

"They can," Col. Bouchard said. "I had my CPA out to the house Thursday. Bernard Jeams confirmed they're his numbers, ranging over the past ten years, put side-by-side, year-after-year, and then graphed. Revenues have climbed in excess of 10 percent each year, margins are well above industry averages, and given present strategies and continued efficiencies, Bernard said, he would be surprised if these trends did not continue."

"Well." Stuart Allen paused and looked around the room, looking each one in the eye. "Fantastic. Management has presented their report. Let's all clap our hands and jump for joy. May we now proceed to the question? Shall we accept Consolidated's tender offer or not? All those in favor, say aye and state your shares."

Randy clasped his hands before him. "Stuart," he said. "You are incorrigible."

They proceeded with the vote.

Col. Bouchard said, "Aye, four hundred ninety-five shares. Sorry, Margaret, it's for the best."

"Opposed?"

Margaret said, "Nay, four hundred twenty-five shares."

Randy cleared his throat and said, "Nay, eighty shares."

"What?" Henry said. "What shares do you own? Can you prove them? Eighty shares? Eighty voting shares?"

"Of course they're voting shares. Look, Dad," Randy said, walking over to Henry's side. He pulled a statement out of his inside sport coat pocket. "Here's my brokerage statement. Read this line here: 'Bouchard Beverage, eighty shares.' In my name, no mention of a secondary position. Any more questions?"

"Is that true, Elijah?" Stuart said. "I thought you had five hundred seventy-five shares. But you only voted four hundred ninety-five."

"I did have five hundred seventy-five. But now I have four hundred ninety-five."

"Huh?" Henry said. "You never told us."

"You never asked, and it looks like the broker never told you either. I've been gifting Randy ten shares a year now for quite some time. The broker took care of it all. Are you sure, Randall, that's the way you want to vote?"

"Yes," Randy said. "It is."

Elijah Bouchard shrugged. "Well, it's settled then. It looks like the younger generation has spoken. Stuart, you can tell your buyer, sorry, no sale. Maybe they'll come back and sweeten their offer."

"No!" Stuart shot to his feet. "We won't stand for that!" He paced. "Henry and I put too much time and effort into this to just walk away. I wasn't going to do what I'm about to do, because of propriety. We respect relationships between fathers and daughters. We acknowledge things are strained between Henry and Margaret, but you leave us no alternative." Here Stuart opened the sliding door to the reception area. "Violet," he said. "Would you please bring the certificate in now?"

Violet entered the room, carrying a framed document. She handed it to Stuart and then quickly turned around and stepped back out.

"I have here a certificate for twelve shares," Stuart said. "I vote aye, twelve for the sale. Let's see. According to my figures, that's four hundred ninety-five and twelve makes five hundred seven *for* the sale and four hundred twenty-five plus eighty against makes five hundred five *against*. Lady and gentlemen, it looks like the sale goes through, by two shares."

"Not so fast," Randy said. "Since when is there a total of one thousand twelve shares? I'd like to see that certificate." Randy got up and grabbed the framed certificate out of Stuart's hands before the lawyer could raise a protest. Then, taking a spoon from the coffee trolley, Randy removed the backing from the frame. He pulled the stock certificate out to look at the back. "Look," he said. "The certificate was signed over to Elijah Bouchard in 1954! That was well before Margaret received her shares. It must have been part of Elijah's five hundred seventy-five after he gifted Margaret and before he gifted me."

His voice sounding pressured, shocked, Stuart asked to see the back-side of the stock certificate. "Col. Bouchard, sir. Can you confirm that outrageous conjecture?"

Paul saw how Col. Bouchard now breathed deeply yet appeared winded. Under his breath, the Colonel said, "Stuart, your mother framed that certificate, in memory of the close relationship between our two families. Allen went partners with me in the company, as I recall, for less than a year, before he died." Did anyone else notice? Paul thought he say the Colonel's limp hand pointing in the direction of his oxygen tank. "When Allen died," the Colonel continued, "I bought his shares back as I carried life insurance on him for that very purpose. If I hear you correctly, you must have taken that certificate to mean something more than the sentimental memento it was to your mother."

"I found it among my mother's things when we sold her house," Stuart said. "So, well. That's quite a surprise. The measure fails. For now. Maybe, just maybe, Consolidated will sweeten the pot. Every-thing, everyone, has their price, right?" Stuart gave his preppy rah-rah smile. "Moving on, we do have one other order of business to discuss today, the Bouchard Trust. It won't be quite as robust without the pro-ceeds of the sale in it, but it will be a great help to you, Col. Elijah, as you enter your, ahem, later years, and also for the family on your pass-ing."

"Go to Hell, Stuart!" The Colonel barked.

Paul saw how the eyes of the others rolled at this. It must have evoked for them a taste of the man's former vitality. The remark stunned him, too.

Col. Bouchard attempted to rise and then relented. Gasping, he said, "I never thought I'd see the day. The world has changed, Stuart, and you're still groveling in the dark." Again, he gestured toward his oxygen. "Air," he said.

Stuart looked taken aback. "Me? Whatever could you mean? How have I offended you, Col. Bouchard?"

Paul and Randy busied themselves bringing the oxygen tank over to be near Col. Elijah. Paul went to get the tubes out of the Colonel's coat pocket. Even as he fitted them to the regulator on the tank and offered the tubes to the Colonel to place under his nose, Col. Elijah spoke: "I've made mistakes in my life, Stuart, to be sure. I was a fool to alienate myself from my daughter and her husband. I take full responsibility for that. Don't think for a minute I absolve myself of that. But you preyed on me, taking advantage of former personal failings, and you betrayed my trust." The Colonel's head began to waver and his voice weakened as he wheezed.

"Now, Elijah, sir," Stuart said. "Don't stress yourself. We only have your interest at heart. For the sake of Allen A. Allen, my father and your dear friend, please consider what you say."

Daddy Bruce saw that, in addition to the modest tube the Colonel used, his oxygen tank also had a thicker tube attached to a latex mask that would cover both mouth and nose. He set up this more generous supply for Col. Elijah.

Elijah took deep breaths from his oxygen tube. He pushed himself back up in his chair, then he pointed a finger, first at Stuart then at Henry.

Paul reached for and held the Colonel's hand in his own. "Save your strength, sir," he said. "Let it go. It doesn't mean a thing. We'll handle it for you." He knelt down. Randy assessed Elijah, taking his pulse, examining the size of his pupils, testing the pinking of his fingertips. "The Colonel needs medical attention everybody," he said. "Give him space. Paul, call 911."

Elijah had been wheezing. Now he began to sputter. He spit up blood. Paul asked Randy and Daddy Bruce to assist him by laying Grand-pere down on the conference table to make him comfortable and so the transfer to a gurney would be easier once the paramedics arrived. Paul elevated his head with the overcoat. Margaret rushed over to sit by him. "Are you comfortable, Grand-pere?" she asked. She looked anything but comfortable herself. Daddy Bruce came over to hold her and offer solace. He reached out to place a hand on the Colonel's shoulder.

On the other side of the table, Paul laid his hand on Eli's other shoulder.

"If they'll release me from the hospital and it's no burden," Grand-pere said, pulling his mask aside, "I'd like to go back to the Bouchard house at Tower Grove Park for my last days."

The paramedics came. After a quiet night at the hospital, the Colonel was discharged the next morning. In keeping with his request, Paul and Linda took Col. Elijah Bouchard to stay with them at the Bouchard house. He remained there for five days, staying in Randy's old room and dying in his sleep Friday night, November 9, 1979.

# EPILOGUE

When Randy visited Paul at the Bouchard house, he liked parking in front of the house. The winding cobblestone path up from the street served as a far nicer approach, he thought, than driving down the alley, garaging the car, and entering through the back door. That's the way he entered the house most days, back in his childhood.

Walking past the expansive lawn, looking up at the towering English oaks, he remembered the day he and his father planted them. Then the stately old colonial itself. The chimneys on either side of the house had their memories, too—of watching the flickering flames dance away the hours on many a timeless winter's night. Little Randy sitting Indian style on the floor, asking the flames, *What is adulthood like? Will I be happy? What will I do to support myself?* It would be funny, wouldn't it, to walk back in time, and update that little dreamy-eyed guy on how it all turned out?

Randy laughed within. He'd joked with others about all that "inner child stuff," but this image seemed particularly indelible. Yes, he'd done all right for himself, his practice, his career in healthcare.

Hastening up the three steps to the gallery, rapping a few times on the massive door, Randy entered the home.

With him, he carried a present for Bruce Jr.

"Hello, everybody! Company's here!"

Linda came down the hallway from the kitchen to greet him. "Come right in," she said. "We were expecting you, though you're a little early." He returned her greeting, and they embraced.

"I'm not officially here," Randy said. "I'll be back. I just need to run something by Paul before the festivities begin. Oh, and where's our young scholar?" Randy asked, seeing Bruce Jr. peeking out from behind the door at the end of the hall.

"Scholar? C'mon now," Linda said. "He's just started kindergarten."

"I know," Randy said. He whispered, "I got him a puzzle game. Shh!" Then louder "Uncle's here, Brucie J."

With a wave of the present, soon Bruce Jr. had his present opened. It was a large puzzle-map of the United States made out of Masonite, the states each enameled one of six colors.

With coaching from Linda, Bruce Jr. thanked his Uncle Randy. Then he raced into the living room, lay on the floor in front of the fireplace, dumped out the pieces of his puzzle, and began playing the game.

By then Paul had come to join Randy and Linda in the front hall. The tallest room in the house, the front hall featured a staircase up to the second floor, a long glass chandelier, and dark oak wainscoting with wallpaper above. The pattern on the flowered green wallpaper was bundled flowers. "So," Paul said after an exchange of pleasantries, "where's Pam?"

"I'll be back with her. I just wanted to run an idea by you first. Now that I'm a full partner in Sherman, Smith and Allen, MDs, I'm feeling bad about all the money I'm making on my Sunny Day stock. I'm wondering if you could help me out. It just doesn't feel right, a passive investor like me, having the ownership stake that I do."

Paul folded his arms across his chest. He pursed his lips and nodded in a mock grave fashion. "That sounds like a tremendous burden for you. However, correct me if I'm wrong, are you asking me if I'd like to buy some of your stock?"

"Yes!" Randy said. "That's exactly it. My, but you are a sharp businessman. Now that all the tenant-friends of Grand-pere have gone to join him in that big bridge game in the sky, Meriwether Manor has all new tenants and a waiting list that doesn't appear to be getting any shorter any time soon. So I'm thinking of buying another house out in Ladue. If you and I can agree on a price and a buy-out process, the proceeds would come in handy when we acquire that second house. Anyway, if buying company stock sounds interesting to you, we should have that conversation."

Paul put a hand on Randy's shoulder. "You're on," he said. "We might be able to work something out. I've already bought some of Margaret's shares. She's offered me very generous terms…"

Randy backed away. "No, no. I don't want to get into the numbers right now. Just floating a trial balloon, as they say. We'll talk about it more later now that I know you'd entertain making me an offer. Listen, I've got to go get Pam. I'll be back."

Randy began excusing himself to go.

Linda said, "Wait. You got your invitation, didn't you? Daddy Bruce and Margaret invited us all to a winter break on Barbados. Are you going?"

"Well, probably. I'd like to talk it over with Pam. She might enjoy the time, too. It does sound like fun, doesn't it?"

"Don't wait too long, Randy. I wouldn't want you to miss the boat."

"Oh, I'll be there, and maybe Pam, too. Hey, Paul, thanks for everything, okay?"

Randy turned and walked back out the door. The leaves had started to turn. A gorgeous fall appeared to be in the making.

www.ingramcontent.com/pod-product-compliance
Lightning Source LLC
Chambersburg PA
CBHW072103170626
46813CB00004B/1438